PARKED

Danielle Svetcov

DIAL BOOKS FOR YOUNG READERS

DIAL BOOKS
An imprint of Penguin Random House LLC, New York

Copyright © 2020 by Danielle Svetcov

Visit us online at penguinrandomhouse.com
Library of Congress Cataloging-in-Publication Data

Names: Svetcov, Danielle, author.
Title: Parked : a novel / Danielle Svetcov.
Description: New York : Dial Books for Young Readers, [2020] | Summary:
"Newly homeless Jeanne Ann and wealthy Cal form a vital friendship as
they both search for stability and community, finding it through love of
books, art, and food"—Provided by publisher.
Identifiers: LCCN 2019021282 (print) | LCCN 2019022313 (ebook) | ISBN
9780399539039 (hardcover)
Subjects: CYAC: Friendship—Fiction. | Homeless persons--Fiction. | Books
and reading—Fiction. | Food—Fiction. | San Francisco
(Calif.)—Fiction.
Classification: LCC PZ7.1.S9 Par 2020 (print) | LCC PZ7.1.S9 (ebook) |
DDC [Fic]—dc23
LC record available at https://lccn.loc.gov/2019021282
LC ebook record available at https://lccn.loc.gov/2019022313
Printed in the United States of America
1 2 3 4 5 6 7 8 9 10

Design by Mina Chung • Text set in Neutraface Text and Slab

For Charlotte and Josephine
and their future wings

"NOBLE DEEDS AND HOT BATHS ARE THE BEST CURES."

—Cassandra Mortmain, *I Capture the Castle*, by Dodie Smith

"YOU'RE JUST JEALOUS BECAUSE YOU DON'T HAVE A FRIEND WHO CAN FLY."

—Fudgie, *Superfudge*, by Judy Blume

DEPARTURES

Chicago Public Library, Sulzer Branch

The following titles were renewed by Jeanne Ann Fellows, and are due June 4.

Mrs. Frisby and the Rats of NIMH

Frankenstein

El Deafo

Oliver Twist

Nooks & Crannies

The Lion, the Witch and the Wardrobe

The Golden Compass

The Night Diary

Hatchet

Dr. Jekyll and Mr. Hyde

The Lottery

The Phantom Tollbooth

The War That Saved My Life

The Wolves of Willoughby Chase

Roll of Thunder, Hear My Cry

A Long Way from Chicago

One Crazy Summer

The BFG

Howl's Moving Castle

When You Reach Me

Pippi Longstocking

Swallows and Amazons

The Little Princess

Born Free

Ballet Shoes

The Penderwicks

The Saturdays

Brown Girl Dreaming

101 Dalmatians

From the Mixed-Up Files of Mrs. Basil E. Frankweiler

Merci Suárez Changes Gears

Redwall

The Railway Children

Adventures of Huckleberry Finn

A Little History of the World

Zen and the Art of Motorcycle Maintenance

The Way Things Work

Finance for Dummies

Jeanne Ann

I don't mind the nights. I stay at the library until it closes, which is ten o'clock on weekdays, eight on weekends. After, outside, it's mostly dark. I slouch on my bike seat and read by the light of the Food-Mart sign next door. Tonight it's *Hatchet*. I've read it a couple times. I like that one tool saves the kid's life in all these ways, and that his biggest threat is his weird mom, not the moose that charged him, or the bloodthirsty mosquitos, or the tornado. I think about this as I wait. Someone on the library staff stays with me out front till Mom shows. Mrs. Jablonsky made it a rule.

Mom usually arrives out of breath, running from the L. I swear the ground shakes as she gets near, like an earth-moving machine. Her shift at the restaurant technically ends at nine on weekdays and seven on weekends, but since her boss is a poisonous Hydra in track pants who inherited the restaurant from his dad, Mom oversees everything, includ-ing the other cooks, most of them Hydras in training who leave for the night without shutting the walk-in fridge or noticing the meat order for the next day never arrived. Mom is always running somewhere to fix everything for someone who doesn't appreciate it "so I can get to you, kid," she reminds me.

We walk the same twelve blocks home every night. Mom

carries my bike on her wide shoulders and sort of tilts over me like the teapot in the song. My book rides in the front pocket of my overalls. It's nice on spring nights like this. We can take our time. The air smells like burnt toast. It's warm. If either of us has breaking news—a guy cooking oatmeal on a camp stove in the library bathroom (really happened), a customer at the restaurant stuffing an entire steak in her purse (really happened)—we share it. But usually we're quiet. That's because I feel like a squeezed-out sponge after a day of sixth grade and just as many hours at the library. And Mom feels way worse after a day at O'Hara's House of Fine Eats.

It's nothing special, but I love this walk. If we stop on the way home, it's super fast, and almost always to look in the window of the travel agency at the foot of our apartment building. The store there has been vacant since somebody invented the Internet in 1990-something, Mom says, but no one ever took down the posters that are taped to the inside of the glass, facing out. There's one of the Eiffel Tower and one of the Taj Mahal. And one of the Golden Gate Bridge. They're all faded like everything else on this block, but Mom likes to tap the glass over the Golden Gate Bridge poster like she's got a plan. Which she does. I know she does. She just hasn't shared it with me yet.

Cal

I can do this.

I have to do this.

Maybe I should've asked to do this.

Just climb, I tell myself.

The bricks are easy once I find the handholds. The wall is only about six feet high. I've studied it for two weeks, after school. The tree growing out of the sidewalk on the street side boosts me past the three-foot mark. Thank you, tree. The harder part is climbing with the paint cans. I need to get up and over quick to not be seen, but the cans in my backpack are like carrying another person.

At the top, I know I'll have to jump.

I pull myself up. Look down. Tug at the knot of my bow tie. I imagine the sound of bones breaking and then someone drawing the outline around my dead, twelve-year-old body.

Then I hug the backpack, open my eyes, and leap.

I wish I didn't have to do this alone.

That thought slips in uninvited as I fall, air whooshing past me—seaweed, sour milk, pine needles—what a San Francisco scratch-'n'-sniff would smell like if cities had scratch-'n'-sniffs. Then: *Fwump!* I'm on the ground and on my feet. It's not graceful, but I'm alive.

Now the good part.

I lay out my panels. The work will cover most of one wall, five feet wide by six feet high. I dig for my brushes and rollers at the bottom of the backpack. I have about eight hours, the length of Mom's shift—if no one catches me. It won't be my best stuff—I don't have enough time—but it *will* be the most public. The four-panel pencil sketch I've put together tells me what I have to do and where, like a map. I've practiced all this in my head and on variously sized pieces of cardboard a hundred times. I dip a brush into the green. If this were a school day, there'd be a roar of kids behind me—yelling, trading cards, candy. Looking past me. But it's Sunday. The courtyard is still and quiet.

I touch the brush to the bricks. They can't look past this.

Jeanne Ann

Mom's beside me on the stoop, leaning over to peek at the note I'm transcribing for her. "That's it. Read it out loud," she orders, and closes her eyes. "Please," she adds.

I read: "*Dear Mr. O'Hara, I quit. The green beans with gorgonzola would've been great on the menu, if you'd had the guts to let me make them. And the lamb croquettes. And the duck legs. You could've just called them 'Specials of the Day.' People would've ordered. Good luck finding another cook with a brain in her head. You're a terrible boss. —Joyce*"

"What do you think?" Mom says, opening her eyes again.

I think duck legs and croquettes sound disgusting, but I've never tried them. Has Mom?

I think everything is moving too fast, that we are playing in quicksand.

She scoots toward me, so we're hip to hip. She's pulled a piece of paper from her back pocket. I sit up straighter. It used to be milky blue, this paper, two months ago when it arrived in the mail, but now it's turned kinda gray. She's read and refolded it so many times, it's got tears along all the creases. I've never read it. And I'm not sure if seeing it again makes me feel left out or just wound up. I lean in to see, but she *tsks* playfully and tucks it back in her pocket, like always.

Fine.

"I dunno," I say about the note she's asked me to help her write. It's not the sort of thing you can apologize for later. I take a deep breath. "It's really final."

Mom nods vigorously. Final is what she's after. "I don't like the *dear* and *Mr.* parts," she says. "Cross those out. They make it sound like I respect him."

I cross out *dear* and *Mr.* "What's gorgonzola?" I ask.

Mom peers at me briefly, then grabs the note and crumples it. All the worry lines in her face have worked themselves out. "You know what?" she says, ignoring my question. "He doesn't deserve an explanation. Come on."

And that's it. She tugs me gently but steadily toward the van parked illegally at the foot of our crumbling stoop. The van matches our apartment building: They both look patched together by Dr. Frankenstein. That's our nickname for it, our building, with the eight-lane expressway running past, and the heat that comes on in summer instead of winter and the showers that leak through the floors: Frank. Mom's already got a nickname for our van: the Carrot. It's orange. Two taped-up seats in front, curtains that might be cut-up bedsheets over half the windows, aluminum everywhere else. We spent almost our entire savings on it today, my last day of sixth grade. I think a better nickname might be: Rash. As in: bought without thinking.

"Why are we doing this again?" I ask.

Mom's opened her door.

She swings her thick arm around me and squeezes. I can smell kitchen grease in her hair. "Dignity, kid, dignity."

And I go to my side and climb in, for that reason only.

Cal

I was eight the first time. I walked out our front door and handed a man at the corner a loaf of Mom's prizewinning lemon-pistachio bread. "Here, sir."

I'd seen the man through the living room window, pacing in his usual spot by the stop sign, clutching his knitting needles. He was talking to himself when I reached him—"an invasion of Alexas," I heard him say—but he stopped long enough to look at me and nod. He had black oceans for eyes. And puffy scabbed hands. And he shivered. I was cold too, even in my footies. This was the closest we'd ever come, but I'd passed him in the neighborhood dozens and dozens of times. On benches and stoops, inside doorways when it rained. He wore a yellow raincoat and red rain boots every day, just in case. I thought that was smart. He accepted the loaf. I returned his nod. "Bye, sir."

Back in the house, I tucked myself into the warm spot on the couch I'd left a second before, next to Mom, who was prepping a menu. She patted my head without looking up. I love Mom, but she hardly ever looks up when prepping a menu. I thought about telling her what I'd just done—I thought about the man's face, his shivering, his hand taking the bread—but I wanted this, whatever it was, for myself. A project that was mine. Mom, of all people, understood about projects.

My mistake.

The conversation on the other side of this door would be going differently, I think, if I'd told her about the first pistachio bread four years ago, and all the others.

Because now I'm stuck in the Point Academy office. It smells like cream of tomato soup, and the school's secretaries are sneaking looks from under lowered eyelids. Like lizards. I wish it were still yesterday.

If it were yesterday, Mom and I would be eating early-bird takeout and watching Julia Child *French Chef* reruns like usual. She'd load up on hot sauce and I'd load up on soy sauce. I'd eat with a fork and she'd eat with chopsticks. After, I'd locate her purse, and we'd cross the street to Greenery, where Mom would ref the dining room like a major-league ump, and I'd settle into a bottomless pineapple juice and my sketchbook at the corner of the bar. We'd wink at each other between "customer relations."

But it's not yesterday. And nothing is usual. Today is the second-to-last day of sixth grade, and the dean of the middle school has just asked my mom what could "possibly be going through" my head. Like I'm a mystery.

They're on the other side of this door. I can picture Mom at the edge of her chair, whapping the toes of her clogs together, waiting for Dean Cappo to take a breath so she can pounce all over him with my defense.

"Cal is a very good boy," I hear Dean Cappo say. Mom knows that. "The teachers all agree. But they also tell me he spends all his time alone—at lunch, at recess. Not talking. Drawing those . . . wings. Kids find them in their books and backpacks. He doesn't seem to have his friends around him anymore."

I hug my backpack tighter. "Oh—" Mom starts. I hate how surprised she sounds.

"And you've likely noticed the brown. And the bow ties."

Beige, not brown!

"I, uh, yes," she says.

"We see this all the time with kids. Just a phase, a dip between peaks," Dean Cappo rushes on. "Cal's got so much going . . . He's, well, he's a wonderful artist." Mom must be silently nodding. Must be. She's offered to hang my work in the restaurant. "If it weren't technically graffiti, I might even like his"—the dean clears his throat—"alterations to the school."

A chair scrapes, like someone's standing. "If I could give you one piece of advice, Lizzie: Get him out of the house, new scenery, a chance to see himself from a different, better angle."

Dean Cappo sounds wise, with his deep voice and personalized "Lizzie," but he doesn't know what he's talking about. *Don't be fooled, Mom! Our house is great. The scenery is great.*

"This all would've gone much differently if he'd spoken to us first," the dean continues. "We don't want the other students getting ideas. The janitorial staff has already begun scrubbing, but we may have to invest in special supplies to complete the job. It's our policy to bill the student's family . . ."

I rise so fast, my chair tips over. *Scrubbing?*

"You can't!" I've flung open the door. "It's not graffiti!"

Dean Cappo is standing with his nostrils squeezed together like he'd rather not breathe this in. Mom jerks around in her chair, a fluff of blond hair catching in her eyelashes, making her blink rapidly.

"Cal," she says, sizing me up in a way she's never done before.

"He can't," I plead, all of me turned toward Mom. I swipe my bangs off my forehead, but they swing back over my eyes. She should be on my side, but she's shaking her head. She's turned down her mouth, like a crescent moon that's slipped its axis.

This can't be. This is the opposite of what was supposed to happen. Mom should be ... We should all be gathered in the courtyard right now, admiring the ... "I'm not the problem," I say. "The problem is—" I can't find the right words. I don't want to find the right words. This is why I draw.

"We will call you in when we're ready, Cal," Dean Cappo says, eyebrows up like arrowheads.

If it were yesterday, the paint on the courtyard would still be drying, and Mom and I would end the night with the classifieds from the free newspaper that gets thrown in our driveway. She'd whisper them in my ear while I'm half asleep, head on pillow: "For sale: partially eaten duck, ten days old. Twenty-four dollars or best offer." We'd laugh so hard, we'd cry. I'd fall asleep smiling.

Jeanne Ann

It's dumping snow when we reach the Beartooth Pass in Wyoming, with winds so strong, the van is rocking side to side like it's in an automatic car wash.

Mom's got the windshield wipers flailing, but we still can't see the road in front of us. I'm wishing I'd said a proper good-bye to my bike. And Lake Michigan. And that I'd written a real letter to the librarians. And to the other volunteers. No one was there but the cleaning crew when we swung through on our way out of town. Now I may never have the chance.

A blizzard in June? This is bad. We don't have four-wheel drive or chains. I lean closer to Mom. Turtling at five miles per hour, one hand on the steering wheel, the other on my knee, she looks at peace, like this is exactly how she imagined our trip to San Francisco would go. Like this is the perfect start to our new life. If we get stuck here, she's probably strong enough to lug me twenty miles on her back through the snow. But still . . .

"What are you looking in the side-view for? Keep reading. Does she get the guy? Will there be kissing? Don't stop for the snow." Mom picks up her hand from my knee and snaps her fingers at the book in my lap. Then she tugs gently on one of my curls. I've been reading to her since we peeled out of Chicago.

"Maybe we should pull over?" I say, but even as the words are coming out, the snow begins to thin, first to a spray, and then a dust, and then—gone—just blue, lunchtime sky with thin wisps of cloud. I can see the road again and the giant trees ushering us along like very tall butlers.

"Well, that was fun," Mom says. She rolls down her window, wipes off her side-view mirror, and wags a finger at the sky. The gesture translates roughly to: *We're not turnin' back, no matter what you throw at us.*

PARKED

Cal

Forty-four pencils. Sixteen sketchbooks. That's all that's left. Paints, pens, brushes: confiscated, an hour ago. My desk looks like an abandoned lot. It's taken Mom six days, but she's had it. She's moved from talk to "consequences." I crank open my window and slide to the floor. A warm breeze slips in.

In San Francisco, a warm night is rare. Freaky rare. The air over the bay turns fuzzy green, and everything it covers looks older, even the Golden Gate Bridge, which hovers like the last remains of an ancient fortress tonight.

On warm nights, everyone goes outside. Happy noises drift up from the street—laughing and wind chimes and hoots. In the playing fields across the street, I can see a pickup soccer game, and, closer to the water, a bunch of tourists photographing an ice-cream cart from all angles like it's the Mars Rover. Even the van-dwellers next to the fields are out in lawn chairs, wiggling their toes.

There's a new van down there. Orange. Illinois plates. Flat tire. Parked across the street at the very front of the line. I should log it in my sketchbook, but I don't have the energy.

"Good luck," I say to the new arrival, fogging up my window. I mean it, but it doesn't sound like I do. If they know anything about this block, they'll leave tomorrow.

I usually like warm nights. Not this one.

"It wasn't your wall to paint," Mom declares daily—in the hallway, by the front door, outside the kitchen, beside my desk. "You've always been so responsible, Cal." Which is all a wind-up to: "There's no good excuse. You will pay for the removal. You will apologize to the janitors, and the principal, and the students."

"I can't," I say. I'm not sorry.

"Cal!"

This morning she covered her face with her hands and groaned. When that didn't help, she reached up and covered my face, until, unhappy and overstretched—I am a foot taller than she is—she covered her own face again.

"You've never talked back to me," she gasped.

"I'm not talking back." I really wasn't.

But the more she insists I'm wrong, the less I want to explain anything.

It's like that time one of her cooks choked on a carrot while testing a recipe and had to be saved by a customer who knew the Heimlich because no one on staff did. The whole thing freaked Mom out so bad, she ordered all her cooks and servers to enroll in advanced CPR, including lifeguard training, and for six months all carrots at the restaurant were served pureed.

"This is my fault," she added this morning. "I didn't give you a normal childhood. You were always at the restaurant, never any trouble. I thought I was paying attention, but clearly..." She looked like she was remembering something happy and sad.

"I love the restaurant. You're a great mom," I said. She really is. "I'm fine. Really. Can we—"

"All your friends?" she interrupted. "Eliot, Miles, Saul . . . ?"

I shrugged. I didn't want to talk about that. It hurt. "That's something else," I said.

"I don't think it *is* something else," she said.

"It is."

"It isn't."

"It is."

That's the loop. She repeats what Dean Cappo said about "new scenery." She says she's going to throw the "kitchen sink" at this problem, that the art supplies are only the start. Her face is always a mix of serious and pumped.

I wonder if it'll ever end. I wonder if it's our new normal.

Mom says she'll return my supplies after I've had time to think about "what I did."

She doesn't get it. I look outside to where the orange van is parked at the front of the line. It's what I *didn't* do that I can't forget.

Jeanne Ann

We wake to a stampede. I look out the van's back window. Hundreds of people are staggering toward us. They're all naked except for short-shorts and tank tops, and they've each got a number pinned to their chests.

"It's a triathlon," Mom says. She's shimmied over to the back window while still in her sleeping bag and is kneeling beside me. She can't stand up in the van without hitting her head. "They'll run a bunch of miles, bike a bunch, swim a bunch." She points to a giant banner over the street that says so.

"Why would they do that when they could be sleeping?" Or eating. We haven't had a proper meal, on plates, with forks, since we got here three days ago.

A runner throws a half-empty water bottle without looking and hits the side of the van. Then another squats and . . . Mom closes the curtains on my nose. This is worse than living next to an expressway in Chicago.

"How long are we going to park here?" I ask. We have other places we could be besides this van, this intersection. Mom's not even bothering to feed money to the meter. How long before someone notices?

We're at the front of a line of vans that look a lot like ours—drained of blood. I thought they were abandoned, but last night I caught sight of an arm popped out of a window two vans back; it dumped something wet and steamy onto the sidewalk. Not a good sign.

Mom shrugs, smiling. A fog horn groans, a sound that exactly matches how I feel. I can see her making calculations in her head: *This is my first vacation in years; let's be low-budget tourists a little longer; we've got the rest of our lives to live indoors, pay bills; and don't forget the flat tire.* She's not minding this at all.

She slips the ragged blue-turned-gray paper from her jeans now, taps it against her forehead, and slides it right back into her pocket. "We won't be here long, kid. There won't be triathlons every day. We've got a view of the Golden Gate Bridge, like we always talked about." She holds out a box of cereal I polished off in Utah, shakes it, frowns, says she'll get to the store again today.

We? I never talked about this view. *She* talked about this view.

The only view I need is of ham and eggs.

Cal

I find Mom's lost purse on the side of the bathtub and something I probably wasn't supposed to find poking out of it.

Cal Adjustments:
School (new scenery)
Job (new scenery)
Art supplies (redirect attention)
Color back in clothes (new scenery)
Friends/social life/sports (new scenery)

I probably shouldn't have looked.

Mom only makes lists for "the big stuff"—a waitstaff mutiny or a health inspector visit. I'm just as important as the restaurant, but my problems have always been small. I've been—I _am_ easy. Like those dogs that fit in a purse and don't make trouble. She's never needed a list for me.

I don't know if this means I've changed or she has.

"Cal! Did you find it?!" Mom calls from the bottom of the stairs. "It's not down here!"

I can hear her clogs clomping across the wood floors. Mom refuses to get ready for work until she's already five minutes late, and then it takes her five minutes to find her purse, so she is at best fifteen minutes late and always blames something or someone besides herself, even if she was napping on the couch right before. Until recently, this was one of her few flaws.

She's mumbling now: "I'm going to be late" and "The new dishwashing guy is coming. He'll use too much soap and the plates will streak and someone will complain about a chemical taste. Cal!"

Usually, I'm happiest at this time of day, right after we've shared an early-bird dinner and right before a shift. The sounds, her racing back and forth across the house like a miniature pony, feel exciting, like a drumroll before a show.

Tonight I wander to my room and stand at the window, nose against the glass. I share a moment with the orange van across the street and its flat tire. *In for it, both of us.*

I sink into my beanbag chair and turn to look up at the heroes on my walls, portraits recently completed. Eleanor Roosevelt, Clark Kent, Gandhi, Harriet Tubman. I was going to sketch Mom next.

She pops her head in. "I'm leaving."

"Okay."

"I found my purse."

"Uh-huh."

As owner, Mom works a bunch of shifts at Greenery, and this is the one I usually join her for. I want to go, but not if it's like this. She must feel the same, because she doesn't invite me along. We just stare at each other, looking for proof that the other person is a fake, a robot with a malfunctioning chip.

All I can think to do once she's gone is roll the garbage cans to the bottom of the driveway. Tomorrow is garbage pickup, and *I am a good son* who always takes out the garbage.

A dirt clod wonks me on the forehead as I'm turning back up the driveway.

Mom?

Through a shower of dirt falling past my eyes, I can just make out our next-door neighbor, Mrs. Paglio, kneeling by the hedge between our yards, surrounded by flower pots. She wears gardening gloves and a matching blue hat. She has flowers in one hand and in the other a chunk of something brown.

"Close your eyes!" she cries. "Oh, dear." I can hear her scrambling to get up and shuffle over. "I'm so sorry."

"You threw dirt at me?"

"Don't speak. It'll get in your mouth."

She has to go to the bottom of her driveway and then up mine to reach me. Her gloved fingers move with a slight tremor as they dust the dirt from my hair, brushing gently at my eyelashes and eyebrows. I feel like a fossil at an excavation.

"You got caught in the crosshairs of my temper tantrum," she says. I spit out some soil. I hear her groan, then a bubble of something—laughter?

"Can I open my eyes?"

"No. Keep them shut, Cal."

She's stopped brushing, and I think she's just staring at me. I peek out of my right eye. The view is blurry at first, then clears with some blinking. Mrs. Paglio's got her hands bunched up by her throat. Her gloves are still on, and she's not facing me like I expect. She's facing the bay. Mom says Mrs. Paglio looks like two cabbages stacked on top of each other. I'd agree if cabbages were a little squishier. Her hair is a white wedge—sharp and blunt like a modern sculpture. I think she's close to seventy. "A person can't just flip a switch and change," she says.

"What?"

She startles, rocking back on her heels. "Oh, that wasn't for you." She pats my head almost like she needs it for balance. "Let's go talk to your mother. I should apologize." She laces her arm through mine and tugs in the direction of my house.

"Mom's at work."

Mrs. Paglio changes course without pausing. We enter her house through a side door. I've never been inside. We're wave-over-the-hedge kinda neighbors.

The outside door has dropped us into a mudroom. We are greeted by bags of garden soil everywhere and pots of flowers. "Yellow carnations," Mrs. Paglio says. She doesn't move for several seconds, just stares at the flowers at her feet, then shifts and startles again when she sees me. "Cal!" She reaches up to squeeze my arm and shakes her head. "There you are." A clump of dirt falls out of my hair onto a throw rug.

The house smells like peaches and vinegar. A large portrait hangs in the hallway outside the mudroom—a man with a moustache sits at his desk, wearing a suit and studying paperwork; behind him a woman who looks a lot like Mrs. Paglio holds out a teacup. Mom and I don't see Mr. Paglio much—Mom says he's a "workaholic"; I think this painting is a portrait of Mr. and Mrs. Paglio when they were younger.

"You give someone yellow carnations when you want to tell them your love is waning. Did you know that?" Mrs. Paglio is leaned over, rubbing the petals of one of her flowers.

"No." I try to step backward without her noticing.

"Yes, all the carnations have meaning. Most flowers. Don't ever accept a begonia bouquet." She shakes a warning finger, then disappears around a corner and returns a moment later with a box of Popsicles. Only now do I read her green smock: GARDENERD.

She hands me a Popsicle. Grape-flavored. "They're my husband's. Go ahead. You can eat it in the house." She watches me like the Popsicle is medicine and I've got to finish it in front of her, then looks down at the box in her hands and shoves it toward me. "Take them all. He doesn't deserve them. He doesn't believe in comforts anymore. Who knows what he believes in." She crosses her arms, angry suddenly. Maybe this was her mood when she threw the dirt.

I am tempted to tell her that hers is not the only family having trouble on the block, but she stops me with a little gasp as we pass through the front door. Her driveway is covered in clumps of dirt. The clod that hit me was one of many. "I'll have nothing left if I keep this up," she says. She's looking right past me, toward the water, like I'm not even there. "I was trying to beautify my little corner of the world." She sighs. "I just despise change."

I try to see what she's seeing—a soccer game tearing up the playing field's grass?—but the only change I can make out is the orange van with the flat tire and the Illinois plates across the street. And I don't know Mrs. Paglio well enough to say "I'm worried about them too."

Jeanne Ann

Mom comes back from wherever the heck she goes in the morning, makes herself some instant coffee, and invites me to join her in our "primo" seats for the "afternoon feature." Her words.

We sit with our backs against the Carrot's front tire to watch the Bumblebee Seaside Summer Camp march across the ball fields. They surface like ants after lunch each day to play capture the flag in the area near the public bathrooms. There are only two counselors for twenty kids—all dressed in yellow-and-black T-shirts, a buzzing mob of Charlie Browns. Lots of shrill whistles and shouts to "stay inside the cones!" One camper—six or seven, high socks, mop top, finger up the nose—is trouble. Mom's started calling him "Bad Chuck."

Bad Chuck starts the game by kicking over the orange cones. Then he tiptoes beyond them, and, eyebrows up, sees which counselor he can get to chase him. "A delinquent in training," Mom says. She would know. I've heard bits and pieces about her checkered past. Emphasis on *past*.

Today, neither counselor takes the bait. Bad Chuck punches his hips and sets off running—smirking like a maniac. He's past the hot dog cart I've been ogling and half-way to the water before either counselor notices. Then he's on the pier, pushing over rental bikes, including one holding a shocked tourist.

"Smug little tyrant," I say, throwing down my book, standing. "Someone needs to wipe the grin off that kid's face."

"Go get'm, tiger," Mom mumbles into her coffee mug, smiling. She likes this Bumblebee Camp routine.

We've been here four days, staring out to sea like a golden egg is going to roll out of the waves and land at our feet. Mom disappears for hours to do who knows what, leaving me with my books, ten bucks for food, and an order to lock the doors. I'm so sick of the four walls plus lid. I could go with her—but it's a city. Not a petting zoo. I know what's out there. And vacation is over. Time to get a job and a real bed. It was fine to sleep in the van on the way across the country. That *was* a vacation. But not anymore. Mom's got a friend we can stay with—in an actual building—and I want to be there already.

She hands me half of a ten-dollar roast beef sandwich she picked up on her ramblings today and smiles. "Nothing to take care of but our backsides," she sighs.

"A sandwich won't enroll me in school," I say.

"September is only two and a half months away," I say.

I crane for a view of the vans behind ours, all still and quiet. Too quiet. Did they drop out of seventh grade? Is that why they're stuck out here?

"Crapinade," I mutter. It's Mom's phrase. A favorite—like, "If life gives you lemons, make lemonade." I adopted it about forty-eight hours after we got here.

Mom calls someone who scratches at the same worry, over and over, a "grinder." I am definitely grinding. But Labor Day is when school starts in Chicago. It's gotta start around the same time here. And I'm pretty sure I can't go without an address. I know I can't check out a library book without one.

"Try to enjoy yourself, kid." Mom chews on a corner of sandwich, looking freakishly satisfied.

She's too happy to notice I'm not.

Bad Chuck clips a guy taking a picture of an ice cream truck.

"Enough already!" This I yell at Bad Chuck *and* Mom. I start running.

Cal

I'M IN THE DRIVEWAY PATCHING BIKE TIRES WHEN A MEGAPHONE somewhere across the street booms, "Bumblebee on the loose!"

I'm supposed to be cleaning out the garage. Mom's specific order was to weed through the clothes bins and keep an eye out for an old bomber jacket—some ex-boyfriend's parting gift—that she wants me to have. It'll give me a "new perspective on myself," she says.

I've chosen bike repair in the driveway instead. Afterward, I'm going to feed the meters across the street.

When I stand, I can see the kid, the Bumblebee, tearing across the playing fields, running dangerously close to the water. He's just a little guy. There's somebody chasing him, but they're not catching him. Not even close.

I think of my Franklin Delano Roosevelt portrait upstairs, just completed. Four-time president. Man of the people. Hero. Bow tie wearer. He wouldn't be stopped by a mother who said "Don't leave the garage until you've got something to show for it." He would gather up his crutches and catch the kid.

I grab Mom's bike. It's two sizes too small but the first one I see. I'm practically kneeing myself in the face as I pedal across the street, dodge picnickers, and angle to cut the kid off.

He's cheetah-fast, darting in one direction, then another, a blur of yellow and black. The quarters for the meters jangle in my pockets. The bike doesn't give me much advantage in the bumpy grass. "Hey!" I abandon it and begin to run. This isn't much better. I come within an inch of the kid, reach out, catch only air. He turns long enough to flash a smile. Ew. He's missing his front teeth.

"Stop!" I hear someone else yell. Can't tell from which direction. No wonder no one's caught this kid.

The sweat in my eyes has started to sting. This is not how I thought the chase would go. The kid's going to hurt himself.

I swerve right just as he brakes left, hard, and steps on a picnicker's hand. "Hey!" the guy shouts.

Then we're back out in the open green.

"You're it!" the kid whoops over his shoulder at me.

It?

What?

Jeanne Ann

I'M RUNNING. I'M REACHING. I'M GONNA GET THE LITTLE punk—but then the weirdest thing: A hand shoots out from near the ground—almost too quick to see—and takes the kid down.

Bad Chuck crashes to earth with an "Awww, come on!" and, half a second later, a brown streak flies through the air and lands like a bundle of sticks on top of him.

I hear "Ow!" then: "Gotcha!"

Time slows as I'm falling. Someone's foot has caught mine and—like a bowling pin—whacked me sideways onto the heap.

I land on a leg. Not sure whose.

Something wriggles under me. "Hey!"

My shin is screaming, but I silently peel off the pileup and limp a quick step back. The bundle of sticks—a kid about my age who didn't consult a mirror before he left the house (brown pants, shirt, socks, *and* sneakers)—sits up. He's got Bad Chuck pinned under his butt.

"He tripped me! He tripped me!" Chuck hollers.

The boy on top of Chuck rises, keeping one foot on the

ground, the other on the kid's chest. He brushes aside his sweaty blond bangs, but they just flop back over his eyes. "I didn't trip you."

"Whoa. You're tall." Bad Chuck gapes at him. "Like a giraffe!" He sounds gravelly.

"Very original. You're short," the bundle of sticks says. "Like a broken crayon."

"You're a menace to society," I add, noting the grass stains on my knees. Those aren't coming out with wet wipes and elbow grease.

Bad Chuck bends a smirk into a grimace. "Am not. *He* is. He tripped me."

We follow Bad Chuck's pointer finger: A few feet off to the right, an old guy sits crisscross-applesauce in a lawn chair, whistling. His eyes are closed and his hands—cupping his knees a second ago—have reached up to scratch his beard. It's more like fur than a beard, really—across his cheeks, around his eyes, down his neck all the way to the top of a tie-dye T-shirt that reads JENIUS. He peeks open an eye and quickly closes it. I think he's . . . homeless.

"You dirty rat." A teenager in an oversized Bumblebee shirt jogs over, swinging a megaphone, pigtails poking from under her baseball cap. Bad Chuck's smile grows when he sees her. "You bilious creature born of the sea muck!" she bellows into her megaphone. "Thank you, Sea Pirates"— she looks from me to the bundle of sticks—"for capturing him. Now he's going to walk the plank." She's really mixing her metaphors, but Bad Chuck cheers. The counselor lowers the megaphone and leans toward me. "We usually let him run till he passes out from exhaustion, but he *usually* stays inside the cones." She pats Bad Chuck on the head, then squats beside him. "Ready?"

Bad Chuck sticks his tongue out at the bearded man who tripped him, then at us, then follows his counselor, rolling away like a commando evading sniper fire.

"So I chased him for nothing." Even slouched, the bundle of sticks is really tall. Maybe six feet. My head would hit his armpit. *A rail, like Oscar Wilde*, my librarian, Mrs. Jablonsky, would say if she were here; she knows all the famous authors' heights. When we're settled, when I have something good to say, I'm going to write Mrs. J a letter.

The bundle of sticks turns toward me, finally brushing aside enough bangs. He stands a little funny, sort of sideways, like he'd rather not face me straight on. He's got deep-set eyes, wide, that he blinks slowly. There's something about the way he looks at me—studies me ear to ear, forehead to chin—I think he's memorizing my face.

"I thought *you* were a counselor," I say, noting his bow tie.

"Me? Nah. I'm nobody."

A gust of foggy air blows me a little backward as it sweeps in from the water. "Me too."

From: Chicago Public Library, Sulzer Branch

Re. Notice of Overdue Books

Date: June 5

To: Jeanne Ann Fellows, 798 W. Wilson, Chicago, IL 60622

This is a notice to inform you that the following books, checked out on May 8, are overdue:

Mrs. Frisby and the Rats of NIMH

Frankenstein

El Deafo

Oliver Twist

Nooks & Crannies

The Lion, the Witch and the Wardrobe

The Golden Compass

The Night Diary

Hatchet

Dr. Jekyll and Mr. Hyde

The Lottery

The Phantom Tollbooth

The War That Saved My Life

The Wolves of Willoughby Chase

Roll of Thunder, Hear My Cry

A Long Way from Chicago

One Crazy Summer

The BFG

Howl's Moving Castle

When You Reach Me

Pippi Longstocking

Swallows and Amazons

The Little Princess

Born Free

Ballet Shoes

The Penderwicks

The Saturdays

Brown Girl Dreaming

101 Dalmatians

From the Mixed-Up Files of Mrs. Basil E. Frankweiler

Merci Suárez Changes Gears

Redwall

The Railway Children

Adventures of Huckleberry Finn   The Way Things Work

A Little History of the World   Finance for Dummies

Zen and the Art of Motorcycle
Maintenance

———————————————————————

Your fine is 25 cents a book, per day, or $9.50 total.
If the books are not returned within 8 weeks, you will
be fined for their entire value. Please call this branch
library if you cannot locate the missing items or if you
need to renew. Thank you, The Chicago Librarians

Jeanne Ann,

I was almost happy to see this overdue notice for you and pulled
it out of the sorter so I could add a personal touch. Where have
you been? I don't think you've ever missed an entire week before,
or even a day . . . And, records show, this is your first overdue
notice. What?! . . . Meanwhile, the place is coming apart at the
seams without you. My candy bowl is overflowing. I've got no one
to review the new releases. And the Help Desk Ladies are arguing
about the ideal temperature in the stacks again; we always
count on you to break that tie. I hope you don't have a summer
cold. Those are the worst. Remember when you raked through the
library archives for ancient "common cold" remedies and found
some? Nobody else would think to look, Jeanne Ann, nobody.

—Alphabetical Love, Marilyn Jablonsky (who's considering reading
the entire Stephen King canon, despite my fear of the dark, and
needs your thoughts on this delicate matter)

Cal

It's *her* van. The van at the corner. The van at the front.

I raise Mom's opera glasses and thumb the focus till the blurry smudge—parked on the street below—sharpens. Then I flip to a blank page and reach for a pencil, a deep shader. The streetlamp helps—night shadows are the toughest.

I'm finally getting to the detail work. It's an orange Chevrolet Astro with a "Land of Lincoln" license plate, a giant outline of a happy face painted in black on the roof, and a Chicago Bears decal on the front left bumper. There are two occupants: the driver, who's built like a refrigerator and owns three army fatigue tank tops (or hasn't changed clothes since she arrived), and the passenger—twelve? daughter?—who scowls so hard, it's like its own energy source—I can see it in the dark.

That's the girl. From earlier. Shiny brown curls, snarled in places. A gray-green streak down the front of her overalls that I'd rather not think about. Royal chin. If that chin knows it's living in a van, it's showing no signs. It's a high-on-a-hill-looking-down-at-all-of-us kind of chin.

But they've parked in the absolute worst place—at the front of the vans-in-residence line, closest to the intersection.

By "in residence," I mean that these people are living in their vehicles. Sleeping, eating, fighting, watching TV, suntanning, admiring the bay view, hanging their clothes to dry on fenders. They use the public restroom in the adjacent playing fields for all their ... um, private business.

The orange van is in the spot the police always tow. If she were just one spot back—where the guy in the red van is now—that would make all the difference.

I squeeze my eyes shut.

If she doesn't move, it could happen.

While I'm sitting here, even.

Again.

My guts give a little kick. She needs to find a new spot.

I open my eyes. I scan the street for police cruisers, but they must be towing in another part of town. The night's quiet. Just streetlamps, swishing trees, and a deep darkness where the bay is. Everyone's inside.

I should turn off my lights, put down the spyglasses, get into bed.

... I've never seen a *girl*-in-residence. Only grown-ups.

2,138 miles between Chicago and here. I looked it up.

She's a long way from home. If she has one.

Jeanne Ann

One a.m. shadows are only slightly less creepy than twelve a.m. shadows.

Mom's beside me in her sleeping bag, mumbling insults at the passing cars. They're louder than ever tonight—at least it seems that way. "Mufflers, you idiots." I take it as a good sign that she's having trouble sleeping too. Finally. This is our fifth night.

The inflatable mattress beneath me sighs out its air.

I remember falling asleep to the sound of water lapping against rock. And—connected in a straight line to that thought is this one:

We are in San Francisco. And we are not going back.

I sit up and squint at the dark. I can just make out the frame of our bookshelf beside me.

Something appropriately bleak tonight. *Dracula? The Shining?*

I turn on the flashlight that lives in my sleeping bag full-time. *Short Order,* one of Mom's cookbooks, stares back at me from the shelf; pancakes slathered in syrup.

I hop the sleeping bag to the front seat. If I'm lucky, I'll find a stale cracker jammed between the front seat and seat belt clip. Mom's between shopping runs.

A truck rumbles by, a four-hundred-wheeler by the sound

of it. It sends shudders through the van. I hear a sniffle and then Mom's sleeping bag unzips.

"Bathroom," she announces. "Keep the doors locked," and she's up and out before I can say *Wait!*, slamming the door behind her.

I pull aside the window curtains to watch her go. She lumbers from the sidewalk to the grassy field, and on into blackness.

"Crapinade," I mutter.

Of all the places we could've parked, Mom had to choose the *actual* end of the road. Where dry land stops. This family is not light on symbolism.

I wipe the window where I've breathed on it—then move to Mom's side of the van, stepping over our jerry-rigged cooktop—a battery-powered toaster, formerly the cupholder thing between the seats—and flop into the driver's seat. This view is better. It's of houses, mostly. A line of giants that goes for at least a mile. They're bigger somehow in the middle of the night than they are in the day. Each has a straight-on view of the water. There's a square one, like a giant glass Rubik's Cube—right across the street. And next to it, a light green house, stacked like a fancy cake. It's got a driveway lined with flower pots that looks like a hotel entrance—a car can enter from two directions—and an actual working fountain in the middle, lit from below.

In a house the size of those, there's gotta be a spare bedroom . . . maybe a bathroom nobody uses . . . white towels that smell like flowers . . . fruit bowls filled with cherries, ovens that don't leak black gunk like roof tar . . .

Mom returns, slips back into her bag.

"You okay?" she asks before she sets her head down. She reaches up and squeezes my arm.

No. "Yeah." I want to tell her that everything feels more real at night, that her grand plan, our new life, is a box of rotten teeth. But I know I have to give it a chance, and this, the van, isn't forever.

I fall back into the seat, turn off the flashlight.

It's just camping . . . in a van . . . in the middle of the city . . . We won't park here forever. We'll move into an apartment as soon as Mom gets a job. I'll enroll in school. Everything is going to be fine. The van is perfectly safe for now. Mom is reliable. Mom has a plan.

I will hug my book—*Dracula*—and repeat these thoughts until I fall back to sleep.

I shut my eyes. I listen to Mom breathe.

There.

There.

Drifting off . . .

HONKKKKKKKKKKKK! Screeeeeeech!

My lids snap open and my heart jumps from one side of my chest to the other.

The angry cars move on. *Swooooosh.* Then silence.

It's just camping . . . in a van . . . in the middle of the city . . . It's just camping . . . in a van . . . in the middle of the city . . . It's just camping... in a van... in the middle of the city... without a campfire... or a plan to go home.

It's like I'm in a game of musical chairs and I can't find a seat when the music stops. We lived in Chicago, we bought a van, and beelined west, we ate popcorn at the Corn Palace, we counted 422 of 11,623 pipes in the Mormon Tabernacle organ, we wolf-howled at the resting place of Jack London, we sighed at the Golden Gate Bridge. And then we yanked up the hand brake.

It was sorta fun until the music stopped.

Now I wish Mom would squeeze my arm again.

"I'll make some calls tomorrow," she whispers instead.

I wait for a flood of relief, but it's just a drip, a steady drip. I'll take it.

I settle my eyes on the homes across the street. To them, looking down, we're just a shadowy crease, like in the fold of my book. Everything that matters is off to the sides of us—the water and bridge out my window, the mansions and hills out Mom's. We're in the no-place place.

Cal

Rebeautify the Marina!
Demand the removal of curb-side squatters—vans, RVs,
ne'er-do-wells—who mar our breathtaking view for months at
a time. Join our monthly meeting at 200 Marina Blvd. on June
21, 5 p.m., to discuss PERMANENT eviction strategies.
☺ Snacks provided. ☺
—The Marina Beautification Committee

The flier is at the top of the morning mail stack, printed on bright blue paper. I crumple it up, then reconsider and flatten it back out. Two hundred Marina Boulevard is right next door—the Paglios' house. I try to picture Mrs. Paglio with her wedge hair and GARDENERD smock and purple Popsicles writing this. I don't know her that well, but I can't really see it. On the other hand, she *was* throwing a lot of dirt around . . .

Jeanne Ann

It's time to go, vans, RVs, and curb-side squatters.
You've overstayed your welcome.
Authorities have been notified.

—The Marina Beautification Committee

I find this flier tucked under our windshield wiper blade with a twenty-dollar bill. I guess this is San Francisco's version of "Welcome to the neighborhood."

Cal

It's a little early for the doorbell to be ringing—seven thirty—and when I open it, no one is there.

Instead, I find a five-dollar bill sticking out from under our doormat and a note from Mrs. Paglio with instructions. I'm supposed to take a pot of pink rhododendrons from outside her mudroom and deposit them directly across the street. "Directly" is underlined twice. That would put them right between the orange van and the red one behind it.

Flowers for the vans she wants removed?

I walk the pot across the street slowly, wondering the entire way why I'm doing it. I pause outside the orange van. The girl is asleep with her head against the window glass. Hair smashed all over. That can't be comfortable. We have so many spare pillows she could borrow.

This is the closest I've been to her in two days. I want to knock on the glass but know I shouldn't.

The pot has gone cold and heavy in my hands. I set it down but don't feel right just turning back. I usually come out here with a few tea cakes from the restaurant, change for the meters, socks to give away. I'm not thinking straight.

I tuck the five-dollar bill under the girl's windshield wiper. Then I turn and see Mrs. Paglio watching—she's in her green-framed upstairs window, with her hands clasped under her chin like she's praying for something. Has she been watching the whole time? I get that heart beat-in-the-mouth feeling, like when I'm called on in class and don't know the answer but should. I glance over my shoulder, unsure. Why didn't Mrs. Paglio just make the delivery herself?

Jeanne Ann

We're turning into Popsicles on the sidewalk. I fold and unfold the five bucks I found on our windshield this morning and fantasize I've swapped it for a scalding hot cocoa topped with a skyscraper of whipped cream. The money is jammed into one of my overalls pockets along with my freezing right hand. I just want to go inside. Any minute, someone at this joint is going to yell at us to quit breathing on the windows and get lost. *I'd* yell at us if I thought Mom would listen. But she doesn't want to be hurried. On the other side of the window glass—cut to look like a porthole—cooks in white jackets shake pots, wave tongs. They appear to be vibrating. It looks warm in there. Sweaty-upper-lip warm.

"Let's go in," I say, "let's get Sam." And the keys to his apartment . . . and blast the heat to eighty degrees. We're going to stay with this Sam person till we've got enough money to pay for our own place—Mom doesn't want another day in the van any more than I do now. Thank you, thank you, thank you, God.

But she hasn't moved any closer to the door. "It's one of the best restaurants in the city," she says for the third time, rubbing my free hand between hers. Each time, she says it with a little less pep than the last. The waiters passing through the kitchen all wear camouflage baseball hats, like as uniforms. It's a little cheesy. So is the restaurant name: MEAT-HED. "You see how that guy is holding his knife?" Mom raps her knuckles on the window. "He's gonna cut off one of his fingers doing that. None of my boys would ever cut like that." By "boys" she means all the cooks she trained at O'Hara's House of Fine Eats in Chicago. Like Sam. "I can't believe he works here."

"Mom?"

"What?"

I make a shoving motion toward the door. She tucks in her lips, like I've annoyed her but she's not going get into it with me, then turns back to the kitchen window.

We're twelve blocks from the van. The wind is picking up confidence and, with it, bits of trash, blowing it around our ankles. This is San Francisco's version of summer? At this hour, back home, Chicago is so hot, you can smell the chemicals steaming out of vinyl siding.

"You see that? That big haunch?" Mom taps at the window. "That's venison. Fancy name for deer. I always wanted to serve it at O'Hara's. People woulda loved it. Deer. What's more American than deer?"

"I dunno." Hot dogs. Ketchup. Chicago. I wanna go home.

While I shiver, I try to remember this Sam guy. Cooks at O'Hara's were pretty much a revolving door. But if you were good, Mom fought for you to stay. If Mr. O'Hara threatened to fire you, Mom would stand like a shield while the Hydra spat. If you burnt a nine-dollar steak into coal dust,

Mom would take the blame. If you were kicked out of the house by your parents, she'd let you sleep on our floor. Sam must've been good.

"Nobody helped me out when I was that age, when I was a mess," Mom would tell me when I'd complain about visitors. I didn't want more people in our place. It was tight enough with just the two of us.

I think Sam stayed with us once. I think he's the guy who folded our laundry. He put my socks together into matching sets. I thought socks were meant to live mismatched at the bottom of a drawer, so his approach was memorable, even if he wasn't. I think that was Sam. To be honest, I try not to remember the good boys. They always left eventually. And every time they did, Mom would come home and say "There's been another prison break." She'd get kinda sad for a week, drag her feet across the apartment. Then she'd forget them, or pretend to.

But this Sam guy, he'd sent Mom a letter after he'd gone. Blue envelope, blue stationery—postmarked San Francisco. This is the paper falling apart in her back pocket. Mom has never read it to me, but I've gotten the gist from her since we've been parked: It's raining kitchen jobs in San Francisco . . . seven days a week; the sun never stops shining and everybody's smiling; slay the nine-headed snake and come on out.

"Mom." I want to point out that it's five p.m., June, and the sun is *not* shining. I can't feel my right pinky toe.

She folds her arms across her chest, deciding something. "Sam must be in the walk-in fridge." She doesn't see him through the porthole. She takes a step toward the door. Thank you, god of small merciful acts. This, I've decided, marks the real beginning of our time here, a new Day #1. Because of you, Sam, I will never have to use an ice-cold cement toilet at six o'clock in the morning or fall asleep an inch from a fire-truck siren. I promise to remember your name.

"That kid loved to take breaks in the walk-in fridge," Mom says, leaning closer to the porthole glass to make sure she's not missing anything. "He runs hot, like a lava monster."

"Uh-huh." I am rocking foot to foot, rubbing my arms. This whole town is like a walk-in refrigerator.

"Okay. Okay." She yanks open the front door. "This is gonna be great. He's never gonna believe I made the move."

She's gone for less than two minutes. "His day off," she says, blowing back through the doors. She stands close to me, closer than she needs to.

"I thought you said he works seven days a week."

"Musta got one off," she says. "Lucky him." Which by the inverse property means: unlucky us.

Cal

"I need you, Cal!" Mom shakes me awake.

A counter-person has quit at the restaurant, she says—and I'm needed to fill in . . . for the rest of the summer.

A smock lands on my head. Then a jacket I've never seen before. I think it's leather. We don't even believe in leather.

Mom's restaurant—Greenery—is across the street, down a block. We're in the intersection before I fully digest what Mom's said: "The rest of the summer." I slow my pace and fall in step behind her.

I think this is more "consequences."

The trees by the water slap their limbs as the wind picks up. I glance at the line of vans, cold and quiet. Does Mom even see them? Does she know there's a bearded guy in the red van? He lies in the sun when it's warm and gets lots of visitors. Or the couple in the RV at the end of the block? I'm pretty sure they're students—they're always at a picnic table with a stack of highlighter pens and a textbook between them.

I stop for a second at the orange van. It's sunk deeper into its flat tire. I reach out to touch the worn rubber but am clipped by a runner dashing by. There's a race on—there's always a race on—and the area is swarming with athletes who'd prefer the rest of us get our soft bodies out of their way.

Inside Greenery, sun is blasting through skylights, making

all the silverware shine. The counter-staff is stocking pastries and waking up the espresso machine. It doesn't look like we're short a server. I point this out to Mom.

"This'll be good for you. Just a few mornings a week. You'll stay busy. New scenery, I mean, a new perspective—from behind the counter. I'll get you a cell phone so you can reach me . . . or anyone."

She's behind me now, pushing. I turn to face her.

"I don't want a cell phone." She knows this. I'm the one who convinced her to put up tasteful PHONE-FREE ZONE signs in the restaurant. Not that it helped. The phones still creep out of purses and pockets, like spiders, ruining the main reason a person comes to a restaurant—to notice everything with all the senses. Mom caved to customer pressure recently and took the signs down. She said, "We should stop fighting the modern way of the world." So I adopted the color beige. Why bother with bright colors if no one sees anyone anyway? Now I just blend in. I put color into my portraits instead. And I put my portraits where a person can't look away. Or I was trying to.

Mom strides to the counter, rubbing clear a smudge on the display case with the edge of her sleeve. This is the side of the restaurant that sells to-go items for people who don't want a sit-down meal in the main dining room. Usually, I admire the case—a little thatch village of sugar and fat—and compliment its brilliant creator—Mom—but not this morning.

I've only worked behind the Greenery counter once before, and the staff and I agreed we should never try it again.

"Maybe you'll see an old friend come through," Mom says, brushing my bangs out of my eyes, "or make a new one." We stop to stare at each other. We have the same eyes, blue-gray with long, blond eyelashes that Mom says make us look a little dopey.

"Maybe." Or maybe I'll turn into a dragon and spit hot whipped cream out of my nose.

Mom reaches one hand up to my shoulder and beckons Mac over with the other. Mac is our head chef, Greenery's unlicensed plumber, and my surrogate aunt. She's got pink hair and lipstick and clogs to match (against the all-green Greenery dress code). When she's annoyed—which she must be now—she stands with her legs wide, hands on hips, like she's about to demonstrate a wrestling move.

If Mac's a bowling ball, Mom's a marble.

Mac took charge of Greenery when I was nine months old, approximately eleven years ago. Instead of cooking, Mom handles "diplomatic matters" now—training servers, making sure farmers give us their best stuff, guiding patrons by the elbow to the tables they love best. She also passes through the kitchen a few times a day, sniffing and tsk-ing and pointing out things she'd do differently if she were still Greenery's head chef.

"What's this doing in here?" Mom mutters to no one in particular now, removing a tray of powdered snickerdoodles from the case. "These get stale quicker inside the case." Mac watches, shaking her head and letting her eyes drift up to the ceiling. I think she wishes Mom would take up a hobby in Patagonia or Alaska or Timbuktu.

With her free hand, Mom presses me forward. "Here he is!" She sets down the tray of snickerdoodles and laces one arm through Mac's, releasing mine. Mom leads her to the very end of the counter to conference in private. They're only two feet away.

"Is this really necessary, Lizzie?" Mac mutters, looking over Mom's head and making a funny gag face at me. I guess they discussed this in advance.

"New scenery will be good for him," Mom says.

"I can hear you!" I shout. And it's not new scenery!

Mom tucks in her lips, like she's trying hard not to reply. She nudges Mac toward me, or tries to. "I'm going to let Mac address that."

Mac comes to stand by me. "I'm so confused," she leans close to whisper, scratching her pink head. "You're a twelve-year-old boy. She's your neurotic mother. You're supposed to be pushing *her* away, not the other way around." I halfway shrug. "We'll make this good," she says, "somehow. And, if not, there's free brownies."

I jam a hand into my pants pocket and feel the seam rip. I thought this couldn't get worse, but it has. I love my mom. I don't want her to take up a hobby in Alaska. But she's got this all wrong.

Jeanne Ann

"What're you doing?"

The tall kid with the floppy hair from the other day is squatted on the sidewalk near our front fender, a leather bomber jacket over his head like he'd rather not be seen, and a piece of chalk in each hand.

"Um." He swallows, looking up. Except for the jacket and bow tie, he's dressed in brown again. His skinny arms and legs really do look like a bundle of sticks.

I'm hanging out the van's open window above him. Mom's gone already, doing her thing. The van's doors are locked. Usually, the windows are up. But I don't think this kid is a risk.

"Decorating?" he says. He looks unsure. He slides the jacket off his head.

"At seven in the morning?" I smell breakfast cooking nearby—bacon. It's like Chicago has come to San Francisco in the form of a pig.

"I was on my way to . . ." He gestures to someplace down the road. "And the sidewalk looked"—he remains crouched as he shoves chunks of chalk into his pockets—"sad."

I can't argue with this. The sidewalk is littered with half-gnawed chicken bones, empty bottles of Gatorade, Popsicle sticks, and trash I can't even identify. I push open the passenger-side door and stand beside him. We study his work. He's managed to swerve his chalk lines around the garbage. Impressive. But also super *weird*.

"Streets are cleaner in Chicago," I volunteer.

"Are they?" He stands. "There're supposed to be great restaurants in Chicago . . . My mom says it's too cold for vegetarians, though. We're vegetarians."

I raise my eyebrows. *Weirder.*

"That's a lot of butterflies." I point to the many sets of orange-and-purple chalk wings, running from our van to halfway down the block. He must've been here, drawing, for an hour.

He shifts from foot to foot, considering his work. "They're not butterflies. They're arrows . . . with wings." He scuffs at one with a shoe.

"Oh."

He looks down at himself, wipes his hands on his jacket, sneaks one last look at me, and skulks in the direction of his arrows, then doubles back the other way. He drops a quarter in our meter as he passes.

Super, super weird.

Cal

I march back to the house.

This can't go on. I can't sell pastries at Greenery. I have more important work to do.

I'd tell Mom right now that she needs to put things back the way they were—if her eyes weren't closed and her head weren't resting against the living room couch like that. It's her "everything hurts" pose, usually the result of filling in as late-shift dinner maître d'. Her frizzed-out hair looks like it was rubbed against a balloon.

I hesitate, then sit. Maybe we could just watch a Julia Child episode this morning and—PING! Her eyelids flip up and in one swift motion she's grabbed my chalk-covered hand and slid off the couch to kneel at my feet, pulling her sweater tighter around her shoulders. Like she knows I didn't show up for work. Like it's time for a reckoning.

I stare at her scalp a second too long; she has gray hairs sprouting, which has nothing to do with anything, except when you're a portraitist you notice these things.

"Just remember I love you and that what I'm about to say is not another consequence," she says, glancing at a piece of paper, then standing.

Wait. This was going to be my turn to lecture *her*. "Mom—"

"I cannot rewind the tape," she says, glancing at her paper

again. "Yesterday, you were in diapers. Today, you're almost in seventh grade and pee with the door closed. Don't make that face, Cal. This is hard. Let me get it out." She places the paper in her mouth for a second and laces and unlaces her fingers. She takes it out again and says, "I know how to raise a restaurant. I'm less sure about a boy. I've kept you close, but I haven't really steered. And that worked for a while, but you've lashed out"—she flings out her hand to illustrate—"and now things have to change."

"Lashed? No, I . . ."

"A single mom can't be expected to get everything right," she continues. "What I'm trying to do is a quick correction. The Greenery job, this whole summer, it's going to be a dose of"—she sweeps her arm over her head so hard, I think it's going to swing back and whack her in the face—"real life, out there, with me steering but not hovering. So you can find your feet without me tripping you. You've got to stick with the program. No skipping work."

"Mom."

But she keeps going. I hear "earn your own keep" and "road to manhood" and "color swaps" and "making friends again" and "the school of hard knocks." The lecture is several minutes along when I realize she means an *actual* school.

She's transferring me out of Point Academy.

There's more, but I can't hear with all the internal screaming.

Jeanne Ann

Mom is watching me eat. She keeps sliding bits of her meal onto my plate, then nudging the bits closer to me, so that I know that *she* knows I haven't eaten them yet. "Mom."

"What?"

"Aren't you hungry?"

She shrugs. "You eat."

She's brought us to a different restaurant, a tiny one, squeezed between a used-book store and a grocery selling bruised fruit. They make these fried bean balls called falafel here. When we ate out in Chicago, which wasn't often, it was usually this. Cheap and filling. It's the first meal we've eaten outside the van since we got to San Francisco eight days ago. The windows look steamed. Grease coats the walls. Just like joints we went to in Chicago. "Trust me, this'll be good," Mom said when we walked in.

Trust me, you'll love San Francisco. Trust me, it's all gonna work out. Trust me, our future is West. Trust me, trust me, trust me.

Our food came a few minutes ago, mounded on paper plates. It's yummy. Not that it matters. I'd eat salty dirt. The walk here nearly killed me. Hills, hills, hills, hills, hills. They're everywhere—one after the other, like a kick-line of sleeping volcanoes. They start climbing almost immediately after you get beyond the block of mansions across the street from the vans and RVs. A person without enough money to take a bus or trolley is either rolling down one hill or crawling up another. I need food. *More* food.

While I stuff myself, the chef marches over with extra sauce and stares at Mom. We're not much to look at on a good day—neither of us has ever bothered much with hair or makeup or socks for that matter—and after almost two weeks in the van, well . . . *crapinade.* Is he going to kick us out?

"I think you have spent time in kitchens," the chef says, pointing at one of several scars on Mom's arms. "You suffered so others could eat." He pulls up his food-stained sleeves to show us his burn scars. I relax. A little. Mom's response—a tenth of a smile—would barely register under a microscope. She has him beat—twice as many scars—and that's just on her arms. A weird kind of victory, but we'll take it.

He offers us a honey-and-nuts thing called baklava—free—on his next pass. I wait for Mom to push it back toward him. Mom refused a birthday cake from the Chicago librarians once—called it "charity we didn't need"—but she surprises me now and slides the baklava to the center of our table. I eat my half fast, before she can change her mind. Mom watches, then skids her chair back from the table, grabs a book from her purse, and dumps it in my lap. I've never seen it before. It's called *Eating Your Way*

Through the Golden Gates. I've flipped through thinner encyclopedias.

"You've dog-eared half the book," I say. Mrs. Jablonsky does *not* approve of dog-earing. She does not approve of gum-chewing or self-help books by movie stars either. "So many vegetarian restaurants. Doesn't anyone like salami in this town?" I think of that boy I keep seeing, with the chalk and the owl eyes hiding behind all that hair. "Are there fewer vegetarians in Chicago because of the cold?"

Mom looks at me like I'm cracked, then slides the second half of the baklava toward me. "Really?" I hold it up to my mouth to give her a chance to change her mind.

She nods, then grabs my wrist before I can pop in the last bite. "I gotta ask a favor, kid."

Her face goes kinda stony.

"Okay," I say.

She lets go of my wrist. "I need to find a job."

"Okay." This is not exactly breaking news. It's not like we're waiting on a trust fund.

"And I need you to be patient while I look."

When am I ever not patient?

"I don't know people here," she says. "It might take a while."

"You know that guy Sam," I point out.

"Yeah." She looks down at her book. "Right. I do." She fans the pages. "The thing is, I already interviewed at a few places, and they turned me down."

"You did? They did? When?"

"Where do you think I've been going every day?" She falls back in her plastic chair, like she's spent.

I shrug. "You said you were being a tourist."

She looks at me like I should know better. "I didn't want you to worry," she says, "if I didn't get one in the first couple of days."

When I just stare at her, she adds, "It doesn't matter. Look, Jeanne Ann. I need you to understand, we don't have a place to stay. Just the van."

I am suddenly, ferociously thirsty. I look past her to the exit, to the air outside the window that is in extremely short supply in here. "But what about . . . ?" My voice sounds squeaky, parched. There's not enough water on earth for the fire inside me.

"Sam won't work. He's—he's on vacation."

"For how long? How do you know? Did you go back?"

Mom pauses, twists her mouth down. "I called."

"When?"

"Found a pay phone. He says he's out, three weeks. And his roommates aren't into strangers being there without him."

"Three weeks? Mom!"

"It'll be okay. We've done fine so far. We just need to keep thinking of it as an adventure."

"I don't need any more adventure."

She gets quiet. "I know. I'm sorry."

"After he comes back, we can move in with him?" She stares at me instead of answering. Too long. "Mom?"

"Yes, if we need to."

The fire has run up my neck to my ears.

"Why didn't you call him *before* we came all this way?"

She leans forward so our faces are close. "I should've. But I didn't want to slow down. I needed to just go. If I slowed down, we'd still be there."

I feel like crying. I think I am crying. I'd rather *still be there*.

"We're low on funds," she adds, squeezing my hands. Like it's an afterthought. "So we're going to start, you know, being careful."

Now the table is wet. Now my nose is running. "Why did we splurge on this food? How much do we have left?" Did she spend the money that got tucked under our windshield wipers? I hold up my paper plate and slap it down. How many mistakes can one person make? *Crapinade*.

She doesn't answer right away, long enough for me to figure out the answer for myself: I should be as full and as happy as possible when receiving bad news.

"I budgeted for a few weeks," she finally says. "I didn't think . . . I didn't plan past that. Jeanne Ann, don't."

I have my arms pulled over my head, as if I can hide from this.

"Don't be mad. That's the favor I'm asking. Don't be too mad. Give me a little time."

That's asking a lot. That's asking so much. I've given her time already.

She leads me outside to a nearby stoop. The city's summer cold finds my bones. I hug my knees and face away from her. A group of girls with pierced noses and thigh-high boots walks past, followed by a mumbler in an old yellow raincoat and red rain boots, poking at the back side of a flip phone. Mom looks at me sideways, concerned, sits up a little straighter and tightens her ponytail. "We should wash up when we get back to the Carrot," she says. We haven't showered since Donner Pass. Donner Pass was over a week ago. I nod at her, though I don't think I will—I was going to shower in our new apartment. I was waiting to celebrate with shampoo and conditioner.

I peek at Mom. She looks pretty crushed, which must be how I look too.

"This reminds me of home . . . if I squint my eyes super tight . . . and cross them," I say, watching the city stomp by. I want to be hopeful. I want to try. The alternatives stink.

"But brighter," Mom says, patting my back, scooting closer.

"And with hills." I clench my toes.

"And without overhead trains."

A guy snapping photos of himself nearly trips over Mom's feet.

"And with . . ." I am tempted to say *prospects*, but don't. We are a jinx-accustomed family.

"Did you apply at any restaurants you liked?"

She smiles for a second.

"I liked them all." She leans closer. "They just didn't like me."

Cal

"A.R.E. Y.O.U. O.K. O.U.T. T.H.E.R.E.?"

I'm reading a book on Morse code while trying to send my first Morse message. It's a lot of flashlight work. My thumb is spasming. "A.R.E. Y.O.U. O.K. O.U.T. T.H.E.R.E.?" takes me five minutes to send.

I scan the dark outside my window. It's ten p.m. I know the girl in the van has a flashlight. I can see it moving inside. She's probably reading. During the day, if her mom's around, she's always sitting on the sidewalk, reading.

It's stupid that I thought she'd know Morse. I just *wanted* her to know it.

Di-di-dah-dit, di-dit.

A flashlight is sending back a message, but not the right flashlight. The Morse reply is coming from the van parked behind hers, the red one. The bearded guy lives in that one. He's outside his van more than any of the van-dwellers, lounging in lawn chairs, like the sidewalk and grass are his yard.

I scribble out his message in my sketchbook. It takes forever, but I translate it to "F.I.G.U.R.E. O.U.T. T.H.E. R.E.M.O.T.E. C.O.N.T.R.O.L. Y.O.U.R.S.E.L.F."

Maybe it's a riddle?

Maybe he's mentally, um, unwell.

I snap off my flashlight. Maybe I am.

JUNE 18

Jeanne Ann

Someone is knocking on the back doors of the Carrot when we return from the public bathroom this morning.

His green T-shirt reads: DILL WITH IT.

Mom and I hang back, eyeing him from a not very hidden spot at the Carrot's front fender. A thick beard threaded with gray drapes over the top half of his shirt. He sways slightly on two knobby and sunburnt knees, wiggling his toes in flip-flops. When no one answers his knock, he rests his belly—Santa XX large—against the van, cups his hands around his eyes, and peers in our window. I know this guy. His is the hand that tripped the kid from Bumblebee Camp the other week.

He knocks again, then mumbles something and looks up. He catches us staring.

I turn away, though I know it's too late.

"Oh! Thank goodness!" he shouts, and barrels forward with one arm outstretched, the other tugging an overstuffed suitcase.

Mom and I edge backward along the lip of the sidewalk.

"Sandy," he says, pointing to himself, and then to the van behind ours. "I'm your next-door neighbor." He runs back and whacks his red camper van on the hood. "Oh, hallelujah. You're home."

He brings his arm down, but his face—the little of it I can see through his beard—is still lit up. I look away. I'm embarrassed for him. But that feels wrong too.

"I saw you pull in," he says, "but I've been so busy with this event I'm, ah, catering that I just pretended it was okay to be rude for a brief spell and not introduce myself. But it wasn't okay. I can see that now."

He knocks on his skull, gently, jiggling a huge ring of keys that's dangling off a belt hook on his shorts. "What you must think of me. And now, I'm about to double down on rudeness." He stops and assesses us. "Do you have a whisk I could borrow?"

Neither of us moves.

There's something about the way he's smiling. Something . . . I look him over again. This time my eyes catch a flash of light coming from his wrist. A reflection off a watch band. Gold?

I look back at his face.

His van is a little wider and higher than ours, and the tires look new. The exterior paint hasn't rusted yet.

"I couldn't help but notice your array of cooking tools in there." He leans on The Carrot and peeks in again. "It's like a kitchen on wheels. Remarkable."

He is not exaggerating. There is a pot rack hanging from the ceiling, a knife block jammed with blades by the spare tire at the rear, and behind the driver's seat, a cardboard box overflowing with wooden spoons, spatulas, measuring

70

cups, garlic presses, smocks, mixing bowls . . . all of which Mom may or may not have lifted from O'Hara's House of Fine Eats when she marched off the job.

He lets go of his suitcase and claps his hands together. "You know, I could use a rubber spatula too. It's for a good cause."

Mom and Sandy lock eyes. He grins, she snarls.

High noon for the homeless.

I guess that's what we are now.

Cal

They're making . . . smoothies? An extension cord runs from the orange van to a blender on the table behind it. I passed them on the way to Greenery this morning.

The bearded guy in the red camper van looked to be in charge. He had the tall lady in camo washing greens—spinach, chard, parsley?—in a metal bowl. The girl was close by, reading a book in a lawn chair. The camo lady walked over a test-sip on a spoon, and the girl accepted it without looking up.

I slump across the Greenery counter, sketching the scene from memory, then set aside my pencil. I tear at an almond croissant, lay a shred on my tongue; the butter in it curdles somewhere between my mouth and my stomach.

They're all friends now?

"Cal, buddy, serve the customer his croissant." Mac bumps me with her hip as she passes by. "He'll be right with you, sir."

Do people living outside make friends faster than people living inside?

I can't imagine running an extension cord from our house to the Paglios' next door so we could make bright green smooth-ies together in their blender. I mean, we have our own blender, our own kitchen, and our own electricity. Mom would probably sniff and *tsk* anyway and point out all the ways they'd turned out wrong. It would be easier to just stay home.

Jeanne Ann

A criminal, but perhaps not a mastermind, is what I think of Sandy, while wrapping the twenty-dollar bill he gave me around my thumb and sipping my smoothie. It tastes like frozen spinach and oatmeal cut with Bit-O-Honey. He gave us twenty each for helping out. Crisp bills. Mom didn't stop him; I'm trying not to dwell on what this means.

She told me to sip mine slowly and took hers with her to get peanut butter, jelly, bread, and a can of scurvy-fighting pineapple. And then she came right back. No job search today. Yesterday she tried eight places. No dice. She sharpened her knives to murderous points afterward; she doesn't want to talk about it. I know she's trying. I know she's mad. I prefer smiling Mom, barreling through Beartooth Pass after the snow cleared. It wasn't that long ago.

I'm back in Sandy's "living room"—between the tail of the Carrot and the front of his red camper van, sitting in a lawn chair. His card table is between us.

"Is that sunset a knockout or what?" he declares, slapping a magazine against the suitcase that always seems to be right beside him. The magazine looks brand-new—probably lifted from a nearby mailbox. He's got his feet kicked up on the cooler that holds the smoothies.

The sun is streaking the sky orange sherbet. I'm reading

the part in *Cheaper by the Dozen* when twelve kids pile into the family car for a joyride, no seat belts, kids stacked on kids, and I'm feeling something in my chest, but I'm not convinced it's awe. I want eleven brothers and sisters. A huge family could not live inside a van . . .

I *will* admit this sunset tops the ones over the Holiday Inn in Uptown; no one pulled up a chair to watch those. Still, what I would give to be back in Chicago, defrosting a waffle over the radiator . . .

Sandy talks in a loud voice Mom may or may not be hearing from inside the van. Somewhere nearby someone is frying bacon. *Torture.*

"I've lived the indoor, every-day-the-same life," Sandy says, fondling the pink petals of a potted plant beside his chair. "Too many rules. Too much clutter." He grabs at the air. "This is freedom; this is the way. A life under the stars and sky. Nature's confrontation."

Anyone who has used the cement toilets in the public restrooms and still says "this is the way" has seriously lost his way.

He tells me he's a serial entrepreneur and shakes his giant key ring. I think it's more likely that he mugged a janitor. He tells me the smoothies are a "trend" investment; he tells me that the first rule of business is "buy low, sell high"; he waves to the hot dog vendor—"Bob"—who pushes past us with his cart twelve times a day, leaving a trail of salty smoky steam that smells so good, the CIA could use it to pry secrets out of prisoners; he palms a twenty from a tattooed bike messenger who lives four vans back; he raises a thumb at the man in the yellow raincoat and red boots—"beautiful day, Gus!" He tells me he plans to "pull up stakes" as soon as he can implement his "big plan"—to drive around the world with his "best mate," leaving any day.

"In the meantime, we are going to have a great time, neighbor," he says. He uses "we" like Mom and I have been absorbed into a group, his group; I think he means all the people living outside. He talks as fast as a rushing river.

"And you?" he asks, gesturing to the Carrot. He leans back in his chair.

"What?" I ask.

"Are you free?"

I laugh out loud. I think I hear Mom laughing inside the Carrot too.

Cal

The sirens wake me. I fell asleep sketching. Now I sprint out the front door and across the street. I knew this would happen. I just didn't know when.

It's nearly dark. The police have started their ticketing at the back of the line of vans, near Greenery. They're scribbling fast on clipboards and banging on windows. I'll just speak to whoever is in charge, explain that . . . this has to stop. I look down at the pavement and my feet walking in the opposite direction I've instructed them to go.

I reach the orange van. I'm standing as far back from it as I can without stepping in the wet grass.

I should've put on a sweatshirt. It's foggy, the halo kind that's impossible to draw.

From up in the house, the vans look farther away, but they are so very, very close, really. Just three stories, a pebble driveway, two lanes of asphalt, two sidewalks.

I wonder if the girl's inside. If she cannot afford an apartment, she cannot afford a ticket or a tow. When she's around, the big lady in the camo tank top sits on the curb sharpening knives and staring at the water. The girl just walks and reads . . . and reads . . . and reads. It doesn't look like vacation.

I turn back to face my house. It rises up up up into the fog. The windows are a warm, gauzy yellow, like a lighthouse.

I knock on the van's passenger door and then hear a voice. Someone is fumbling with the window crank.

"What?" It's the lady. Her face and shoulders fill the entire window. Up close, she resembles a giant, hunched vulture. But I think she's younger than my mom. Almost no wrinkles.

My tongue feels suddenly heavy.

The girl peeks out from behind her. She's got a dictionary-sized book in her hands. Her curls brush the sharp line of her jaw.

"Tickets," I choke out, pointing down the street. I sound like a street vendor. "*Parking* tickets," I cry, this time hitting an adjective that means something. "You gotta move your van. You really shouldn't park here."

"Jeanne Ann, get your head back inside!"

She has a name. Jeanne Ann.

Jeanne Ann has leaned over the vulture-faced woman and out the window so far, only her knees and feet are still inside the van. Her head nearly grazes my arm.

"I knew we shouldn't ignore those sirens," she says.

"If you go now and come back in half an hour, you'll be fine." I dig out the words. "They don't do this more than once a week. This spot gets it the worst."

The police are getting closer.

"Mom!" she shouts, sliding her upper half back into the van.

So the big lady *is* her mom.

"We're out of gas, kid; the tire's flat." Jeanne Ann's mom raises her hands up and lets them drop in surrender.

"Sometimes they tow," I insert.

"Crapinade," Jeanne Ann groans.

Crapinade!

I shove my hands in my pockets, and when I look up again, Jeanne Ann and her mom are staring at each other—one face stony and huge, the other shuffling through a dark rainbow of scowls. Neither is leaping to action.

"You live in one of the vans too?" Jeanne Ann says, turning toward me.

"No." I pivot away slightly. "I—I just see how it goes here sometimes."

She narrows her eyes. "Wait, I know you," she says. "You're the kid in brown. The sidewalk-chalk guy."

"It's beige," I mumble, not quite sure I like her descriptions but glad I'm at least sort of memorable. I look up again, just in time to see her shrink into shadow.

A hand falls on my shoulder.

"License and registration," the police officer says.

I flinch and my heart kicks up. But then I feel my feet, solid, beneath me. I breathe in—seaweed and saltwater and something sour. I stand up straighter.

This is where I'm meant to be.

Jeanne Ann

Attention vibrant residents of the Green Adjacent Area! A strategy is needed to combat the aggressive ticketing tactics employed by local police. All ideas welcome.
Meeting time: now.

—Sandy

I find the pink flier under our windshield wiper this morning and show it to Mom, who takes one look, then resumes staring at the Golden Gate Bridge. It smells like old gym clothes in here and recycled breath. Mom's got her mostly empty wallet on her lap. The parking ticket hasn't improved her mood.

Mom's wallet—full or empty—usually cues The Speech. It goes: *If you want credit cards when you're thirty-five, Jeanne Ann, don't break into a convenience store and steal soda and steaks when you're eighteen while participating in truth or dare with fellow high school dropouts. And, when you're twenty-one, don't make it worse by whacking the boss's favorite bartender with a frying pan, no matter how often he tries to kiss you. Just report him.*

Credit card companies aren't fans of felons, which is what Mom technically is. Was. They make felons check a special box on applications. Mom refuses. The past is past, she likes to say, though I don't think she believes it. If the application asked: "Are you a totally different person from the one who committed those crimes?" it would be better.

The absence of a credit card is like the absence of a thumb, Mom says. You can't grip things tightly. We lived in a crummy apartment in Chicago because of the absence of a credit card. We live in this van because of the absence of a credit card. We can't pay this new parking ticket. Missing a thumb is something you notice quick.

She must be too tired to give The Speech, which scares me a little. She's exhaling in huffs.

"You okay?" I ask.

"For sure," she says, sounding the opposite.

I note the return of dark shadows under her eyes. She had them in Chicago. She lost them on the road trip. There's a new vertical line of worry between her eyebrows too.

"Have a seat," Sandy says, pulling over his spare lawn chair. I sink low. This is better than inside but only by a hair. His living room has moved to the grass beside our vans. The air smells like bacon again.

I've brought along a book, a pen, the flier, and another peanut butter sandwich—I'm averaging two a day since our falafel feast. We've got bread again thanks to the smoothie money. I'm reading *The Outsiders*, starring Ponyboy, the gang member with a heart of gold. He would know what to do in my situation; he'd get all the greasers together and rumble till somebody felt bloody but better. I want a gang. Instead I've got:

$5.45: amount remaining in Mom's wallet
$150: cost of parking ticket
45+/-: number of days till summer is over and I'm officially a 7th-grade dropout
0: number of jobs for Mom
2: number of people who've shown up for this meeting

"Tea?" Sandy nods at a blue teapot on his table. "A kukicha blend. Not my best stuff, but it does the job. Pairs well with indignity."

"No thank you," I say.

He pats the teapot, as if I've hurt its feelings.

"Do you think they got your flier?" I say, tipping my head in the direction of the other vans and RVs.

Sandy cleans out a fingernail with a dented pocketknife, then leans back in his lawn chair to get a better view of the vehicles behind his. Several of them have cracked windshields and tinfoil radio antennae. "Swing shifts, medical exams, muscle fatigue, retirement"—he points to the vans behind me as he goes down his list; he makes my nearest neighbors sound almost normal. "Yes, I do, but, they're not a 'right now' kinda crowd."

He slices a peach into four wedges with his pocketknife.

He sees me staring. I can't help it. I now think with my stomach all day.

"How many tickets have you gotten since you moved here?" I manage to say.

Sandy laughs quietly. He's wearing a tie-dyed T-shirt that hugs his belly. It reads: I SWALLOWED A SEED AND LOOK WHAT HAPPENED.

"I could pay your way through college with the money I owe the San Francisco Municipal Transportation Agency," Sandy says.

"You never pay?"

He shakes his head.

I guess that makes sense. Why would a criminal pay his parking tickets?

"So why do you need a strategy to combat ticketing?"

He sits up straighter, pulling his suitcase close. "They don't ticket those people in the houses across the street for blocking sidewalks with their hired cars. They ticket us, and sometimes they tow us too. And when that happens, we have to fork over real cash to get our vehicles back. Hundreds of bucks to get our homes returned. It's not right. The whole city is against us. You can't park anywhere long-term. Not this block. Not any block. You must sometimes fight the principle of a thing, not just the thing itself."

Sandy pats my hand. "Relax your eyebrows. You won't get towed. I can teach you a few tricks. We'll be careful together."

We will? I don't even know this person. I pull my hand away and begin folding the flier into smaller and smaller squares, as if I can make it disappear, along with the police, our ticket, this entire month . . .

I look across the street at the houses—the glass Rubik's Cube, the green layer cake. Chicago had fancy houses too, but they weren't across the street from our creaky two-flat, looking down at us all day.

Sandy has followed my gaze. "They're ornaments that people live in."

"Yeah." I sigh. "I'd like one."

"No, you wouldn't. They're filled with stuff that will ruin your life."

"Like couches?"

"And self-timing ovens that cost six months' mortgage, and armoires from France, and TVs bigger than king-sized beds, and antique vases that can't be moved except by professionals with insurance."

"And that's bad?"

"You can't leave. You're constantly worried about your stuff—if you have enough, who has more, where to get the best. And you forget to go outside and breathe."

"The couch sounds nice."

"They're not happier, those people."

I look at the limp peanut butter sandwich in my hands and at Sandy and his peach. How would he know if they're happier? "That's baloney," I say; it's a favorite expression of Mrs. Jablonsky's.

I take a bite of the sandwich, gag a little, then swallow. I wish this sandwich *were* baloney.

By the time I look up again, Sandy has disappeared into his camper van. The meeting attendance has now shrunk to one. I push up out of the lawn chair and am, in four steps, at the door of the Carrot.

"Wait, wait," Sandy calls from his passenger window. He's got a bulging plastic bag in his hand and shakes it. "For you."

I trudge back to him. He has exited and emptied the bag's contents into a lawn chair.

Four peaches.

One half loaf of bread.

Two smocks.

One bag of brown dirt marked TEA. IMPORTED.

"You'll need the smocks Sunday," Sandy says.

"We will?" Sunday is six days away.

"Six a.m. Be up. Be dressed. Be limber."

"For what?"

Sandy disappears into his van again and returns to the window with something wrapped in waxed paper. "You'll need some cheese with that." He points to the loot he's already given me. "It's sheep's cheese, from Spain. Smells like farts, tastes great." He tosses it onto the pile in the lawn chair. "And the tea is just to get you acquainted.

We can discuss its unique qualities after you've tried it."

I hesitate, then blurt, "Is it legal, the thing Sunday?"

He brushes the question aside with a hand. "Just be ready. I'll pay you each twenty dollars. Easy-peasy."

I look down at my chair full of food and back to his face. I don't understand our neighbor. Every crease and wrinkle in his hairy grin hides a story, I think.

I grab a peach from the pile and rub it against my shirt, then look back at the Carrot to make sure Mom isn't watching.

She is, though. Hunched in the window. I quickly set the peach down in the chair. I watch Mom pull in a big breath and hold it. Then she nods—the slightest downward bow—and turns away.

I look back to the peach, grab it.

Now: Eat or save, eat or save?

Oh ha. I take a bite.

Cal

"Visitor!" the bearded guy shouts as Jeanne Ann exits the van.

I stand up from the curb so fast, my backpack slips off my lap.

Jeanne Ann pauses in the doorway, sniffing the cold morning. Her cheeks are still puffy with sleep.

"No thank you," she says in my general direction, hugging a book.

The bearded guy grabs the sides of his lawn chair and stills his bouncing legs. "Hey, it's sweet. An admirer," he says to her, a bit more adamant than I expect. This is the closest I've ever gotten to him. He's shaped sort of like a butternut squash. His clothes are rumpled but not dirty, and he smells more like spearmint than trash. The stuff that looks like dirt from my window is just lots and lots of untamed beard. Even his voice surprises me—it's deep and kinda musical, like someone who reads the news on the radio.

I throw the backpack over my shoulder, stick my hand out toward Jeanne Ann, wonder if it's too formal, and shove it in my pants pocket. "I'm, I mean, my name is Cal."

She half meets my eye, half looks right past me.

"Go home. Please, go home." Her voice cracks, tired.

I point across the street. "I was just there. That's my window."

It feels like a lot to reveal. I glance at the bearded guy again, worried. He's studying his teacup, like there's a mystery to solve at the bottom. I try to inspect his face without staring. I can't remember exactly how long he's been out here. But he's become familiar, a real neighbor.

Jeanne Ann mutters something. It sounds like: "Rubik's Cube."

I pull my sketchbook out from my back pocket and tap it against my thigh. "I was just . . . I wanted to make sure you were . . . after the ticket . . ." My tongue feels like a flopping fish in my mouth. I can't make it work.

She replies with her nuclear scowl.

"No thank you," she says, firm and flat.

I look out to the bay for assistance. It shouts back: *If nothing else, tell her she has to move the van!*

She's crossed her arms.

"I brought chocolate." I reach back into my bag and pull out two bars. Thick ones. Made by hand. Mom serves this chocolate in the restaurant. "And milk."

Off to the side, the bearded guy flaps his arms. "First rule of business," he says, "*accept freebies*. Let the boy swoop in, Jeanne Ann. Take the chocolate, take a walk!"

Jeanne Ann

"THE CHOCOLATE," I SAY WHEN WE SIT DOWN, SHOVING OUT a hand.

I eat half the bar in about thirty seconds, only remembering to keep an eye out for Mom after I've let out a satisfied moan. I have a feeling I'm going to regret this. I know Mom would not approve. Food from Sandy? Maybe. Food from this kid? No.

We're sitting at a picnic table down the shore from the van—there's nothing between us and the water but a square of cement, a pile of rocks mixed with sand, and a seagull pecking at a shell. The sun is trying to find its way through the fog.

Cal's flipping through his sketchbook, which allows me to stare at him. He's got a decent face. I guess. Wide, wet eyes. With this far-off worried kinda stare—like he's working out a big problem in his head. But his expression changes the minute he picks up the pencil. Everything smooths out. This must be the real him, the one that forgets I'm here.

"So," I say. "Why are you everywhere I am?"

Cal sets down his pencil and glances at the second chocolate bar beside him. He slides it over, then pushes up the sleeves of his bomber jacket, which looks like something he pulled out of a costume closet. It's black, but everything else he wears is this washed-out brown, including the bow tie. It's like he stepped out of a confused time machine.

I slip the chocolate into my front pocket while looking

away. I know the answer he's not giving: Mom and I are like sad guppies at the bottom of his fish bowl; he couldn't resist checking to see if we breathe through gills.

"Does this usually work for you?" I say.

"What?"

"Watching someone from your window, then stalking them?"

He pauses, raises a finger like he's going to deny it. "It's my first time."

I look at him a second, then lean over to get a view of his sketch. He's working on my nose. It actually *looks* like my nose. He's drawn wings on my back, though, which, last time I checked, I don't have.

"Don't you have friends you should be drawing, or a family dog?"

He shrugs, keeping his eyes on the page. "I'm between friends right now. No dog."

At least he's honest.

"And you decided to skip summer camp?" He looks like the band-camp type. He erases a part of my hair, then stops to lift his head and squint at the sun. "I tried camp, once. I spent a lot of time at the nurse's station."

I need to stop asking questions. *Just enjoy the chocolate,* I tell myself. I pick at a splinter poking from the bench. Two of my neighbors are at a picnic table nearby, bent over a textbook, arguing about something on the page. I guess they're not seventh-grade dropouts.

I smell bacon again. Bacon and chocolate smell good together.

" . . . They let me handle easy cases—little kids who cut themselves, bumps and bruises and ice packs. That was the only part of camp I liked." He shrugs. "I don't get bored at home. There's lots to do."

He looks less sure of himself all of a sudden, like the last part might not be totally true.

"Stalking is time-consuming," I offer. "You can't really afford other commitments."

Cal looks at me quickly then, and his face changes again—fills with a smile so fast and easy that I start to smile back before I remember to stop.

"Right" is all he says. He pushes his sketchbook toward me, flipping a few pages back and showing me a drawing he's done of the Carrot, as seen from—I guess?—his room. This should freak me out, but it doesn't. The van looks solid and quiet, and kind of peaceful.

"Are you visiting friends out here or something? A grandma?" he says.

I shoo away a seagull, then shake my head. No grandma, no daddy, no sugar-daddy, no aunt, no uncle, no family. No good one, at least. And no time for friends.

Nobody to owe, nobody to kick us out, is how Mom spins our loner status. She says people can have a hard time seeing you as anything other than what you used to be.

"So you just live in the van?"

I glare at him, like he's thrown a rock through our window. "So you just live in a gigantic house?"

He leans away. "I didn't mean—I'm . . ." He looks across the street to his house. "It can get lonely with just two of us. Lately, we don't say much. I stare out the windows a lot."

I can't believe he's complaining. "Thanks for the chocolate," I say, standing. I sound the opposite of thankful. But who cares? I'm just a fish in a bowl he decided to feed. Everyone knows the guppies don't make it.

Cal

The doorbell rings late the same day, and I'm certain it's her. She's come to tell me to never speak to her again, that she prefers chocolate from someone who talks less about his *gigantic, lonely* house.

I drag my feet to the front door, passing Mom's purse, upside down on the living room couch.

Two women, like a celery stick beside a stack of cabbage, stand in a huddle on our front step with the toothless kid from Bumblebee Camp between them. A sideways wind catches the women's blue sun visors and they reach up to press them to their heads. The kid yanks at a polka-dot bow tie around his neck. I give him a point for good fashion. The cabbage is Mrs. Paglio from next door, but the tall woman beside her is a stranger. She's wearing a long, narrow skirt with running shoes, like she's just walked home from work; her hair swings from a tight ponytail threaded through the back of the cap. "Good evening! I'm Lily, Lily Caspernoff." She gestures to herself, wipes a mist of sweat from her upper lip, then points down the street. "We live at one hundred Marina Boulevard. This is my son, Nathan. And you know Anna Paglio."

"The Giraffe's house!" Nathan slides forward for a better view of the living room. "Wow."

"Is your mom home, Cal?" Mrs. Paglio leans with Nathan to

see past me. She smells like her house: peaches. Her white wedge of hair looks more stiff and creamy than before, like it's turned to butter.

"She's at work," I say.

"Oh." Mrs. Caspernoff and Mrs. Paglio sink a little.

"They want your money!" Nathan shouts. "Give'm all your money!"

Mrs. Caspernoff pulls her son against her legs and covers his mouth. "Ha-ha. He's just turned seven. Nathan—*shhhhhh*." Nathan shakes a metal bucket filled with coins. He tips it forward to show me the contents. "We're here to talk to your mom about what's been going on across the street," Mrs. Caspernoff adds, lowering her voice. She and Mrs. Paglio turn halfway toward the street, then back. "The Marina Beautification Committee has made those"—she tracks her eyes to the left—"*vehicles* our number one priority. We are here to rally neighbor support to get them removed."

Mrs. Paglio clasps her hands together at her waist, closes her eyes, and sort of sways to the sound of Mrs. Caspernoff's words, like she's trying to memorize them for later. I recall the blue flier I found in our kitchen a few days ago. I study Mrs. Paglio's face. She opens her eyes, smiles at me, and winks. She once brought Mom a garden-themed bumper sticker that read: I WET MY PLANTS. Maybe she's a spy, fighting the committee from the inside.

"Yes. Yes," she says now. "Just that." She sounds like she's reading a script.

"Please tell your mother we came by?" Mrs. Caspernoff says.

"But why?" I ask.

The boy, Nathan, removes his tie with a yank and stuffs it in the money bucket. So much for fashion.

Mrs. Paglio raises her eyebrows, sending her frown lines running into her forehead. Mrs. Caspernoff scrunches her nose. "Why? We just explained . . ."

"No—why do the vans need to be removed?"

Mrs. Caspernoff clears her throat and grips Nathan's elbow.

"They're not doing anything wrong," I point out.

"Your mother will understand the seriousness of the . . ." Mrs. Caspernoff dips her head to acknowledge the vans again. "There are neighborhood committees like ours all over the city, trying to clean up the streets. Sidewalks were not made for people to live on. Those—they need services, care. They can be dangerous, unstable. Anything could happen."

"And they're ugly!" Nathan declares, zipping between his Mom's legs.

"Nathan!" She loses hold of him, grabs for his shirt, misses.

"That's what you say. 'Ugly, ugly vans!'"

Mrs. Caspernoff smiles stiffly. Nathan is sidestepping down the driveway.

"We'll return another time," Mrs. Paglio says, glancing at the chase behind her. She holds out a flier to me and slips a twenty-dollar bill into my palm with it, raising her eyebrows again in a "you know what to do with this" way. And I do. I think.

"There are safer, cleaner places to stay than in a van in a city," she adds in a solemn voice. "Facilities for those who can't care for themselves properly, and for their *children*." She makes sure to look me in the eye on *children*. "For the others who are merely avoiding responsibilities, well, they need to quit their carousing and return home."

I shut the door a little too hard after they leave, then, through the living room window, watch them shuffle down the driveway.

Dangerous? Carousing? I look at the twenty in my hand. *Return home?*

They'd need to have a home to return *to*.

"I.M. S.O.R.R.Y."

I Morse it over and over in different variations. *Sorry. So sorry. Very sorry. Soooooooooooooorry.*

She doesn't even need to know Morse to just flash me a sign—anything to show she sees me. But there's no reply.

The bearded man living in the red van behind her responds again instead.

"M.O.R.E. C.H.O.C.O.L.A.T.E.", he says. And then: "O.F. C.O.U.R.S.E. I. T.I.P.P.E.D. T.H.E. C.L.E.A.N.I.N.G. L.A.D.Y."

It makes no sense unless he's—what did the celery stick at the door say? *Unstable.* Unless he's unstable or I'm unstable or ... there's someone else Morse-ing besides just him and me.

Jeanne Ann

"**K**eep up, kid!"

I knew things were different this morning when Mom took time to braid her hair.

Her wide back blocks my view of the sidewalk ahead. She's got *Eating Your Way Through the Golden Gates* tucked under her arm. At the intersection, she stops to consult the book, harrumphing at passersby who bump her as they scoot to get past. She has more in common with telephone poles than people. A hair escapes the braid she's wrapped around her head, and somehow she tucks it back into place, perfectly, with thick and nimble fingers.

Sandy's freedom talk inspired her, or, possibly, the parking ticket we can't afford. The free food she saw him give me probably didn't hurt either.

I've been invited along for good luck today. "But stay quiet," Mom says as she J-walks, crosses on red, and makes lewd gestures at walkers who slow us down. *Boom, boom, boom*—her feet pound the pavement. I'm huffing but thrilled.

So you just live in the van?

No, Cal, we're just exploring options. That's what I should've said to him.

We're going to knock on the doors of dog-eared restaurants

in *Eating Your Way Through the Golden Gates*. They have names like Café Plunder, Chez Zoop, Frangalu. "Don't laugh," Mom barks as we march. I wouldn't. I haven't. I'm sure they're all better than O'Hara's House of Fine Eats, where the most beloved dish is deep-fried dinner rolls, where waiters call all diners "pal" or "bub," and where the owner—who knows Mom's police record—considers a "raise" a free bowl of spaghetti on Christmas and a whack to the back. It wasn't the sort of place a kid hung out except in an extreme emergency. Mom stayed as long as she did because they paid in cash, "under the table," no questions asked—and because, she says, "I didn't think I could do better."

"What's your name?" the chef at the first restaurant asks.

Mom doesn't answer, just shifts her knife case to her other hip. I didn't know it was possible, but she's nervous.

"Hello? Is this an audition or a knife massage?" The chef, whose legs are too short for his body, sits on a stool by the sink, feet kicking over open air.

We're in a basement kitchen with no windows, or it feels that way. Mom has to duck to avoid hitting a sprinkler head on the ceiling. "We wear white here," a woman informed us when we entered the dining room, then cringed as she led us here. We are in our usual uniforms. Me: overalls, Converse high-tops, and a formerly clean T-shirt from a library fundraiser. Mom: black O'Hara's House of Fine Eats camo tank top, work boots, and tight jeans that stop at the calf.

"Joyce Fellows," I shout from my corner by the fridge, where I'm supposed to be inconspicuous.

The chef pinches the bridge of his nose like he's got a killer headache. I already don't like him, but we're not here to like him. He just needs to hire Mom and pay her every other Friday so we can rent an apartment. He checks his watch, then nods at two eggs on a plate, near Mom. "Okay. Improvise, Ms. Fellows."

Mom unrolls her knife case, adjusts the pan already on the stove, and turns on the flame. In two strides she's at the fridge, making split-second choices about what she needs: butter, some green stuff that looks like weeds, cheese. "You got this?" I whisper.

"Can I throw the omelet in his face when I'm done?" she whispers back, then spins toward the stove. The cooking goes fast: sizzling, cracking, beating, pouring, nudging, inspecting, sprinkling, pushing. It's like ballet over fire. She smiles without meaning to, I think—not in an "I'm happy" way, but in an "I've got this" way. I've seen Mom do this a million times—we lived on eggs in Chicago—but I don't get tired of it. I can't believe this is the audition test. I thought he'd have her hanging upside down from the ceiling, deep-frying fish eyes or something.

When she's done, she doesn't say a word, just holds the plate out to the chef.

He looks down at it, pokes at the edge, then pulls a fork out of his front pocket and takes a bite.

"It's good, right?" I say, stepping out of the fridge's shadow.

"Who referred you to me, again?" He's jumped off his stool and stepped forward to study Mom. He seems stuck on her eyebrows—which meet in a thick V—and her nose, which looks like a medieval weapon. Lots of people get stuck on Mom's face.

"No one," Mom says. She's staring at her eggs. I get the sense she wants them back. I get the sense she's impressed him in ways he didn't expect and maybe she didn't expect either.

"Tell him how you read about his food in that book, Mom," I call out. I know I should be quiet, but I'm afraid she won't brag for herself. "She has this giant book called—"

Mom lifts her narrowed eyebrows, which stops me short.

"So, what else can you do?" the chef asks.

Mom shrugs. "The line." I think "the line" means working at the stove.

"Pastry?" he asks.

Mom grimaces like she's spied roadkill just past his right ear.

"You see this kitchen." The chef gestures to our surroundings. "It's a closet. To cut down on bodies, we need cooks who can do everything: dance, sing, strum the guitar. Know what I'm saying?" The chef is staring at Mom's knives while he speaks and wrinkling his nose.

"I've only done the line," Mom says, tapping the side of the stove with a spatula. "Just the line."

"We need our chefs to be flexible, nimble. You'd have to do pastry sometimes, maybe a lot of the time." He waits a beat, but Mom doesn't leap. The chef pulls a face—impatience? He sighs. "Well, leave me something. A number. A résumé. Things go sideways . . . if we get desperate enough . . . you never know." He heads toward the swinging door that leads to the dining room. He hits it, then turns back and glances at Mom's eggs. "And, if you know anybody looking to dishwash, that's a post we need filled ASAP."

The door squeaks on its hinges as he passes through.

Mom is already shoving her knives in their carrying case. "Come on."

"Wait. What?" I sprint across the kitchen to stand in front of her. "You have to go after him. He liked your eggs. Just go tell him you'll do the pastry."

Mom shakes her head. "Pastry is formulas."

"Who cares?"

"I do. I don't know them."

"So you'll learn."

"No. I won't. Pastry is for prisses who can't think on their feet. It's not cooking."

I pick up the chef's used fork and point at the swinging door that's still creaking a little. "That's two different things. Which is it—you don't know how, or you don't want to?"

"Jeanne Ann."

"Couldn't you have *lied*?"

"He wasn't going to hire me anyway." Her voice is low and tired.

"I think he was."

She shoots a look at her knife case, then me. "It's not a fit. And he was a jerk." The kitchen door squeaks again as she smacks through to the other side.

I take one last look at the spotless floors, the bare counters, the greaseless stove. Unlike O'Hara's House of Fine Eats, no one's at risk of catching tetanus here.

I feel nauseated and hungry at the same time. We just hit the jackpot, and she chucked the winning ticket. I pull the plate of eggs toward me, rub the chef's fork on my shirt. The eggs are still steaming.

I want to scream, and I want to eat.

The first bite makes me almost forgive her. The eggs taste like lightly salted clouds . . . of butter. I want to eat ten more. I want to run a crust of bread across the plate. But I have no bread and no choice but to lick the plate clean. This could've been her kitchen. But it wasn't a fit. She says it wasn't. And I believe her?

At an A-frame restaurant resembling the house in *Hansel and Gretel*, a chef races around a stove, talking to Mom without actually looking at her. "Chicago? You people know how to work." He fondles his ponytail and attempts to smile but seems unused to the effort.

"Tell me, have you ever been a chef de cuisine?" he says.

Mom hesitates. "No."

"A sous chef?"

"No."

"A chef de partie?

"No."

"A saucier?"

"No."

"A potager?"

"No."

"A poissonier?"

"No."

"A entremetier?"

"No."

"A garde manger?"

"No."

"Well, what rank have you achieved in a kitchen?"

"Cook," she says, without hesitating.

His ponytail disappears into the walk-in fridge and does not come out.

Next.

"What's an entremetier, anyway?" I ask. We're on the curb. I can feel a blister forming on my heel. The eggs from earlier have burnt up and I have a scorching cauldron in my stomach where lunch should be. A food cart passes by, trailing a delicious smog of salt and burger. Cruel! Three meals a day has turned into one and a half. The fog is starting to thin, leaving us exposed.

"I don't know."

"But you said you weren't one?"

"Yeah."

"Mom! Maybe you were and just don't know it."

I thought she'd hear this as I intended it—annoyed—but she looks at me and her face alters for a second, her eyes widening to reveal the blue that's always there if you look hard enough. And I swear, in that second, she's remembering something good and wants to tell me about it, but then her eyes dim to gray, her face hardens again, a door closing.

"You keep that faith, kid. Keep that faith."

Ten restaurants. Three auditions. No job.

Downhill should be a relief, but it's not. The tips of my toes rub against the fronts of my shoes. Now I'll have blisters on both ends.

How long will this take? What will be right enough?

I'd give anything for peanut butter right now and sticky heat that makes shivering impossible. The sky has cleared, but the wind is still slicing cold.

More than ever I want to know why we had to come to San Francisco for this. We could've stayed put in Chicago and looked for something new. There were plenty of restaurants there . . . even in our neighborhood . . . some of them were even getting tablecloths. She could've taken as much time as she needed looking for a new job while she kept her old one. I could've helped. I could've researched candidates at the library.

At a busy intersection, we stop and wait for the light to turn green. I can see rows and rows of houses at the bottom of the hill, and behind them the bay spreading out, blue and sparkly. It doesn't seem right to be living in a van in a city this rich, this dazzling.

I don't think Mom imagined how badly this could go for us. I think she only pictured good. *I* can imagine how bad, though. I read *Oliver Twist* in fourth grade. I can imagine a lot.

"What about the falafel place? The one we ate at? The cook there liked you," I say. "You could do that job easy, right?" It's not fancy, but it's better than nothing. "Mom?"

"What?" She sounds gravelly.

I pause a second, then grab her shoulder and pull her back to face me. It's like trying to move a tree stump. "He would hire you. I know he would. And he seems nice."

She rolls out of my grip. "Absolutely not." It's a whisper with a knife cutting through it. "I didn't come all the way out here for that."

What did falafel ever do to us? The light turns green and we cross. She's walking so fast, I nearly lose sight of her halfway down the next block. "Mom!" I call, stopping.

She backtracks and kneels right there on the sidewalk, facing me. Her expression is—I'm not sure—like someone begging, but also demanding. "I need more time, kid."

Even kneeling, she's almost as tall as me.

"How much more?"

She just stares. "You said you'd be patient," she says, finally.

"I lied!"

"Jeanne Ann, you know I'm good for it."

I do know that. I do know that. No one works harder than Mom. But what if she's wrong? What if more time isn't what she needs? What if . . .

I've only ever known employed Mom, responsible Mom, can't-get-ahead-but-won't-fall-behind Mom. But that's not who she's always been. There was a version of her, before me, who made big mistakes. Who was reckless and tore things down.

"A week, tops," she says.

"Okay," I say. But I don't want to. "Okay" is not what I feel.

Cal

"Hi." I wave from across the street—big circles.

Hi, she mouths, raising her hand and resting it back in her lap.

I feel little sparks in my fingertips.

I'm at the bottom of my driveway, dragging garbage cans back up to the house before dinner.

Jeanne Ann's in a lawn chair, twenty feet away, facing my house, cradling a book.

She waved back.

She points her royal chin at a spot just over my shoulder.

I turn. The bearded man who lives in the camper behind Jeanne Ann's is pushing a grocery cart full of green bottles straight for me.

He's dressed all in black today, beard and hair combed, face shaded by a black baseball cap.

"Thanks for the flowers," he booms as he passes, then swings a sudden right into the Paglios' driveway.

My legs go soft. I want to run, but I'm already in the safest place—home.

Last night he Morsed: "E.N.O.U.G.H. W.I.T.H. T.H.E. F.L.O.W.E.R. I.N.T.I.M.I.D.A.T.I.O.N." and "M.A.Y.B.E. W.E. D.O. N.E.E.D. T.O. T.A.L.K.," but now he's thanking me?

I didn't even know he knew I'd delivered the flowers.

What would we talk about?

Now he's walking up Mrs. Paglio's driveway. He's smiling. Maybe he plans to confront her but be nice about it. Maybe he's bypassing me and going straight to the flower source. I try to make out what's in the cart. It looks like bottled barf.

The Paglios must have people over. Their horseshoe driveway is clogged with cars, each one displaying a blue PROUD MEMBER OF THE MARINA BEAUTIFICATION COMMITTEE sticker. If it's a committee meeting, they're not going to like this visitor at all.

He reaches the Paglios' side gate, pulls down his cap, and pushes through to the backyard. "Smoothie delivery!" he announces. "Did someone order smoothies?"

I let go of the garbage lid and spin back toward Jeanne Ann. But she's not in the lawn chair anymore. She's in the grass, running after a Bumblebee armed with a double-action Super Soaker.

I can't help it—I smile.

Jeanne Ann

"WHAT'S HIS DEAL?" I SAY, SQUEEZING WATER OUT OF MY shirt. We're standing next to the Carrot. The bundle of sticks—okay, fine, *Cal*—is facing the water, and I'm facing the houses across the street. Mom missed the whole thing. She's out buying more peanut butter and pineapple with our remaining funds.

"Yeah, he's so fast," Cal says, gasping, hands on his knees. Cal did not catch Bad Chuck—possibly because Cal was having too much fun getting wet, possibly because he looks like a warped windmill when he runs, possibly because the camp counselors tackled Bad Chuck first.

"I don't mean the kid," I say, staring at the backyard Sandy entered.

Cal turns to see what I see. "Oh, yeah. What's he doing over there?"

"He's gonna get himself arrested." No wonder no one wants us here. My hairy neighbor is making house calls.

"The Paglios. Yeah. They're gonna freak out. They're not fans of—you know—the v—"

"I think he steals their flowers too," I say, and nod to the flower pot on the curb. Some kind of pink poofy thing that's sagging from neglect. The lady across the street has flower pots just like it lining her driveway. "Who steals flowers and then doesn't water them? Who steals flowers and then puts them on display right across from where he stole them?"

Cal coughs. He's moved closer to the Carrot and is sorta tilted awkwardly over the hood and windshield, like a bent hanger. "Huh. Um. Yeah, that's a weird thing to do. Oh. Hey, your book!" He's just noticed *Jane Eyre*, bloated with Super Soaker water, clutched in my arms. His face, usually a little loose and goofy, pulls into a surprised snarl. I didn't know he had it in him. "That gap-toothed—"

"It's still readable," I interrupt, though I'm not entirely

sure. Mrs. Jablonsky would be chewing her knuckles if she saw this—water is a librarian's worst nightmare. "I mean, Jane Eyre *is* more durable than other leading ladies . . . She survived Mr. Rochester."

Cal looks confused. Not a *Jane Eyre* reader, clearly.

I pull open my door, climb in, roll down the window. It's warm enough. I will sit here and dry by evaporation. There's a new twenty-dollar bill under the windshield wiper. I reach around and grab it, flicking a glance at Cal, who's thankfully looking away. I don't know who's leaving this money and I don't want to know and I don't want anyone asking. I shove it into my pocket and am about to say "See ya" when a lady with a bandana tied around her head walks up to Sandy's camper, unlocks the side door, and lets herself in. She's carrying two heavy-looking plastic buckets.

"Who's that?" I whisper.

"Dunno," Cal says. His eyes have gotten bigger, if that's possible. "But I think I've seen her before."

"What's in the buckets?"

He shrugs. "Dunno."

We watch her slide shut the door and disappear inside. We stare, waiting for her to reappear.

"You should keep an eye on him," I say, breaking the silence. I appreciate the food Sandy gives us—to supplement the peanut butter—but where does it come from?

"Me?" Cal stands a little taller. He's wearing a new brown ensemble today with bright yellow socks, dotted with lightning bolts that match his bow tie. "Sure. Okay." He brushes his bangs to the side; they fall right back into his eyes. "Do you . . . you don't think he's dangerous?"

I shrug for an answer. It seems silly. Sandy, dangerous? He still hasn't come back from his trip across the street, though. Maybe the lady in the bandana is his pickpocket partner? Maybe the people across the street are future victims he's casing?

Cal looks lost as I crank the window closed between us, like he doesn't know the way home. I am tempted to ask if he's okay, but then, there it is again—bacon—as though a hot pan of fried . . . "Pig," I say, stopping mid-crank. The window is only halfway up. I inhale a big breath.

"What?"

"Can you smell that?"

Cal raises his nose. "I dunno. What? Maybe."

I exit the van and sniff my way west, toward the water. Cal follows. I stop in front of a large wood shed marked PRIVATE: MARINA BEAUTIFICATION COMMITTEE GARDEN SUPPLY ANNEX, which shares a wall with a larger brick building marked SAN FRANCISCO CITY AND COUNTY FIELD MAINTENANCE OUTBUILDING B. The restrooms we use are on the far side of this building. The bacon scent is strongest near the shed.

"You can't *maybe* smell bacon," I say. The wind shifts and I lose the scent, which is a relief. It's like an invasion when it comes. I get so I can't think.

"We're vegetarian," Cal says, like he's really sorry this time. He sinks deeper into his pockets.

"Right." I glance across the street again. All that house and no bacon cheeseburgers. Jeez, that's sad.

We watch a group of shirtless guys jog by, muscles bouncing, sweat flying. They look ridiculous. Cal kicks a rock in their direction after they pass, then pinches the fleshy part of his arm, near the elbow. He tries to flex his biceps while squatting and gritting his teeth.

"Keep your shirt on, please," I say, swatting him on the arm where his muscle should be.

Cal

She's not mad at me.

She touched my arm.

I flexed my nonexistent muscle in front of Jeanne Ann and *she touched my arm and laughed.* Nice-laughed. Not mean-laughed.

I didn't even think—I just did it. And it was okay.

I hold on to this memory as I finish replacing the batteries in the flashlight—my hands are all sweaty—and point it toward the window.

I take a deep breath. I tap out:

"I. M.E.A.N. Y.O.U. N.O. H.A.R.M."

This takes me ten minutes to Morse, not because it's hard, but because I'm not sure it's a wise idea.

We learned about appeasement in sixth-grade world history with Mr. Ruiz; it's the military strategy of giving your enemies what they want so they'll leave you alone. It almost never works.

The bearded guy in the red van receives and replies: "Y.O.U. A.R.E. S.O. F.U.N.N.Y."

Jeanne Ann

I wake up to whispers. It's early morning. Gray dark, with pops of light from the broken streetlamp above us. I rub my ear. It's sore, throbbing, and kinda itchy. I think I slept on it wrong. Everything feels a little sore, sleeping on this deflated mattress.

"Hang in there."

"Got to."

The whispers float in through the window on my side of the van, which is cracked to let in air. I scoot toward it, lift my eyes to the glass. I recognize the wide rectangular shoulders in the nearest lawn chair. I look over my shoulder at Mom's sleeping bag, empty. In the lawn chair facing me: Sandy. They're both stretched long, ankles crossed. Mom is sipping something. Sandy's hands rest on his belly. He chuckles. They could be old friends talking low over a campfire. Comfy. Except there's no campfire and they're not friends.

"I can't tell her," Mom says. A car backfires. I miss half a sentence. "I'm asking too much already," she adds.

I slip out of my bag in search of my shoes. I don't like this. Not one bit. Sandy's probably talking her into something. Bad enough we're burying bodies for him on Sunday. Maybe he's killed someone across the street and was visiting the body yesterday . . . I roll my eyes at myself. Ridiculous. I've met scarier librarians than Sandy. But still. She shouldn't be talking to him like . . . this.

"You just got ahead of yourself," Sandy says. "First rule of business, don't get ahead of yourself."

"You're generous," Mom says.

"Hmph. Tell my wife."

I pull on my right shoe. *Wife?*

A chair scrapes the pavement, feet shuffle. "Keep an eye on things—her—for me?"

I freeze.

I hear Mom's hand on the door. I don't know what I want to say yet. I tear off my shoe and slide back into the sleeping bag.

"Hey," she says, grabbing her purse. "You okay?"

How does she know I'm awake?

"Yes. No." I turn on my flashlight, get it close up to her face. "When can we move in with Sam, again?"

"Oh." She opens her purse like she's looking for something. "I told you. Soon."

"You're sure?" It's all that matters. If real walls are in our future, I can handle anything.

She climbs into the front seat, adjusts the rearview mirror. She never does say she's sure.

Cal

"You can't serve customers from down there, Cal." Mac is standing over me with needle-nose pliers she's been using to take apart a toaster. I look up, but it hurts my neck, so I stare at her pink clogs instead.

"There's a"—I lower my voice—"there's a person in line I don't want to see me." I'm sitting cross-legged behind the Greenery counter, facing the display window. Servers are tripping over me. Coffee grounds are falling in my hair. This is the best hiding place I could come up with on short notice: The bearded guy from the red van—who Morses weird stuff and seems to know all about me—is in line, five people back from the counter. This is his second time here in three days. I've tried pretending it's a coincidence. "I didn't have time to hide in the bathroom," I say.

"I don't think hiding from customers is the gig your mom had in mind for you." Mac squats for a face-to-face. "She gave me a list. You sitting on the floor is definitely not on it."

"I'll just be here another minute. What's he doing now?"

"Who?"

"The guy. In line."

"There are ten guys in line."

"The hairy one. With the suitcase."

"Cal."

"Hey—I know that girl." I point outside, beyond the display window. "That's Jeanne Ann." Right there, behind the glass. "Jeanne Ann!" I reach past the pastries and knock on the window. Did she follow my arrows?

"You know a girl?" Mac peers around the croissants to see.

I begin waving. Then harder.

"She sees me." I try to keep the excitement out of my voice, but it's hard.

Mac rises and pats my head. "Never mind. As you were, soldier."

Jeanne Ann

"Do you know that boy?" Mom says. "Hey, you okay? You seem upset."

"I'm fine." I don't feel like sharing. I wish Mom hadn't followed me. She keeps reaching for my hand and squeezing, like she's asking for forgiveness for something. I think this is related to what I overheard earlier this morning. I'm not squeezing back.

I woke up five minutes ago to Sandy whistling the Star-Spangled Banner in his "living room." He had his rolling suitcase and his wide grin, and when he started down the sidewalk on one of his "errands," I just—I followed him. Now I'm standing on the sidewalk in front of a wall of glass that separates me from pastries that might as well be jewels.

Cal's in there, on the other side of the glass, flapping like a penguin, and Sandy too, rifling through his wallet unaware that he's got a tail.

"Tell me what's going on, kid," Mom says, facing me.

"I'm hungry." It's not a lie but it's not the whole truth either. I know I shouldn't be as mad as I am at her—I wasn't supposed to overhear her this morning. But Sandy—keep an eye on *me*? Ha. Other way around, Mom.

The sign over us reads GREENERY: VEGETARIAN RESTAURANT AND BAKERY. Sandy's waiting in line. Cal—I don't know what Cal's doing, but he's wearing a smock that reads GREENERY, so my guess is he works here, but if he stays on the floor like that, waving, this job won't last long.

"Just hungry?" Mom tries again. "Is this about—?"

"What? I'm— Look." I point at the window, glad to have her eyes off me.

The pastries on display are like the Sirens of Greek myth, luring in underfed passersby, and it's hard to concentrate on Sandy or Cal with all that butter and sugar staring back. The croissants alone could feed a small town—almond, chocolate-filled, and plain. My jaw aches from lack of use and over-salivation. This is the closest restaurant to us, I think, but we've never stopped here, maybe for this reason: It's too much.

Mom stands with her hands jammed into her armpits, trying to appear unimpressed. A slice of toast costs five dollars, a fancy coffee costs four dollars, and a sandwich with avocado costs fifteen. And that's just breakfast. There's a whole other menu and dining area for lunch and dinner. We could afford crusts from this place, maybe. So, what's our scrappy neighbor Sandy doing here?

Every item is accompanied by a sign that includes the pastry name, its price, and a sketch with, weirdly, wings. They resemble the butterflies—the arrows with wings—that Cal was drawing on the sidewalk a week ago, pointed in this direction.

Oh.

Click.

Now I stare at Cal.

What's this kid's deal?

"Is he deranged?" Mom says. She doesn't recognize him from our ticket night.

"Dunno."

"Do you think he gets paid to do that?"

"Dunno."

Cal is stuffing his face, mime-style, on the other side of the Greenery display glass. It's very distracting. I've lost sight of Sandy.

Cal begins tipping pastries in our direction and raising his eyebrows to near his hairline after each tip. First an éclair, then a cinnamon roll, now a cupcake. He's really going to get himself fired. He must guess that we prefer the cupcake (I do), because suddenly it's flying through the air and—splat—crashing against the display glass.

"Cupcake giveaway! Damaged goods. Totally unsalable!"

He's slipped the smashed thing into a bag and is now leaning out the front door, pretending to look both ways for a taker.

"You work here?" I say, sliding toward the door.

"Sometimes. When I have to." He looks from Mom to me. I can feel her eyes on my back. "It's sort of a punishment."

I can't imagine this kid making trouble. I can't imagine food as punishment. "For what?"

He looks at the clean-swept cement—"Painting stuff," he answers, shifting his hips, holding out the cupcake bag.

Mom grunts and turns away. Cal takes a small step back into the restaurant, pushing the bag into my hands in one last effort to make me take it. I want to, but if I do, something will become official. I won't be taking it as a bribe or because he's just being nice. I won't be taking it because he's curious about me. He'll be giving it out of pity, and I'll be taking it out of desperation.

"You were sitting on the floor," I say, stepping back.

Cal flicks his eyes side to side like he might be under surveillance. "Your next-door neighbor. He was in line."

"Yeah." I push the bag away one last time. "He's my new babysitter."

Cal returns to the counter, and Mom and I find a seat at a picnic table, facing the water and bridge. This is the back side of Greenery. Nearby, a man dressed in a rubber smock hoses down the restaurant's floor mats, and a delivery person unloads sacks of flour.

"I thought you were hungry," she says.

I shrug.

"You didn't take the cupcake."

"It didn't seem right."

Mom nods. "Yeah. But." She doesn't finish the thought. A moment later she says, "A waste of a beautiful location," and pulls at her lower lip. I think she's trying to lighten the mood. "No meat."

Just as she says it, the hot dog cart rolls by, turning the air savory. Mom and I give it an approving nod. I look around for Sandy—disappeared like a fly in the dark. Mom pokes a finger through a curl of my hair.

I wish she wouldn't do that. It makes resentment very hard.

Behind us, someone harrumphs. We twist around. A pink-haired woman in a green apron is standing with her legs spread apart, leaning her back against the building, pliers in one hand, mug in the other—like she just hotwired the place. She looks like a punk Rosie the Riveter. She and Mom could be cousins. "When I lived in Ohio," she says, "I used to think there was no point in going to a baseball game if you couldn't order a hot dog or a sausage. But then I moved to San Francisco, where the vegetable is king."

"We're from Chicago," I say. I feel a sideways pull toward this wide and sturdy person from Ohio. Ohio isn't so far from Illinois.

"It's cold there. People think they need the extra meat

layer. What they really need are thicker sweaters and better vegetables."

I am offended by this remark. I am offended on behalf of Illinois, brats, and salami.

Mom grunts.

The woman smiles and hums out a high laugh that sounds like it comes from the top of her head.

We turn away but are interrupted a second later by a terrible screeching. The pink-haired lady has pulled a wire from a ten-slot toaster.

"We're lookin' for a line cook." She snaps a part into place, then wipes a bit of grease on her apron. "In case you know anyone in need of a job." She's studying Mom, like maybe she wants to challenge her to an arm-wrestle or something. She points to the scars on Mom's arms. "I can always tell."

She holds out her hand, wide as a baseball mitt. "Come on. You can wash off my vegetarian germs after."

Her name is Mac Papideux. Her office looks like someone built a janitor closet around a desk. It's not big enough for two people to stand in. A string dangles from a plain bulb in the ceiling. Mom's in the doorway with me tucked in behind her, trying to see around. An ocean breeze passes over the empty tables behind us, mixing salt and sun.

"What's going on?" Cal whispers; he's abandoned his post again and stands behind me, craning for a view.

"Shhhh," I say.

Mac sits at her desk, leafing through papers. She finds what she's looking for and lifts her head. "So," she says—directing all of her attention to Mom—"you wanna talk for real about this job?"

I pinch the side of Mom's leg, which earns no response. I think Mom will know how to talk to Mac. I think this could go well.

"You can start by giving me your name," Mac says, then stands and points at Cal: "You! Back to the mines!"

Mom glances back at me. Neither of us expected this. Maybe we're lucky after all.

I wait outside. I climb onto an old wooden railing near the restaurant; it separates land from sea. I lean out over the foamy water and catch a breeze. I can see a mountain, a bridge, an island, and a bazillion sailboats. A pelican or something lands on a buoy a few feet beyond me, its long beak dipping in and out of the water.

A pelican!

Sailboats!

A city on water!

A restaurant at the edge of the city!

This feeling is dangerous, but leaning out over the wood railing, I give in to it. I let myself imagine a normal life. *A normal life.* Instead of working from eight a.m. to ten p.m., Mom will work at Greenery from eight thirty a.m. to four thirty p.m. She'll drop me at school on her way to work and pick me up on her way home. We'll eat in front of the TV together and laugh at the bad commercials. I'll have friends over, at a real apartment with one room for sleeping and one for eating. And we won't share a bathroom with any-one! She'll make me lunches! She'll attend PTA meetings and make friends with the other mothers. They'll call her Joyce and invite her over for coffee. She'll hate the being-friendly part, but she'll go along, because it will be her nor-mal life too.

I wait thirty minutes, going back the way Mac led us before, through the kitchen. The chefs are hovered over a menu. I hear the words *deglaze* and *julienne,* and then someone orders someone else to "prepare the stock."

I like the sound of this, whatever it means.

I pass through and out to the other side of the dining room, and around to the café entrance. Cal is working. His eyes are on his book, sketching something. He looks up, waves, but there's something about the way his hand rises—like in slow motion—stops, and then sinks, that gives me a bad feeling.

"Is the interview over?" I ask Mac. I look for Mom behind the office door.

Mac stands, hitting her head on the lightbulb string and swatting it away. "She left ten minutes ago."

"Oh." I look at the employee roster taped behind her head and pull at my overalls, which suddenly itch. "Did she get the job?" I meet her eye for just a second, which is all it takes.

"She wouldn't fill out this work-history form. She got half-way through it and then took off." Mac holds it up. "We just need to know what she's been up to, you know, in life."

I find Mom in the van, stretched out on her sleeping bag. I slam the door.

She's staring at the pots and pans dangling from the ceiling.

I fall cross-legged on the floor and wait to burst. I glance over at my books. I could use one right about now—a *Pride and Prejudice* or a Harry Potter, where everything magically turns out all right, against the odds.

"I didn't want to work there anyway," she says, anticipating my complaint.

"You wouldn't fill out the forms."

"That—that was just the last straw. You know how I feel about forms."

"Mom!"

"Don't yell." She pushes herself up by her elbows. Her face looks like it's going to crack. The top layer hard like marble and the under-layer trembling.

"You're not even trying! You turn them down before they do anything."

"I *am* trying. I'm trying so hard. But . . . they know." The marble layer slides off. "They know."

"Know what?"

She shrugs an inch, looks away. "Nothing."

"Mom."

She exhales a huff. "That I'm nobody, from no place." She speaks with her teeth clenched tight. "I doesn't matter what I do—balance a ball on my nose, complete their forms—because they already know. They can see it, smell it. They'll never hire me, kid."

"Who's 'they'? What will they see?" She's scaring me.

"All of it."

I don't understand. "Mom. Mom, did someone say something to you?" She's still got her head down, but she's shaking it. "Mom." I lean forward. "You're definitely somebody, from *someplace*."

We should've never left *that* place. We didn't have a perfect life, but we were hanging in there. Chicago was sturdy, predictable. Nothing to climb except the flight of stairs to our apartment. Chicago had its glamorous side—the lake, jingly sailboats, the Magnificent Mile, skyscrapers. But it was rusty too. We were rusty. It worked. I miss the screech of L trains. I miss the mid-afternoon thunderstorms that washed the gutters clean. I miss Vienna Beef on every corner. I miss the free butterscotch candies at the branch library and the pillow waiting for me under Mrs. Jablonsky's desk. Oh, Mrs. Jablonsky! She said I was reading at a twelfth-grade level and should probably just skip middle school and the zits that come with it.

I miss knowing how it would go. Every day. Every hour. Back home, I always knew what would happen next. Good or bad.

Mom's closed her eyes.

I would like to close mine too, but we can't both do it.

"I want to go home," I say. I want it to sound final.

She shakes her head. "No." She raises a hand. The marble face is back on, eyes up. "I just need a minute to feel sorry for myself." She reaches for and pats the shelf behind me. "Read."

"Mom."

"It's gonna be okay."

"How can it be okay?" She won't take the job she knows she can do, she won't take the job where the chefs ask too many questions or speak French, or where she has to make pastry, or work with more vegetables than meat. She won't even fill out the forms. That doesn't leave *anything*.

"Read." It's somewhere between a plea and an order. "The one about the girl in the falling-down house."

"I don't want to."

"Jeanne Ann." She sounds firm. "I'll sort this out. I'll sort myself out. I promise."

More promises.

I would rather hear what happens to *us* now—but I find the book on the shelf. *I Capture the Castle*. It's the cover with a close-up of the turret, every window backlit and aglow against the creeping night. This is what we read on the road trip here, when I thought some variety of castle might be in our future. I glare at it now.

"It's gonna be okay," she says.

I want to agree. I do. But if this is her taking care of things, I'm on my own. This thought presses me down into the floor.

She rests a hand on the book. She bought it for me before we left. She'd seen me borrow it from the library so many times and said she "felt sorry" for all the "chumps" who wanted to check it out but couldn't because of me. But that's not the real reason. She bought it because she loves me. It says so in the inside cover. I stare at her handwriting where she signed it. The letters blur.

Let me do the talking next time, I want to say, and, *You're supposed to protect us!* and, *How could you not know it'd be like this?* And so many other things.

Instead, I place my hand inside Mom's, flipping it palm up, palm down, palm up until she squeezes it still. Then I begin to read.

FEEDING
THE METER

From: Chicago Public Library, Sulzer Branch

Re. Notice of Overdue Books

Date: June 23

To: Jeanne Ann Fellows, 798 W. Wilson, Chicago, IL 60622

This is a notice to inform you that the following books, checked out on May 8, are overdue:

Mrs. Frisby and the Rats of NIMH

Frankenstein

El Deafo

Oliver Twist

Nooks & Crannies

The Lion, the Witch and the Wardrobe

The Golden Compass

The Night Diary

Hatchet

Dr. Jekyll and Mr. Hyde

The Lottery

The Phantom Tollbooth

The War That Saved My Life

The Wolves of Willoughby Chase

Roll of Thunder, Hear My Cry

A Long Way from Chicago

One Crazy Summer

The BFG

Howl's Moving Castle

When You Reach Me

Pippi Longstocking

Swallows and Amazons

The Little Princess

Born Free

Ballet Shoes

The Penderwicks

The Saturdays

Brown Girl Dreaming

101 Dalmatians

From the Mixed-Up Files of Mrs. Basil E. Frankweiler

Merci Suárez Changes Gears

Redwall

The Railway Children

Adventures of Huckleberry Finn

A Little History of the World   The Way Things Work

Zen and the Art of Motorcycle   Finance for Dummies
Maintenance

Your fine is 25 cents a book, per day, or $180.50 total.
If the books are not returned within 8 weeks, you will
be fined for their entire value. Please call this branch
library if you cannot locate the missing items or if you
need to renew. Thank you, The Chicago Librarians

JA, I would file this note under "Rather Concerned," if we still
had a card catalog. Our recent late notice to you came back
with an "Addressee Incorrect" stamp across the top. That must
be an error. Must be . . . But, where are you? Yesterday was
our all-day reading of *Matilda*, and only five kids showed. You
never miss the all-day readings. You would have rolled your eyes
at this one, though. I did my best impression of Miss Trunchbull,
but you're so much better at it. We were hoping you'd re-create
the chokey in the storage closet, like last year. Such a hit.
I can empathize with that Trunchbull woman on some days,
though . . . Did you know I found gum in 24 books last week?
Appalling. We miss you terribly. Nobody reshelves like you.

—Books with hooks, Marilyn Jablonsky

P.S. if you call in, I can give you a two-week extension on *The Lottery*.
You're likely reading it for the 400th time, and who can blame you.

Cal

*Jeanne Ann, meet me at Greenery, 9:30 a.m.,
tomorrow. —Cal*

I fold the note into a bird and tuck it under her windshield
wiper.

*Jeanne Ann, I think my last note blew away. Meet
me at Greenery, 9:40, today. —Cal*

I wait an hour. Only pelicans show.

"Why won't your mom fill out the work form?" I ask Jeanne
Ann, tripping into the intersection alongside her. She's lug-
ging two canvas totes bulging with books. I've been waiting
all morning for her to exit the van. I was prepared to wait all
summer.

Her expression is weird, like there's something in her mouth
that she's trying to grind into dust.

She stops mid-crosswalk. I stop mid-crosswalk.

"Are you going to spit on me? You look like you're going to
spit on me," I say.

She doesn't answer.

"Maybe aim thataway," I say, indicating her other side. "But take the job application forms. I can help you fill them out." I shake the paperwork.

She ignores my offer, clomping ahead.

"Those bags look heavy," I say. We've begun to climb.

She moves the bags to her left shoulder, away from me.

At the top of the hill, she lets the bags fall to the ground and curls over them, wheezing. Finally she speaks. "Don't come in." She holds out a hand. "Promise."

We're standing in front of a used-book store.

A bell rings as Jeanne Ann enters. I watch the transaction through the window, sitting on the neighboring stoop.

When she's done—the doorbell rings again—she exits with a fistful of cash and sagging, empty totes.

"Your mom make you do that?" I say. Jeanne Ann's frozen on the sidewalk, staring at the traffic whizzing by. I really don't like her mom.

"She doesn't know. I'm buying us more time."

Oh.

She inches closer, then lowers herself to the stoop beside me. Faint music comes from the falafel place next door.

I want to say something but can't think of what.

Her royal chin falls to her chest. Then she folds in half, cheek to knees, and closes her eyes.

Jeanne Ann

Turns out, we are not burying bodies for Sandy today. We're hocking his smoothies at a farmers' market.

"The keys to upselling . . ." Sandy begins his speech and does not stop, even when our eyes drift sideways. He's really stepped into his role: Chairman of the Homeless.

It's six a.m., Sunday, dark. My eyeballs hurt. We're standing beneath four posts and a flimsy sheet. The market is held in the Greenery parking lot. Sandy's paying us to set up smoothies, sell smoothies, and clean up smoothies. He says it's a fund-raiser for his upcoming road trip. I wonder if his wife knows, the one I'm not supposed to know about. I wonder if she's aware he'll be taking off soon with his "best mate."

Mom glances down at me, exhales something that sounds a lot like defeat, then shrugs like she knew this was the gig all along and simply didn't care.

Around us, farmers unload boxes of fruits and vegetables from the beds of dented pickup trucks. They look as dirty as we look, and as tired, but they've done something—work—to earn their appearance, and they will shower later.

I reach for the paperback in my back pocket and remember, too late, that it's not there.

"Last points of order," Sandy says, raising his voice. "Keep those smiles tight and keep your eyes peeled for a group of matrons in matching blue hats and shirts. They will require VIP treatment."

I adjust my seat on the crate. "Why?"

"Long story. Big misunderstanding. We should put our best feet forward."

"You pick their pockets or something?"

Sandy grins, cocks his head and blinks rapidly, mock-innocent. I'll take it as confirmation. I roll my eyes for Mom, but she's gazing at a bunch of men in white chef coats, pawing cucumbers one stall over.

"Jeanne Ann, help me here." Sandy taps my elbow. I squeeze the wad of cash in the front pocket of my overalls. I'm never taking off these overalls—they are our bank. Another reason never to bathe. When we finish here, we will have more than one hundred dollars: about forty from the mystery person who keeps leaving money under our windshield wipers—I think it's probably Cal because who else could it be?—forty from Sandy, and sixty-two fifty from my books. That's two bucks per hardback and seventy-five cents per paperback. Sixty-two fifty in exchange for a whole life of scavenging and collecting and repairing and alphabetizing . . . The used-book store owner said I wouldn't earn more for my books anywhere else in the city. He said books don't retain their original value once they've been read. I told him that didn't make any sense. I told the salesman that books should increase in value once they've been read a whole bunch. At the library, the most-read books are the most beloved. He said that was "an economic theory for romantics."

Sandy sets me in front of the display cooler to pick out the dirty ice. I do as ordered while stealing glances at Greenery. The lights are on inside. I can see someone pulling down chairs.

"I could use some signage, next," Sandy says, handing me a Sharpie, paper, and tape. I consider a few signs I'd like to hold up:

Lost!
Girl, 12. Workhorse mom, 31.
Last seen "getting by" in Chicago.
Hire her!

Mother, cook, loyal friend.
Can fry, grill, and boil. Cheap labor.
Daughter tags along.

Map needed: out of this situation.
In any language!

Sandy suggests a simple: SMOOTHIES FOR SALE, $8 PER BOTTLE FOR A LEANER, HAPPIER YOU.

I write it. I am being paid for cooperation.

Customers, it turns out, are awful. They pay with money

soaked in joggers' sweat. They ask for two-for-one deals when none is offered. They hold up a line to complain about a "funny aftertaste."

You've got to eat something to get an aftertaste!—I want to scream. I'd give anything for an aftertaste right now. Hunger is like a rug burn on the inside.

The matrons in blue pass by with their noses turned up. They move as a pack, glare, but do not stop. Their T-shirts read: MARINA BEAUTIFICATION COMMITTEE. These are the people who want us gone. That is more than a "misunderstanding," I think, turning my own glare on Sandy. I look both ways and hurl a small ice cube in their path.

"Jeanne Ann!" Sandy sees and scurries over. "You and your mother are not built for sales!" I can tell he wants to say more. He looks sincerely upset, like I've tarnished his reputation as an upstanding homeless citizen. I feel heat rising from my toes, and a few seconds later a cackle escapes my throat, a sound I don't even recognize as me. Sandy stares, then insists I take a short break. "Here, wear this," he says, taping a new paper sign to my shoulder: IT'S GONNA BE OKAY.

Now I'm standing in front of Greenery, light-headed, with a dry mouth. I don't think the fruit and bread and peanut butter I've been living on are reaching my joints. I feel brittle, like a piece of chalk.

"Hi," I say. To Cal. At the counter.

"Hi," he says, and immediately begins stabbing holes in

perfectly good pastries and throwing them in a box for me.

"Stop," I say.

"Why?" He holds up the box; it's nearly full.

"I can't take it."

"Why?"

I groan. "Can't you just be normal?" I feel bad instantly, but I also mean it. I want something normal so badly.

He twists his face up for a second, grabs his sketchbook out of his smock, and whacks it against the counter a few times. I think I've offended him, but then he looks right at me. "I don't know. I thought so?" A wall of hair falls across his face as he looks down. "But now my mom makes me wear this jacket and she's sending me to the school of quote-unquote hard knocks."

"The school of . . . ?"

Cal grabs the box, tapes it shut, and pushes it across the counter to me. He shakes his hair out of his eyes, beams at me, and says, "This is as normal as I get."

And maybe it's because of this that I say yes when he offers to show me his new school.

Cal

58 DAYS TILL SCHOOL STARTS!

At the fence surrounding the building, we come to a hard stop. It's early afternoon. Warm. Below us: faded basketball-court lines, rusty hoops, puddles that've been breeding mosquitoes since the Paleolithic era.

"This is the 'school of hard knocks'?" Jeanne Ann laughs pretty hard. "This is just a public school, Cal." She has a nice laugh. "It's paaaaradiiiise." She stretches the word. "Look over there—a dark corner where you'll soon be mugged for your milk money. Ha!"

I'm glad she's having fun at my expense, but being here is making me queasy. It seemed like a good idea a half hour ago. This is what Mom wants for me? "I think I smell blood," I say.

It's only three blocks from home, but Jeanne Ann and I took twenty minutes to climb the hill, me dragging my feet the whole way.

A banner hangs over the front entrance of the building:

58 DAYS TILL SCHOOL STARTS!
Marina Pacific Middle School Mixer
June 30, 4-6 p.m.
Meet teachers and future B.F.F.'s.
Return for tours and registration: July 5, 1-5 p.m.

"That's soon," I say. I take a deep breath. "We can go together." I cut my eyes to her.

Jeanne Ann punches me in the arm.

"Warming you up for seventh grade," she says with a grim smile.

"This is terrible."

"Nah. You just need a book and an angry resting face," she says. "You'll be fine." She smiles for real. "'School of hard knocks.'" She bursts out laughing again. It really is a great laugh.

But I feel my guts drop to my knees. At Point Academy, I spent recess in a flower garden, drawing. When it rained, the principal piped big-band numbers through the school PA and taught us to swing dance.

"See that corner over there," she says, "where the two buildings meet, near the shrub, sorta by the window? That's where I'd stash myself at recess and lunch, if I were you. Avoid the foot traffic. Gets some radiant heat from the building in winter. Shade in summer. Invisible except from up here."

"You found that spot fast."

"A lifetime of scouting for the best place to read in a crowd." She smiles but has her arms crossed now, hands tucked tight in her armpits.

"You'll do great here," I say.

"I won't be here."

"Why not?"

141

"Because you need an address to go to school, Cal, and I don't have one."

"Oh." I hadn't thought of that. I can't believe I hadn't thought of that.

I glance at her profile, her royal chin. "But you would want to go here if you could?"

She brings her shoulder to her ear like, *I could take it or leave it.* I don't believe that for a second.

"We could read together at lunch," I say, eyes on the yard again.

She turns her back and falls against the fence, making it rattle, and stares across the street.

"Or I could draw, and you could read," I continue, speeding up. "We'll have a book club. I'll draw my book critiques. You can write yours."

She pushes her heel into the fence. She's squinting at me through one eye.

"*Dune.* That'll be our first lunchtime book pick," I say. I read it last year for school; I've sketched a ton of characters from it.

She shakes her head. Then her chin drops and she stares at something near her feet that I can't see. "*Dune* is pretty great," she says, kicking at the invisible thing. "Survival against all odds."

I nod, pleased.

"I sold it," she says.

Jeanne Ann

Got job. 555-8990, 8 a.m. to 10 p.m. $10/hr or $400 week. Less than minimum wage, but I won't complain. Yet. Now, just need some time. —Mom

P.S. Don't forget to brush your teeth. And wash up. And please change clothes. We'll do laundry with first proceeds.

P.P.S. Your books? All of them? You didn't need to do that. I wish you hadn't done that.

This is all I see of Mom for the next few days, scribbled on the back of a pink receipt, laid on a pillow that smells like unwashed hair. She's gone before I wake up, home after dark. Just like Chicago . . . but totally different.

Also, I don't think she really has a job.

Cal cranes for a view of the note over my shoulder. I crumple it up, shove it in a pocket, then reconsider and hand it to him. He keeps showing up. I don't think it's right, his nosiness, but he's a minor aggravation compared to the rest of my aggravations.

We're sitting with our backs against the Carrot's bum tire, knees bent, looking out to sea. It's morning but the moon is still up, admiring itself in the bay's big watery mirror. "The bay"—that's what Cal calls it. The shed with the phantom bacon scent is on the edge of our sightline. The doors to it are open, and a woman has just exited carrying a shovel.

"That's good, right?" he says, handing the note back. After the farmers' market, Mom told me she'd do "whatever it takes" to get us out of the van. It was what I wanted to hear, but if she's not willing to sling falafel or "julienne" vegetables or roll out pie dough, what does "do whatever it takes" actually mean?

"I wonder what restaurant it is," he says.

"It's probably not a restaurant."

"How do you know? That's what she is, right—a cook?"

"So?" I wish he'd change the subject.

He leans away like he's read my thoughts, then unzips his backpack. He extracts a brown paper bag with a grease spot on the bottom and holds it out. "They're still warm."

I peek. Donuts. Jeez. I feel a little bad now, ignoring his notes from earlier in the week. But sometimes he's like waking up to too much sunlight.

"And milk. Here."

"Are they from Greenery?" I ask.

"These? No. These are made with lard."

I grab the bag and plunge my hand inside, clamp onto a donut. Is it possible for intestines to cry? I will never spend my book money on something this decadent.

"You're welcome," he says, looking satisfied with himself.

It's annoying. We stare at the Golden Gate Bridge, the parts of it that aren't hidden in a gray gauze of fog. Two of my neighbors—the ones always studying at the picnic tables—scoot by with matching caddies filled with soap, toothpaste, washcloths—a bathroom run. They've each brought a textbook along and are reading while they walk.

I hold the donut in front of my face, inhale it, then slide it back into the bag. I can't do it. I want to eat it. But . . . We have a full jar of peanut butter. And Sandy's supplemental grub . . . And I did some figures this morning. If I take a spoonful of peanut butter at nine a.m., eleven a.m., two p.m., five p.m., and nine p.m., I can make a jar last for seven days. I don't actually *need* Cal's donuts.

Cal watches me let go of the donut but doesn't say anything.

"These smell like Chicago." I hold up the bag.

"Yeah?"

"My mom worked a swing shift on Saturdays and would bring home donuts on Sunday mornings. We'd eat them together. And then she'd go to bed."

"What did you do?"

"Read. Solitaire. Library. Library. Library. Sometimes I'd sit on our stoop and watch people."

He follows my hand as I reach into the donut bag again.

"You want to go back, don't you?"

I flick at a grain of donut sugar-dust. "Anything would be better than this."

We both scan the scene. Does he see what I see? The guy two vans down who dotes on his grocery cart, filled to the brim with tin cans and fastened with a bike lock to his cracked fender? Sandy refers to him as Mr. Rews—Retired Without Savings. Or the guy in the yellow raincoat, the Where's Waldo? of the block, popping up from behind shrubs and waving hello, always to a person just behind me, who, when I turn to look, isn't there. At the Chicago library we talked about people like this—like us now—all the time, how they smelled and what was safe to say or do around them. Most just wanted a place to sit, but some had that desperate edge, that destroyed look. Our orders were to "stand clear" of those people. They were unpredictable.

Cal grabs the door handle above his head and pulls himself to standing. I'm left staring at his sandals; he's wearing them with orange socks. I guess it's better than all brown—or *beige*, as Cal insists. When I look up, he's shaded his eyes and pressed them to our window.

"Can I see inside?"

Is this what the donuts were for—a bribe, so I'd give him a close-up of my pathetic home?

"Would that satisfy your curiosity?" I say. It sounds mean. I want it to. Now I'm extra glad I didn't taste the donuts.

"No. Yes. It's all right. Forget it."

I shrug and stalk around to the back. The closer we get to the doors, the more I don't want to open them.

Sandy exits his van just then, followed by the bandana

lady and her buckets. They pass by without raising their heads, deep in conversation.

The donut bag tears where I'm holding it too tightly. A donut falls out.

They. Are. All. So. Infuriating. Sandy, who always seems to know where he's going. Cal, who finds us all so *interesting*—I fling open our back doors.

"Ow," Cal says. "Ouuuuuuch."

"Crapinade." The door handle has hit him on the chin on its bounce-back.

"Am I . . . ?" Bleeding. Yes.

I go to dab at the blood with the elbow of my sweatshirt; he flinches and takes a step back.

"I'm sorry," I say. I am.

He touches his face and looks at the blood on his hand, then he turns toward his house.

"Come on." I tug him back. "You can lie down on my sleeping bag. We've got some wet wipes in here somewhere."

I open all the doors and windows so he's not suffocated by the smell of dirty laundry, feet, and peanut butter.

Laid flat, Cal's a foot too long for the van, ankles and shoes dangling out the back doors. He'd never survive in here as long as I have.

Cal

I TRY TO SIT UP, BUT SHE GLARES AT ME UNTIL I LIE BACK AGAIN.

"It's just a cut," she says, adjusting my backpack under my head. But I know it's bleeding like crazy. I can feel a drip. She hands me another moist towelette. "I'm sorry."

I think she is. She's kneeling next to me, searching for damage. "You got some blood on your jacket."

I shrug. It's not the worst news. "It's not my jacket. My mom gave it to me. Some old boyfriend's, I think. If I don't wear it, she won't give my paints back." The words just slip out one after another.

Jeanne Ann's face twists into a question mark.

"Mom's decided I need 'adjustments.'"

"What? Nah." She flicks my sleeve. That's the second time she's touched me. I am suddenly warm, and the dent in my face doesn't hurt. Jeanne Ann's on my side.

I shrug again. "It's mostly—it's just a big misunderstanding."

She leans way over, her nose hovering close to my forehead so that I have to close my eyes for a second and seal my lips, because I could easily tell her everything. I want to. It would feel good. The vans, the sketchbook, the wings project, the mural and everything that led up to it and everything that's happened since. I could tell her—about my allowance. How I've given it away every month since I turned eight. About my portraits—how I choose each person, why. About—

"Are you dead?" she says, poking my forehead.

Touch three.

I open my eyes. "There was this time when I was eight," I start to say, and I mean to tell the story of the lemon-pistachio loaf and the man in the yellow raincoat, but the first words are so strange in my mouth. What if this all comes out wrong? It's happened before. Or what if she doesn't actually get what I'm doing, thinks it's all stupid? Or what if she's annoyed? That seems very likely; she's already made it clear it's annoying when I ask about her life out here . . .

"You've got a history of bang-ups," she says, when I don't say anything more. She touches a spot on my forehead, near the hairline. Her fingers are cool and dry. Fourth touch.

"I—um," I say, rubbing the place her fingertips were. "Some hot oil jumped out of a frying pan and got me. I was a baby, in one of those baskets on the floor."

Jeanne Ann doesn't look particularly impressed, like maybe I should've jumped out of the way.

"I don't remember it. My mom told me. She was frying zucchini."

"She remembers what she was frying?"

"Oh, yeah. She remembers everything she's ever made. She used to be this really great cook." I can tell Jeanne Ann that.

Jeanne Ann looks dubious, like *how can this woman who makes you wear a stupid jacket also be good at something worthwhile?*

"She was," I say, trying to sound convincing. "Now some-one else cooks for us and Mom runs the rest of the house." I realize how obnoxious this sounds the instant after I say it. By *us* and *house*, I mean Greenery, but Jeanne Ann probably thinks I mean *us* as in Mom and me, like we snap our fingers and food just arrives on our dinner table, which, I guess, it sort of does, but that's even more confusing. "I mean," I say, trying to correct myself—but then I see Jeanne Ann nodding, lost in thought, eyes sorta glazy, maybe not even hearing, and all I feel is relieved, because I'm not ready.

I lie still and let my eyes rove—over the metal walls, which are gray inside, not orange like I expected, to the sheet cov-ering the back window, which makes me think of sleepovers and forts. "It's not so bad in here. Like a little cabin." I feel safer than I thought I would.

From my back pocket, I slide out two twenty-dollar bills—given to me by Mrs. Paglio—and deposit them under the near-est pillow. Jeanne Ann doesn't see.

"I thought of it that way at first," she says, hearing me again. "On the drive out." Her eyes are roving now too. "Our place in Chicago was a dump, but it couldn't get towed or ticketed or sideswiped."

I imagine what it would feel like—the walls shrinking to fit us. "You guys brought a lot of pots and pans," I say. They dangle over our heads.

Jeanne Ann climbs deeper into the van, leans against a wall. "Mom's."

"That's a big bookshelf." It lines the left side of the van, mostly empty.

"Yeah," she says, sinking, and I cringe. I didn't mean to remind her of her books.

But the shelf isn't totally bare. It still holds about eight cookbooks. My mom's got a lot of the same ones. I turn onto my side, lever my elbow and hand to prop up my head. "So, your mom's a real gourmet, huh?"

Jeanne Ann turns to the cookbooks and blinks. "I have no idea."

I look from her to the shelf and back.

Aha.

I do.

Jeanne Ann

Mom, saw a picture of steak in one of your cookbooks.
Weird green sauce on it, but otherwise looked like steak.
Hope you're not working at a vegan restaurant. —JA

CAL LEAVES AND I DEPOSIT THE NOTE ON MOM'S PILLOW
and wait for her to get home from wherever she's killing
time. I would prefer to deliver the message in person. I
would like to see her reaction to the vegan joke and the
word *working*.

It's getting dark, so I check the locks again. Sandy's outside. He gives me a wave and a nod, so I nod back. I read
Mom's cookbooks to pass time. Cal seemed impressed by
them. Also, I have nothing else to read.

When I look at my watch again, it's ten p.m., and I'm
hungry from looking at all the pictures of food. I know how
to chiffonade lettuce and truss a chicken now. In theory.
And gorgonzola is no longer a mystery. It's a cheese. Moldy
cheese. That's what Mom wanted to serve at O'Hara's House
of Fine Eats before we left. No wonder her boss wouldn't let
her put it on the menu. Gross.

Where is she? Mom's taking her pretend job a little far, I
think as I fall asleep.

Cal

The doorbell rings while Mom is looking for her purse, shouting reminders to me from the kitchen. I was about to leave for school—my new school—on Mom's orders. Orders. Orders. Orders. School hasn't even started. She just wants me to hand-deliver my school registration papers. "To make an impression and get a taste of the new scenery," she says. "And wear your jacket!"

Her purse is next to the refrigerator, behind a plant. She left it there last night. It's going to take her fifteen minutes to find it without my help, which is going to make her twenty minutes late for work. But she doesn't want my help. Apparently, if I am too involved in her life, I'm "tripping" through mine. How that makes any sense when she's got me wearing clothes she picked out and working behind the counter at *her* restaurant is, well, it *doesn't* make sense. Throwing the "kitchen sink" at the problem seems like it'll just . . . ruin the kitchen.

The doorbell rings again.

"Cal!" She's glancing at her watch as she comes around the corner and finds me frozen in place, holding the registration envelope stuffed with my birth certificate, report card, proof of address. Her clogs continue—*clunk-clunk-clunk*—over to where I stand. "Were you going to open the door?"

I really don't want to. I've looked through the spy-hole and seen Mrs. Paglio on the other side. She's carrying a flower pot with two hands, framed in fog. Purple flowers this time. "Do I have to?"

Mom edges past me—a now familiar look of confusion and disappointment on her face—and throws open the door.

Mrs. Paglio steps inside without being invited. She's got a dirt streak across her forehead and wears gardening gloves, a shade hat with a chin strap, and an apron stamped **MARINA BEAUTIFICATION COMMITTEE**. It's possible my face is now communicating a look of confusion and disappointment too.

"Lizzie," she says, giving Mom a quick nod. "Cal." She shuts the door quickly and walks to our front window—the one that looks out at the bay. I think this is the first time Mrs. Paglio has ever been inside our house.

"Everything okay?" Mom says. Mom's peeking over Mrs. Paglio's shoulder, trying to see what part of the view has Mrs. Paglio so upset. All I see is a wall of soupy fog. I can't even make out the vans across the street, let alone the water.

"Not really," Mrs. Paglio says, dragging the *y* through her molars, then cutting it off abruptly when she turns into the room and finds Mom right up in her grill. She zigzags around her and shoves the flower pot into my hands. It bends my registration envelope, soaking the corner where the pot is dripping.

"Zinnias," she says. "For delivery." Mrs. Paglio pulls money from the pocket of her smock, a five and a twenty. I have no free hand, so, after searching me for a spot to stow the bills, she rolls them up and tucks them into the dirt; they look like two little weeds, poking up from the soil.

"That's for"—she glances at Mom, whose mouth hasn't quite closed since Mrs. Paglio arrived—"running my errands." Then Mrs. Paglio signals for me to stoop. She cups her hands around her mouth and whispers in my ear:

"The twenty goes across the street. The five's for you. And there's a message I want you to deliver with the flowers." She stands on tiptoes to lean closer to my ear and continues to whisper.

"Huh?" I say, not understanding anything but the money part.

She frowns. "Never mind," she says, sounding tired. She squeezes my wrist. Her hands are warm and lined with tissue-y wrinkles. "Just deliver the flowers."

Mrs. Paglio leads the way out and I follow. I have no choice with Mom watching.

"Cal—" Mom hails me before I can reach the bottom of the driveway. I stop and wait. Mom's lectures occur practically any time I'm standing still now.

"It's very nice of you to run errands for Mrs. Paglio."

I shrug.

That's who I am: nice. Even to neighbors behaving strangely.

I start again toward the intersection, but I can feel Mom following me with her eyes.

"What happened to your chin?" she shouts.

I stop again and touch the Band-Aid. Smooth plastic. I want

Mom to figure out what's happened—all of it—by herself. I don't answer.

Mrs. Paglio turns right at the bottom of the driveway, shuffling toward home. I go left and head for the crosswalk.

"When you get there, say, 'I miss you.'" That's the message Mrs. Paglio asked me to deliver with the flowers. I wish she'd spent more time explaining. She's watching me from the other side of the street now. When I raise my hand to signal *I got it,* she slips around the side of her house and disappears.

I look at the quiet line of vans. The way the fog flows over and around them, like dry ice—a person could pretend it's all a magic trick. All the vans could disappear, then reappear someplace else, someplace better.

I approach slowly. Which one do I deliver her message to? There's something I'm missing, something obvious, between Mrs. Paglio and the vans, something right in front of my face.

A fast-moving object, about the size of a second grader, tramples my right foot as I stand there.

"Hey!" I wobble, then lose my grip. The flower pot crashes to the ground.

Jeanne Ann

"I caught him red-handed!" Cal announces, striding up to the table between the vans, one finger hooked in Bad

Chuck's collar, the other arm hugging a cracked flower pot topped with a soggy envelope. Cal and Bad Chuck have materialized like phantoms out of the mid-morning fog. Or that's how it seems. I'm still half asleep. A crashing sound woke me up.

Cal's got a new Band-Aid on his chin, Superman-themed, and his weird jacket tied around his waist. Bad Chuck looks like a potato bug curled in on itself.

I fall into a seat next to Sandy, who's grinning into his tea like he knows something I don't. "Your mom left for work early," he reports first thing. He's her secretary now too, apparently—his job description is rapidly expanding. He's deposited food on our windshield the last five mornings and has laid out a platter of cheese on his card table, enough for the whole neighborhood. I wonder what he stole to afford all the grub. But I won't ask. My stomach can't afford to know too much. And we need to save all we can—the cash from the mystery windshield deliveries, the cash from my books, the cash not being spent on food—for future rent.

"Red-handed!" Cal repeats.

"I didn't do anything!" Bad Chuck whines. He looks out toward the garden shed where a bunch of ladies in blue uniforms are milling, fading in and out of the fog. One of them—blond ponytail, sun visor—looks like she could be his mom.

Cal sets the broken flower pot on the ground. It's gushing

dirt. And money. I think I see a twenty and immediately wish I could unsee it. I don't want to know who it's from.

"Show them," Cal orders Chuck.

Sandy sets down his tea to give his full attention. He appears highly entertained.

Bad Chuck's holding a stack of something. He places it on the ground next to the broken pot. They're signs. Each one's got two metal toothpicks sticking out the bottom and reads:

Rebeautify the Marina. 6 p.m., Saturday, July 16.
Join us for an epic yard-sale fund-raiser, followed by a protest to demand the removal of curb-side squatters who mar our breathtaking view!

—The Marina Beautification Committee

"They're everywhere," Cal says, swinging his arm out. Sandy's retracted his grin.

I push back my chair and walk into the grass behind us. There are similar signs in front of benches, and all along the grass perimeter. We couldn't see them before because of the fog, not even two feet away. I keep walking, tracing the whole area. A giant REBEAUTIFY THE MARINA banner hangs over the entrance to the piers.

"Mom said I could run around if I put the signs in the grass. Ask her. I got to run real fast," Bad Chuck's saying when I return. He grabs a sign from Cal and tries to sound out the letters.

His mom must have had him jamming signs in the ground before dawn. I look back to the group of ladies by the shed. The sight of them is suddenly chilling, like a coven of blue garden witches. The fog keeps their secrets.

Sandy yanks a sign out of the nearby grass and makes a low rumbling sound in his throat. Then he squats by the broken pot Cal deposited on the ground and carefully runs his fingers over the flowers. "Zinnias," he says, smiling briefly. "Someone's missing someone."

There goes my theory about Sandy stealing flowers. But why is Cal bringing over potted plants?

I fall back into a chair and take a bite of Sandy's cheese. If this were Chicago, if a library were threatened by an evil real estate developer, if our lean-to building were about to be torn down and replaced with a gas station—I'd be so angry. I'd be marching in the streets, rattling a saber, or at least a broom. Here, I just sit.

"It's going to be okay," Cal says, sounding breathless, sounding as though he believes the opposite.

"Sure," I say. Part of me wants the ladies in blue to win, to drive us out. Maybe Mom will take us back to Chicago if she can't live right here. But the other part of me worries that leaving this spot will unravel the little we've got spooled, that there is no place else for us.

I study the line of vans behind ours: bent antennae, rusty fenders, torn curtains, missing hubcaps. Would I be scared of us if I weren't one of us? Would I want us gone?

Maybe.

Maybe definitely.

Sandy tears up one of the signs he's removed from the grass. *He* has fight. "Bullies," he barks under his breath. He tears up another sign. He believes we deserve this parking spot.

I wonder if he is feeding the other vans on the block.

"Here," Cal says, handing me the twenty-dollar bill I'd spied in the broken pot. "I—I just found it. And this five"—he presses the five into my hand too—"I found them both on the ground. With this, um, broken pot."

"I'm not taking your money," I say, holding it away from my body.

"No, really, it's not mine. I just got lucky. If you'd been on the corner a minute before, you'd have found it yourself."

I set the money on Sandy's table, away from me. I won't take it. But I won't take my eyes off it either.

Bad Chuck sinks into a chair next to Cal—he seems to sense he's done something wrong—but it's a quick remorse, because he suddenly jumps up, runs to the garden shed, and throws himself on the leg of the lady with the blond ponytail—must be his Mom—nearly knocking her over.

Nobody says anything for a while after that. What's there to say: *What's bad is going to get worse?*

An hour goes by. Or maybe ten minutes. It's hard to gauge time out here. It's very slow or very fast, depending on how hungry or tired or exposed you feel. With Cal around I can sometimes lose track of it. I can trick my mind into think-ing we're just meeting in this spot because it's equidistant between our two homes.

Cal's doodling on the back of a manila envelope on the table. Two of the corners are wet.

I pull the envelope toward me and flip it over. "'Registration materials for Cal Porter.'"

"Yeah, just . . ." Cal reaches for it. I break the seal. It's his report card, his birth certificate, and something else. "Mom doesn't want to wait in long lines on the official day," he says. He sounds a little embarrassed.

"You got a B in Reading and Composition," I say, digging into his report card. "I got an A in Reading and Composition." I smile, remembering. The reading was easy, and the com-position—it was like putting together capsule reviews for books at the library, which I already do almost every day. Did. Past tense. Mrs. Jablonsky said I had a "real facility" for it. It was fun to be good at something without even trying hard. I was looking forward to Reading & Comp II.

"You wanna come up with me?" Cal says.

"Where?"

"School."

"Sure," I say, because I have nothing else to do. And I like school.

But then we get there, and I immediately regret it. Really, I would've been better off plunging a Beautification Committee lawn sign into my heart.

Cal

THE SECRETARY AT MARINA PACIFIC MIDDLE SCHOOL WEARS hiking boots and a plaid shirt under suspenders and shakes hands like he's aiming to take my forearm right out of its socket. Even his fingers are muscular. When he pulls the registration materials from my hand, he pulls me right over. I snag my elbow on the edge of a pointy metal desk as I fall. The secretary and nurse—Nurse Meg—help me up. Jeanne Ann watches from a safe distance with her arms crossed, like nothing here is passing her inspection, including my fall. Nurse Meg escorts us through the teachers' lounge toward a first-aid kit, smacking her gum and her flip-flops as she goes, introducing us to anyone we pass, including a speed-walker in squeaky shoes who comes to a screeching halt when he sees us.

"Hello, Principal Dan! We've got our first casualty of the year, and the learning hasn't even started yet," Nurse Meg announces.

Principal Dan strokes his moustache as he gives my cut the briefest inspection. "The patient will survive," he declares. He's not much taller than Jeanne Ann. I have a perfect view of the bald spot at the top of his head.

"It doesn't hurt," I say. Nurse Meg has run ahead and returned with a bandage.

"That's the spirit." Principal Dan whacks my back. "Take his leg while you're at it, Meg." He laughs at his joke, gives us the once-over, and asks what we've got on our summer reading lists.

"Um." I sneak a sideways peek at Jeanne Ann, who's faced anywhere but in our direction. *"Morse Code: The Essential Language?"*

"Oh! Interesting. The whole world is texting, and you go the other way. A nonconformist. I like it. "He rubs his moustache again. And you"—he turns his spotlight on Jeanne Ann—"what's grabbed you lately?"

Jeanne Ann is practically painting the office walls with her shoulder, she's leaned so far away from Principal Dan. She hasn't uncrossed her arms since we got here. "I don't read anymore," she mumbles.

Now Principal Dan crosses his own arms. He slides his narrowed eyes to me, like we both know there's something very wrong here. If only he knew how wrong. "Don't read anymore? That's not going to work," he says. "Step into my office."

His office looks like a garage sale, it's so jammed with mismatched furniture and lamps. We sit. He talks. I nod at everything he says so Jeanne Ann won't have to. I accept his "best of" books list. He must keep a stack of this list in his desk, because it's typed and ready to go.

"Okay, so I have a promise from you both, do I?" I nod one last time. "And what part of the neighborhood will you be reading in? Where do you reside?" he asks, standing.

"The ugly part," Jeanne Ann answers under her breath.

"Down in the Marina, near the piers," I correct.

Principal Dan looks back and forth between us again, as if trying to figure out the match.

"And you came by today to check out the campus, suck up to the principal?" He smiles.

"Drop off registration forms," I say.

"Yes! Right! You won the organized parent lottery."

Jeanne Ann's chin looks like it'll never come up again.

"But I'm afraid there are no shortcuts with registration. You'll still need to get in line on July fifth. The photographer will be there. You don't want to miss your moment under klieg lights!"

He walks us out. "He's way nicer than my last principal," I say to Jeanne Ann, crossing the street. And the school wasn't as scary as I thought it'd be. I was expecting hallways with smashed ceiling lights and blaring metal music.

"He was nosy," she says, stopping.

"A little," I say. "But kinda funny."

"Ha. Ha. Ha." Her eyes are glassy, and even as she's banging out the *"ha's"*, she's sinking, like each one is air out of a balloon. She lands in a cross-legged position on the curb. I sit beside her. We don't say anything. She stares at the signage over Marina Pacific Middle School like she hopes it'll burst into flames with the power of her mind. 56 DAYS TILL SCHOOL STARTS! The countdown number keeps getting replaced, like a baseball scoreboard. Except more ominous.

"I miss my books," Jeanne Ann says, her voice almost a whisper.

I should've never asked her to come on this errand.

"Which ones?" I say.

She pauses, looking up for the first time in a while. "*The*

Secret Garden. Everything was dark and everyone was dead or sad. And then, *poof*, a garden, hiding in plain sight, sun, magic . . ." She goes to cover her smile but places her hand on her heart at the last second, like she's taking a pledge. "I'd give my right arm for a *Treasure Island* or a *Three Musketeers*. Oh, and *Superfudge*. Most people give up Fudgy in, like, third grade. But I reread him every year. Fudgy has no filter." She looks directly at me, speeding up: "*I Capture the Castle*. That's the one I read with Mom the whole way here. The main character lives in a falling-down castle and is basically starving, but she thinks poverty's romantic. She sits in the sink and nibbles biscuits for dinner . . ." Jeanne Ann pulls a bunch of clover out of a crack in the sidewalk and sprinkles it over her face.

"You sound like you're talking about friends."

She sighs heavily.

"We have libraries in San Francisco, you know," I say, in defense of my city.

"Yeah, at the top of a very steep hill, wrapped in razor wire probably . . . I could ride my bike to four different libraries in Chicago. I *lived* at the library. Every day after school, weekends . . . I was practically raised there." She lifts her head. "We couldn't fit my bike in the van . . . I'm never going to read a book again. Mrs. Jablonsky doesn't even know where I am."

"Who's Mrs. Jablonsky?" My voice sounds high and probably jealous. Jeanne Ann's never mentioned a Mrs. Jablonsky before.

"My fairy godmother."

"Really?"

"There's no such thing as fairy godmothers, Cal."

"Sure, okay, but there are nice people..."

"She was a librarian, where I volunteered. I read under her desk. She said I was 'indispensable,' and here I am, vanished, without a word."

I gesture to the sign we're trying to incinerate with our minds. "The school will probably have a good library." Jeanne Ann should have a Mrs. Jablonsky here.

"You're too optimistic, Cal. You need to think worst-case scenario."

"Why?"

"Because it's the most likely one."

"You don't know that for sure. Any librarian is going to love you. You'll probably be deputized or something." The way she's looking at me, I know this is coming out wrong. Like a parent giving a "believe in yourself" lecture to a kid who stopped listening ages ago.

Jeanne Ann

It's not safe for children out here. Your mom knows better. There are places to go.
Call 555-xxx-xxx.

—The Marina Beautification Committee.

I FIND IT TUCKED UNDER THE WINDSHIELD WIPER WHEN WE get back from my not-future school. It's handwritten instead of typed like the signs jammed into the grass. I place the note on Mom's pillow. I wait till nine p.m., hoping to talk about it, but fall asleep. Hours later—I think it's hours—I wake. Outside, a car drags its fender across broken glass. That's what it sounds like. After it passes, I listen for breathing. I turn toward it. "Mom?" I whisper.

"Yup." She sounds wide-awake. I flip over. She's reading one of her cookbooks by flashlight; I think she's been writing in the margins.

"Hi."

"Hi."

And that's it, the whole conversation. Not *Did you see the 'It's not safe for children out here' note?* Not *How are you, Jeanne Ann?* Not *We're moving in with Sam, week after next.* Just dead air. I'm afraid to ask why she's taking this so far, and she's not volunteering to tell me.

The next time I'm awake, it's morning, early, and she's gone. There's a sock sitting unnaturally upright on her pillow where the "get out" note from the committee used to be—I peer inside. A slip of paper sits on top of coins and bills. Lots of bills. *Tips* is all it says on the slip.

I shake the sock, listening to the jingle, feeling the weight.

Now I wish I'd asked questions last night. Is she really working? Where?

Cal

"Too early," Jeanne Ann mumbles, cranking the window open a crack. It's 6:30 a.m. I'm making her van a regular pit stop on my way to work.

"You were up. I saw the shades move before I knocked."

She tumbles out in the overalls she wears night and day. A friend would suggest she change. A friend would mention that she smells like the inside of an old shoe. A friend would bring a bar of soap . . . if he had the guts.

"I was sleepwalking," she mumbles.

"Really?"

She throws her arms up, like it's the dumbest question in the world, which, I guess, it is.

I slap a newspaper into her hands. "I've brought you the classifieds."

"I don't read classifieds."

"You should. I read them all the time . . . I mean, I used to read them, with my mom . . . before . . ." Jeanne Ann is scratching her head and only half listening, so I speed on. "She says you can know the personality of a city by its classifieds." I don't add that they're guaranteed to make her laugh, and Jeanne Ann could use a laugh.

She runs her sleepy eyes over my bandaged chin, across my Greenery T-shirt, down to my hands.

"What?" I say.

"Too peppy, too early, too weird."

I hide myself behind the paper, bringing it to just below my nose.

"Why do you keep coming out here? What do you want?"

I start to say "I want to help," but stop myself after *want*. What can I say that won't infuriate her? I stay hidden behind the newspaper and don't answer.

"My mom just got a job. We'll be moving soon. So . . ." she says.

"That's great." I pull the newspaper down. "Wait, I thought she already had a job."

"She did. She does." Jeanne Ann whips her face away, chin up, done discussing it.

I stick my head back in the paper and scan for something, anything. "Here's a good one," I say. "'Woman seeks roommate, fit vegetarian who can reach hard-to-dust places; no dogs, flying animals, perfumes, or night-crawling; near G.G. Park. Fifteen hundred a month with three-thousand-dollar deposit.'" I laugh. "Flying animals. What does that mean? Seagulls, butterflies, monkeys? See how good these are?"

Jeanne Ann grabs the paper and begins reading at high speed. She slaps it back into my lap when she's done.

"That's the cheapest it gets." She backhands the van, then does some calculations on her fingers. "Fifteen hundred. Mom'll have to work a hundred fifty hours to earn enough for a month's rent. Then another three hundred hours to earn enough for the deposit. That's like twelve forty-hour weeks. That's a quarter of a year. And then she won't be able to afford a second month's rent or food or clothes or books..."

"Whoa." I roll up the paper. Jeanne Ann pats the pocket at the front of her overalls. I think she's got money stashed in there. But I doubt it's thousands.

She drops into one of Sandy's chairs and presses the heels of her hands into her eyes.

At this rate, we'll be neighbors for a long time.

I should say something . . . but not that. I know not that. I look out over the green, the bay, and back to the vans. I forgot to put money in their meters today. "Wanna come over?" I ask.

Jeanne Ann

"I can't go to your house, Cal." This is his second invite of the day. He's come back, after his afternoon shift at Greenery, with more unwanted good cheer.

"You can leave if you don't like it," he says. He's tugging on my arm.

I strangle a cackle. As if I'm *not* going to like it. As if I'm not going to want to stay there the rest of my life. "Not happening," I say.

We're standing at the intersection, on the van side of the

street. I'm gaping at his glassy Rubik's Cube. The walk sign has gone on and off three times since we got here.

"We've got couches, a full fridge. Well, sort of full. Actually, there may not be anything but old takeout. But I could get it full."

I stomp back toward the vans. He runs around to my other side and blocks the path.

I shove him backward. Not hard, but he loses his balance and almost falls. I'm too tired for all of this. I had a nightmare after Mom and I had our not-chat chat last night—she and I kept downsizing: from a van, to a minivan, to a sedan, to a hatchback, to a motorcycle. It was terrifying. And now: $1,500 for a month's rent? That's absurd. We paid $450 in Chicago. Did she know it would cost this much to live here? Did she even check? I feel like a yo-yo: twenty-four hours ago, I was sure she didn't have a job; twelve hours ago, I was sure she had one; five hours ago, I was sure it didn't matter. There's no point in saving up with rent that high.

"You're coming around too much. Just—leave me alone, okay?" I say. "You're—it's not helping." I'm being mean. I know I'm being mean. But I can't help it. I'd like to swing an ax and take down anything in my path.

He makes a weird sound in his throat and steps back. I've never seen blood drain faster from a face. His arms go limp as yarn. I get why his mom gave him the leather jacket: thicker skin.

Now I feel bad. But I'm too tired to feel bad for someone else.

I throw my hands over my head and bring them down slowly over my face. "Caaaaaaal."

"You should see the bathrooms, at least," he says, quieter than before, but still pushy.

"I know I should see your bathrooms." I've imagined them. A million times. "But I just can't. Okay?"

"But why?"

"You don't get it." *Why would he?*

Cal

I REALLY DON'T GET IT. I WILL TRY TO GET IT. I WILL DO ANYTHING to get rid of this heavy feeling. I skulk back an hour later, with pretzels from home she probably won't accept.

Jeanne Ann's rolled down her window and folded her arms over the lowered glass, leaning her head out like she she's been waiting for me to come back. That's what I'm telling myself.

I hold out the pretzels. She rolls her eyes toward the sky. I pull the pretzels away like I wasn't really offering so much as floating them under her nose. I glance down the block, like I'm interested in the view down there. One of her neighbors, the bike messenger who always walks like it hurts, like one leg is partially asleep, is adjusting the coat-hanger antenna mounted unicorn-style to the front of his van.

"You're learning," she says, squinting at me.

I stand there for a minute, just staring at her, while she scoops peanut butter from a jar and takes mouse-sized bites of it. This would be adorable if I weren't worried about how much she has left and where her next meal is coming from. I think Sandy gives her food. But what if his luck runs out too? He seems solid, but then, he's out here, so . . .

"What happens in public school?" I ask.

She looks at me over her spoon, like I'm asking a trick question. I'm not. I'm just approaching from another direction. I think.

"You learn stuff," she says.

"Do the teachers call you by your name?" I scratch the Band-Aid on my chin, step closer to the van.

"No." She kicks her feet onto the dash. "They call you by your Social Security number, which gets branded on your forehead at registration."

I feel my eyes bulge, then relax. "Very funny. There were only three hundred fifty kids in my old school, kindergarten through eighth grade. The teachers knew my name *and* my call sign, which was my favorite animal."

Jeanne Ann almost drops her spoon, swinging her legs down. "Your call sign?"

"Yeah, we all had one. It was like the thing that symbolized each of us."

"You're kidding me." She's smiling so big, and I'll do any-thing to keep her just like this.

"Mine was the emperor penguin."

She bites her lip to stop herself from laughing. Also adorable.

"They're the ones that guard the unhatched eggs while the mom goes to look for food," I continue.

I edge closer and rest my elbows on the open window frame.

"Don't tell anybody at middle school about your penguin thing, okay?" she says.

"Yeah?"

"Yeah. Definitely don't."

"Out of a thousand students at this school, how many do you think will be truly hideous?"

She sits up straighter. "Cal." She's looking at me seriously now. "You gotta stop catastrophizing. They're not going to chase you down with pointy erasers. There were hideous kids at your old school too, right? They're neon-obvious and all the same, everywhere. You'll just walk the other way . . . Or, um, waddle . . ."

I exhale, then laugh. I didn't know I was holding my breath. I didn't know I needed to ask her all this. I'll be looking up *catastrophizing* in the dictionary tonight.

"Kids are probably nicer in California anyway," she tosses out. She surprises me and reaches forward to tap the Band-Aid on my face, inspecting it, I think, to see if the skin has scabbed.

"Yeah? Yeah. I bet that's true." I pull my jacket tighter around my shoulders. "I mean, I bet I'm nicer than any kid you knew in Chicago."

She can't help it: She smiles. Again!

Jeanne Ann

CAL LEAVES THE CLASSIFIEDS, AND BEFORE BED I PLACE them on Mom's sleeping bag.

I leave notes with wage-to-rent analyses.

How long will Sam, the cook we're supposed to stay with—who took vacation at the *exact* wrong moment, eleven days ago—put us up? A week, two? Then what? We'll have to live rent-free for practically six months to save enough for a place with real walls. We'll have to beg Sam to keep us longer. That's the only way, unless . . .

> *Mom, would you be ok if i got a full-time job too?*
> *—JA*

I leave this note on her sleeping bag as well.
I wake up to her reply but not her:

> *Forget it. You're starting school in a month.*
> *—Mom.*

P.S. Hang in there. That's your job. Food in the front seat.

I tuck the note under my pillow. It's the best bad news I've had in weeks.

Cal

"**C**hase me!"

Nathan shows up while Jeanne Ann and I are trying—unsuccessfully—to peer through Sandy's tinted windows. She thinks Sandy may be hoarding bicycles, jewelry, and other stolen goods in his van. But when I think of his face, his tea, the food he leaves for Jeanne Ann, I can't imagine him doing any of those things. When he smiles, he kinda twinkles.

"Chase!" Nathan is wearing an argyle vest over his camp shirt, and a straw hat. He bops me on the head with his hand.

"Hey!" I yelp. "That hurt." I lunge. He sprints out of reach. "Aren't you supposed to be with the Bees over there?" The Bees are playing capture the flag again, and I think I see his mother with other gardeners by the shed. She's always near but never quite near enough. No wonder he's always up in our business.

Nathan loops the van and, coming around, kicks Jeanne Ann's flat tire. "The Bees are boring. Someone's always peeing in their pants." He throws himself in Sandy's vacated lawn chair and kicks the underside of the folding table with a repeating *thunk*. "How come you're always out here anyway?"

Jeanne Ann grimaces, then looks at me. I still get the sense she'd prefer me gone. Nathan *and* me.

"We're undercover investigators," I say. I don't know where this lie comes from. "See those ladies in blue?"

The Marina Beautification Committee is studying a patch of weeds by the bathrooms and occasionally frowning in our direction.

Nathan scowls. "The Blueberries? My mom is the boss. They say I'm not supposed to pull the grass or run over people on the grass or talk to strangers in the grass..." He looks from Jeanne Ann to me, deciding something.

"That's good advice. Don't talk," Jeanne Ann grumbles.

The Blueberries, though. I kind of love that.

"I could watch them for you," he offers. He springs up and runs in a circle around us.

"I'll put 'em in handcuffs. I'll throw 'em in jail." He pulls out his invisible magnifying glass and holds it up to Jeanne Ann's face. "You're dirty," he announces.

I squeeze in between them. "It's her special disguise," I say, and catch the briefest flash of relief on her face.

The afterglow of that look will last me all day.

Jeanne Ann

This morning my stomach wakes me up. When I look for the jar of peanut butter, I find it empty, under the foot of my sleeping bag. I must've polished it off in my sleep. I grip the sides of my bag. I've got nothing to eat for the rest of the week unless Sandy comes through. But I don't want to rely on Sandy. Then I remember Mom's found a job, and there's a bag of groceries under her seat. Chips, pretzels, food that will survive unrefrigerated. I crawl toward it, feeling the blood flow to my head again.

When I slow down my chewing and finally look up, I notice two things. First, the van smells like dish soap and sweat; second, a new parking ticket waves at me from the windshield.

I go out to get it.

$225.

One of my neighbors, the guy in the yellow raincoat—Sandy calls him Gus?—passes by and nods at the ticket in my hand like he's more than familiar with it. Like it's the reason he's endlessly circling the block, preparing for invasion.

Crapinade.

Cal

53 DAYS TILL SCHOOL STARTS!

We pedal past the middle school, and I try to imagine myself in the pinhole windows, behind the concrete cinderblock walls. It's like a little Alcatraz. I'm glad we're not stopping.

"Where are we going? This is hell," Jeanne Ann squawks behind me. She's huffing like it's the two-thousandth mile of the Tour de France. "We don't have uphill in Chicago!"

"It's a surprise."

"I hate surprises."

I had a feeling she'd say that.

"You said you missed your bike." I pedal harder. We lucked out with a foggy morning—natural air-conditioning—otherwise I'd be a puddle of sweat. I swerve around a pedestrian.

"Whose bike am I riding, anyway?" she grumbles. "It's too fancy." I glance back—she's smacking the rear basket of the bike I tuned up the day I met her.

"It's my dad's," I yell.

"Well, nice of him to lend it to me," she adds, pulling alongside.

"He didn't lend it. It's been in the garage forever. I'd have to know his phone number to ask for a loan."

We ride side by side for the next block, straight uphill, then stop at an intersection.

"Bad dads," she wheezes as we wait at the light.

Down the street, a truck honks. We edge out into the intersection.

I turn my head just enough to look at Jeanne Ann without her knowing. Her eyes are fixed on the road ahead, knuckles tight on the handlebars. "That's the nicest thing you've ever said to me," I say.

She smiles without looking my way. "Don't be a sap."

I think she means it as a compliment.

Jeanne Ann

THIS IS THE SURPRISE?

"The library is closing in two minutes!"

I'm at the circulation desk, staring down a guy with long hair who sounds like an amplified Darth Vader over the PA system. The pin on his jacket reads HEAD LIBRARIAN. I don't believe it. He's chewing gum.

The overhead lights flick on and off to signal our time is short. We haven't even picked books yet. I haven't identified a desk that I can read under.

This is Cal's surprise; if only he'd checked the library's hours beforehand.

"Address?" The head librarian lays his hand palm up on

the desk while shuffling papers. I've already told him I don't have an address.

"We just moved," I explain again.

The head librarian rolls his chair a few inches to the right. I slide along with him.

"Driver's license?" he says, messing up the papers he just organized.

Has he looked at my face? "I'm twelve years old."

Mrs. Jablonsky treated new library card registrations like magical events. She'd have released balloons from the ceiling for every single one if the library had had a budget for it.

Cal bounds up, pushes books across the desk, and waves something in front of my face—his library card. "I went to the staff favorites shelf. I grabbed the first two books my hands touched." He's out of breath.

I step out of his way. I can't even check out a book on my own.

This place is too bright. Too hard to get to. Crummy hours. Gum. Desks too wide for curling under . . . Even the smell is wrong—instead of applesauce, it's musty and . . . A draft passes over us. Someone has opened a door. The breeze from outside carries in something ripe and funky, like old cheese mixed with . . . dog. I look around. Another whiff sails over me.

I pull my shirt toward my nose. Then I lean back and let the desk take my weight.

Cal pokes my shoulder. "Jeanne Ann? You okay?"

I close my eyes. I should've let Mom wash my stuff when she went to the Laundromat this week. I thought I could wait it out—take the first bath, wash my stuff, *after* we moved into a real place. I thought we'd already be there.

I touch the money stuffed into my overalls' pocket.

Sam will be back from vacation soon. We will come up with $4,500 for rent. We will move out of the van. I will wash my hair in the ice-cold public bathrooms tonight. I will . . .

I pull my shirt toward my nose again.

This is how the van smells.

This smell is me.

The librarian's chair spins on its wheels, his hair swings. *"The library is closed!"* he squawks. Then the lights blink out and leave us all in the dark.

Cal

She's scowling at the library's front door.

She won't touch the books, she won't roll her eyes, she won't bark out one of those things that sounds mean but is actually nice.

The library was a terrible idea.

"At least it's downhill all the way," I offer, strapping the books to her bike basket. She doesn't blink.

I fumble with the cord. I should've checked the library hours. How could I not have checked the hours? I watch her kick her leg over the bike seat. "Jeanne Ann?" She rotates the pedals twice and disappears over the lip of the hill. "Jeanne Ann?"

I release my brake and start to follow.

"Jeanne Ann?"

That's when I hear it: *"Ayeeeeeeeeeeeeeeeee!"*

The sound of Jeanne Ann flying home on two wheels.

I pedal to catch up.

"Whooooohaaaaaaaaaaah!"

That's the sound of me listening to the sound of her.

In my mind it lasts hours. In reality, more like two minutes.

When we reach her van, she jumps off the bike and throws herself into the grass. Her cheeks are wind-streaked and her eyes are wide when she announces: "We don't have downhill in Chicago!"

Finally, a point for San Francisco.

Jeanne Ann

I STARE AT THE HILL I JUST FLEW DOWN. NEXT TO ME, CAL'S talking.

"Do you ever wonder how these people got together?" he says. We're slouched in Sandy's chairs. Cal's watching the throngs of people on the marina green. Bad Chuck stomps by, led by his mom, who's telling him in an exhausted voice how long grass takes to regrow.

Cal's sketchbook's open, but he's not drawing. He's rolling

and unrolling a questionnaire from Marina Pacific Middle School that he'd been hiding in his backpack, afraid to show me, I think, which is polite, I guess, but also kind of dumb. I can survive hearing about school. The questionnaire asks if he's allergic to nuts, fish, undercooked hamburgers, nitrates, bullies, etc.

In a little bit, I will have to slink away to the public bathroom, hover over the sink, and plunge parts of my body into ice-cold water to get marginally cleaner.

But for now I'm replaying the ride home—*Wheeeeeeeeeeeeeeeeeeeeeeeeeeee*—and wondering when I'll get a chance to ride down that hill again. It is the only thing I can say for sure I'm looking forward to doing again in this town. That and reading the books Cal picked out. I have never been to a library before and *not* picked out my own books. But they're still books. And I'll read them cover to cover, a dozen times—I'd do it even if they were phonebooks. I will never go back to that library, though. Cal will have to return them.

"Which people?" I say.

"All of them. That soccer team over there. That group by the barbecues." He points.

I think I understand. "Somebody sends a text to somebody?"

"No. I mean, what did they say to each other, the first time they met? And what kept the conversation going . . . for—for forever?"

I pick up my lawn chair, turn it to face Cal, and let it drop. "What *happened* to you?"

He straightens. "What do you mean?"

"Why are you like this? Where are your friends?"

He lays a pencil on his open sketchbook and spins it. "I told you, I'm between friends."

"Yeah, but, what does that even mean?"

He half shrugs. "A few of us—we used to draw, like as a group—on weekends, at lunch, after school." He stops the spinning pencil, leans over to inspect his shoes. "We swapped lunches. Everybody was nice. We hung out like that for a while, and then—I don't know." He looks at me and sort of through me at the same time. "It was like I missed a signal, and they went one way and I went another."

I'm tempted to interrupt, but I don't.

"I'm not sure if I was officially, like, shunned? Or if we just disbanded, because all last year I didn't see any of them together. I still can't figure it out. Maybe we should've named our group. Maybe that's what went wrong."

"Maybe they didn't like something you drew."

Cal's eyes grow wide, like I might have a clue.

"That's a joke," I tell him.

"I'd rather talk to someone at school than no one," he says.

I wouldn't.

"So, then what happened?"

"What?"

"After you lost your friends."

"Oh." He flips a few pages in his sketchbook. "I started drawing and painting more."

"Uh-huh."

"Like a lot lot more."

There's something missing from this story. I readjust my chair so it's facing the same direction as his again—then raise one of my library books and poke at the cover. "Best friend you could ever have. No missed signals, only missed pages."

He smiles, but I can tell it takes effort. "That's why I like you, Jeanne Ann. You say exactly what you think."

"No, I don't." *He likes me?*

He looks surprised. "Yes, you do."

"What am I thinking right now?" I say.

"I dunno, but you're going to tell me."

"Crapinade."

"See?"

I think he'll be smiling when I turn to glance at him, but his face is slack and his eyes have a gray weather system passing over. "It's just me and my mom," he says. "And now not even that, really."

I whack him on the back. "Join the club."

Cal

The Marina Pacific Middle School gym is buzzing.

"Is it me, or does it smell like French-fried armpit in here?" Jeanne Ann says, ducking behind me as we approach the crowd at mid-court.

I still can't believe she came to the mixer. "You'd hide in a corner if I didn't come along," she said before we entered, but that's not true and she knows it. She got kinda dressed up too—dressed up for Jeanne Ann. She's wearing a clean shirt and overalls and smells like soap-dispenser soap. Also her hair is bouncier. Maybe she washed it? I try not to think too hard about what washing hair must be like in the public restroom.

We've brought a board game—Monopoly—which we're supposed to play with the kids we meet, and two servings of dessert, which we just placed in the middle of the gym floor, on plates with labels. Later, there's going to be a white elephant dessert swap.

"You won't be trading lemon cake with these kids when school starts. Why are they having you do it now?"

She's made this point three times since we left the van.

51 DAYS TILL SCHOOL STARTS! A duplicate countdown banner hangs over the scoreboard on the far wall. I really don't like that banner.

I set up Monopoly while Jeanne Ann leans against a wall,

looking bored already. She brought one of the library books I got her, "just in case the party's a bust"—but I told her we'd leave before things got that terrible.

There aren't many kids here—maybe sixty—and most have come with parents. Mom says she'd have come along if she didn't have a shift at work that no one else could cover. I believe her. I don't think she wants to miss this sort of thing; I don't think our separate "spheres" stretch this far.

I walk a circuit around the gym. A lot of kids are playing SPIT, the card game. A few look up and smile as I pass. Principal Dan waves me over from a spot near the beverage table.

"Morse Man! Wound check," he says when I reach him, bending for a look at my elbow.

"Mostly healed," I say.

"And your friend, the non-reader—is she healed?" He is looking at me, serious.

"She's probably read the entire library, actually."

I watch Jeanne Ann kick her heel against the wall on the other side of the gym, nose buried in her book. Principal Dan follows my stare. "Huh. Interesting."

"She had to sell all her books."

"Had to?" His face goes still.

I nod. "That one she's got, that's from me, from the library," I make clear, not wanting to say more.

"Well, she needs you over there, then, for moral support." He gives my arm a pat.

"There's a chocolate mousse layered with cherries and cream," I report to Jeanne Ann when I'm back. "I think it might be crème fraiche, not cream, which Mac at Greenery says is way more interesting. And, someone brought bananas foster. I'm going for that one. They soak it in rum. I hope this place is flame retardant. Greenery used to make a bananas foster, tableside, but they had to stop when someone's fur coat caught on fire. It might not have been an accident . . . Mac doesn't approve of fur coats."

Jeanne Ann sticks a finger in her library book to hold the page. She looks up, heavy-eyed. "Sounds like you've found your people."

"Yeah, if it's just *these* kids, I'm going to be okay," I say. Jeanne Ann cracks a weak smile. I make a quick correction: "*We're* going to be okay."

Jeanne Ann

CAL THINKS MONOPOLY WILL CHEER ME UP.

"You haven't bought a single property," he says, like it's a real tragedy.

"I know."

"You're hoarding cash," he says.

"I know."

"It's not really Monopoly if you just go around the board

collecting two hundred dollars at Go and never spending anything."

"I don't mind." I roll the dice. I didn't want to play in the first place. Clearly no one else did either. We're the only ones sitting around the board after the dessert exchange. I got a brownie; he lost out on the bananas thing and landed a stale granola cookie. I washed up in the public bathroom three hours ago, next to a lady tourist from a country that apparently encourages staring—and for what? For this? "If they play the YMCA song one more time," I say, "I'm going to rip the countdown banner off the wall, wrap myself up in it, and walk back to the van."

Cal laughs, lit up, and I can't help it—I smile. Briefly. Then he looks at the board, serious again, and up at me. "Don't you want to own a hotel strip, charge rent, bankrupt me?"

"I can't really get into that." I roll the dice.

"There—you just landed on Park Place. Buy it. That's a great property."

"It's expensive. How come they don't cover the cost of eating in Monopoly?"

"That's a good point."

"I know it's a good point." I move my piece—the beggar's hat—off to the edge of the board, to the no-place place. "This is where I live," I say. And I dare him to argue with me.

Cal

Nathan shakes the money can before the front door is even open all the way. The sunset is streaking oranges and pinks behind him. "Ugly, ugly, ugly vans!" he sings in rhythm with his shakes. His mom, Mrs. Caspernoff, puts her hand on his head and presses down. Mrs. Paglio shuffles in place and looks over her shoulder as if she's being watched.

"You remember us from last time?" Mrs. Caspernoff holds out a familiar flier from the Marina Beautification Committee. She and Mrs. Paglio are in their blue uniforms again—matching hats, gardening aprons, shoes. They've made Nathan wear a blue shirt and shorts with a delivery-boy cap.

I push the flier back.

"Oh, dear," Mrs. Paglio says, humming like there's a pigeon in her throat.

"This really would be better directed at your mother. We need her signature on our petition." Mrs. Caspernoff leans her head into the doorway. "Hello? Hello! Lizzie! We've finally caught you at home."

Mom has just tried to slide behind me without being seen. She's late to work and has been looking for her purse for the last fifteen minutes. (It's underneath the kitchen island, where she leaves it when she comes home late and snacks over the sink before bed.) She recognizes Mrs. Paglio and nods. Mrs.

Caspernoff shoves the flier forward again, bouncing on the toes of her sneakers.

No one says anything while Mom reads. Nathan tries to rocket into the house but is stopped by my leg. I'm beginning to like him, but if he comes, so does his mom, and I *don't* like her.

"Gosh, it's a complicated situation." Mom hands the flier to me, like it's a hot potato. "I'm late for work, but I promise to think it through." She smiles extra big. If this were the restaurant, and these were disgruntled patrons, she'd offer them a free tiramisu for dessert and wish them a good night.

I edge the door closed an inch.

"Very complicated," Mrs. Paglio replies, almost in a gasp, pinching the collar of her shirt. Mrs. Caspernoff steps forward, whipping her ponytail around to her front. I *really* don't like her.

"We would prefer your signature *now*, Lizzie."

Mom fidgets with the door handle. "To be honest, I don't really see the vans when I look out there. They've become part of the landscape. Have they done something wrong?"

I'm going to slam the door!

Nathan has pulled out his imaginary spyglass and is looming over the threshold, inspecting my pants.

"Is that the question to be asking?" Mrs. Caspernoff says. "Vans are not homes. The curb is not an address. I bought my home with the idea that the bay was my nearest neighbor across the street. This affects our property values."

No wonder Jeanne Ann didn't like Monopoly, yesterday.

Mrs. Paglio is somehow nodding and shaking her head at the same time.

"They have names!" I say, loudly, leaning forward. "They like donuts!"

"Cal." Mom reaches to pull me back, but I blow past her and up the stairs. I linger on the landing, out of sight. She better not sign anything.

"My sensitive boy," Mom whispers to our guests.

"The Giraffe?" Nathan whines. "Nu-uh."

Jeanne Ann

I thought for sure the Monopoly game would scare Cal off, but he's back.

"You really need to move the van. A spot back, even, would be much better," he says, pleading a little.

"That's Sandy's spot. He's not moving." What part of desperation does Cal think is optional?

We walk to Greenery for his morning shift and sit on crates at the back entrance. Gus, the everywhere man in the yellow raincoat, is back here too, pulling odds and ends out of his deep pockets and examining them like treasure. Cal waves—a quick wag of the hand—and starts to get up, then sits again. He looks at me with this worried expression like he forgot to turn the stove off back home. "What?" I say.

"Nothing."

I've brought along *Ender's Game*, one of the library books Cal picked out, and crack it open. "A sci-fi classic," according to the cover. It's not bad. There's this boy who tries to save the world through a video game. The bad guys are insect-shaped aliens called "buggers." My kind of problems don't exist . . . there are no vans in *Ender's Game*.

"Listen," Cal says. "I'm worried. You're going to get towed. Like the last guy."

I look up from the book. "What *last*?"

Cal stares down and away. "The last guy who stayed in your spot too long. I told you before—people get towed."

I place a finger in the book to hold my place. "You said *sometimes.*"

"All the time!"

I want to stick my head back in *Ender's Game* and never come out.

"He had a parrot."

"Who?"

"The last guy." Cal sounds a little exasperated. He risks a glance at me, then looks back out to the bay. "Young guy. He parked for about a month. He sold paintings on the sidewalk. The bird sat on his shoulder. It could say, 'Major talent! Major talent!' Then they got towed. Right before Christmas." Cal sinks into his crate. "The bird was trapped inside. It screeched the whole time. I could hear it in my room. I watched the spot until the guy, the driver, came back from wherever he'd gone"—Cal turns toward his house—"he sat on the curb and looked right up at me, like I should've done something. Jeanne Ann, the bird might still be in that van, in some ice-cold garage?" Cal looks sick. "I painted it. So other people would see. So I'd remember."

"That's a terrible story," I say. "The bird got away. I'm sure it flew home through the open window."

"There were others. Before him." Cal tugs at his bandage, a new one white with skulls. "It's a thing I do—keep track." He looks squashed by an invisible load.

"I've told Mom we have to move," I say. "She says it'll be the same everywhere, and at least we have a view."

He adjusts the crate again, closer.

"Is she good?"

"Who?"

"Your mom. Is she a good cook?"

I think he means *good enough to get you out of here?*

"Yeah. She works hard," I say.

"What's her best dish?"

I shrug. "Food."

"Can you be more specific?"

"Sure: edible food."

He shifts his crate even closer. His Band-Aid bounces up and down on his chin every time he speaks. No one is going to tip Cal today, looking like that.

"Okay. What did she cook for you at home?"

"You mean what did the microwave cook while Mom worked? Boxes of stuff. When she was home, mostly eggs."

He straightens up—full length—pulls out his sketchbook and pats it against his thigh. *Rat-a-tat-tat.* I can see by his face that he doesn't like what he's hearing.

"Food is food," I grumble, but if I'm being totally honest, I can't say for sure that's true. Eggs, scraps of chops and steaks from O'Hara's, frozen stuff—that's what I know. Mom had her cookbooks, her special pots and pans, but I never saw her do more than look at them.

He taps the sketchbook against his thigh faster. "So, how

do you know she's any good?" *How do you know you won't be the squawking parrot in a few weeks, towed to some icy garage?*

I feel something lurch inside me. He's staring at me, and I want to look away, but I know this is a valid question. I know Mom's good, but I hate that I don't know if she's good *enough*. "It doesn't matter. She's got a job." I want it to sound final and true.

"Yeah, but—?" He blazes at me with his eyebrows. Then he stands, pushes Greenery's swinging service door, and walks through. For a second, after it swings back but right before it closes, I think Cal's turned to face me, to wave goodbye, but it's just his arms overhead—like, *How can you not know this about your own mom?*

Cal

I feel instantly terrible about the look I gave Jeanne Ann and go straight to my sketchbook to make it up to her. Like I understand my own mom any better than she understands hers.

"Scary man in line again?" Mac asks, looming over me with a screwdriver and a cup of coffee. Five minutes seated behind the counter, and Greenery's waffle-weave rubber floor mat is already digging into my butt.

"Um, no." I glance up from my sketch.

"What's the drama? Mom sign you up for the Marines or somethin'?" She reaches for a sugar packet on the Greenery counter and empties it into her coffee.

"Just public school for now."

"Well, you need to have a good reason to be down on the floor again. Your mom expects... You know, I don't know what she expects..."

I chew on the end of my shading pencil.

Mac leans in for a closer look. "Oh, I like what you've done with the girl's chin," she says, tapping the edge of the sketchbook with the screwdriver.

"Me too." I flip back to show Mac older versions of Jeanne Ann. Mac *hmmms* and *mmmms*. "The wings really do add something. Your mom see this stuff?"

I ignore the question.

"I'm getting better at her face," I think aloud. As I shade, I tell Mac about Jeanne Ann, my throat tightening.

"It feels terrible. I wanna do more," I say, lifting my pencil. I must look tortured, because Mac *hmmphs*, sips her coffee. Nods.

"Imagine how she feels," she says. Then she orders the Greenery servers to step over me. "Boy's doing important work!"

But not enough.

Jeanne Ann

Cal's leaving me alone about my mom. He's shifting his attention to his neighbors—the ones in houses. He's saved the light-green house next to his for last. I watch from the curb in front of the Carrot as he rings the doorbell, then takes two large steps back. He clutches his bag full of fliers to his chest.

The woman who answers has thick ankles, an intense hairstyle, and a kind grandma's face, which is not exactly how I pictured the person trying to get me removed from the neighborhood. Cal has told me about her visits to his house.

He thrusts forward his flier. It reads: PARK IN PEACE IN THE MARINA. LEAVE THE VANS ALONE. I winced as he made them after his shift, and now I wince as I watch his neighbor's jaw lock.

I told Cal this was a bad idea. I told him I wouldn't help. It's too . . . He hand-drew the fliers with a red cross in the middle—he had to borrow a red marker from work. It looks like it was made by one of those charities that help with natural disasters. I wish I'd stopped him. I'm getting a throbbing pain in my forehead, watching this.

I can't hear what the lady's saying, but she's rolling her shoulders back, which is universal body language for *prepare for battle, buddy.*

Crapinade.

I expect her to start wagging her finger, to call for the husband or the butler.

Instead, she gazes past him, as if at the horizon line. Cal looks over his shoulder like he's missed something, and I follow. Sandy is sitting in his lawn chair in the "living room" between our vans, waving. He's being his weirdo self. Nobody waves back.

Then the lady in the green house leans close to Cal and says something, holding his hand.

As I watch, I try to think who Cal reminds me of—someone from back in Chicago or in one of my books?—but no single person comes to mind. He's not like anyone.

"What'd she say?" Cal meets me at the crosswalk, on the van side of the street.

"Hello, team." Sandy shouts from his table as he pours himself tea.

Cal and I ignore him and settle on the lip of the curb.

"She said," Cal whispers, "'You're young and can't see all the sides of the situation.'" He looks dumbstruck.

"What did you expect her to say?"

"I expected her to take our side. I thought she already *was* working for our side. Sort of."

I shake my head. I swear, Cal would take candy from a guy actively mugging him.

"She also said, 'People do all kinds of unlikely things

when they think they're going to lose something.' What's that mean?"

I look at the lady's closed door. She's right about that.

"And she said I was valiant," Cal says.

"Why'd she say that?"

Cal shrugs with his mouth in this funny pucker, like, *I know but I'm not telling.*

"She also thinks you and I are friends," he says.

"You are," Sandy chimes in from his living room.

Cal

WE END THE DAY WITH JEANNE ANN SITTING IN MY OPEN doorway, looking into the house. It's as close as she'll come to entering. And even there, it's costing her something. I can tell. She's calculating in her head: a quick glance to the right and left, followed by a grinding of teeth.

Mom's at work. I run to the kitchen and return with Popsicles, the grape ones Mrs. Paglio gave me. Jeanne Ann *can't* say no to a Popsicle, I tell myself. And I definitely need one. Protesting is hard work. Many of the neighbors did not take our flier and were not interested in hearing our side. One of them told me I was a communist. I'm not even sure what that means.

Jeanne Ann pushes away the Popsicle. She's focused on the TV, which I turned on when we got here—I'm trying everything.

"Who's that woman?" she says, pointing. "With the froggy voice and the huge hands?"

"Julia Child?"

Julia's rolling out dough on the TV screen, saying: "Beat it up a little bit just to soften it."

"Mom's got all the reruns recorded. We watch them over breakfast and dinner. Or we used to." The queue is exactly as Mom and I left it, weeks ago.

"I thought your mom doesn't cook anymore."

"She doesn't."

"So why do you watch?"

"It's exciting?"

Jeanne Ann pulls a "huh?" face, her right cheek scrunched up.

"Okay, it's . . . satisfying, I guess? Haven't you ever watched a cooking show?"

Jeanne doesn't answer. I think the answer is no. Maybe she never had a TV?

"She looks like my mom." Jeanne Ann leans toward the screen.

"Who?"

"The lady."

"Um . . . sure." Julia looks like a large marshmallow; Jeanne Ann's mom looks like a large hammer.

"She's a pastry chef?"

"Yes. No. She cooks everything."

"Oh." Jeanne Ann scrunches up her face like she's doubting me again. "You think my mom knows who she is?"

I hit pause. "Your mom has one of her cookbooks, Jeanne Ann. Everyone knows who she is."

I turn up the volume. Jeanne Ann really doesn't *get* food.

Jeanne Ann

I wake to marching tubas and familiar grouchy murmuring very close to my ear: "We *had* to park near a parade route."

"You got a day off!"

Mom's here *and* it's the Fourth of July.

I move to the front seat in my bag. Mom groans but meets my high five.

A river of red, white, and blue flows by the nose of the van.

I swing back and forth between the main attractions: Mom, parade, Mom, parade . . .

I want to ask, right away, about her job, but she throws an envelope of cash into my lap and falls back onto her bag, like, *Here you go, here's what you wanted,* and I realize maybe it's not any of my business how she's earning it. If there were no me, she'd still be looking for her dream job. Maybe she'd have it. Maybe she just needed more time to look. I count the money. It's not nearly enough for a person who's always working, never sleeping. It won't pay a month's rent.

She's closed her eyes again. When she wakes up, we'll talk. Sam will be back from vacation tomorrow, and we'll get out of here. I want to hear about that, and what she knows about Julia Child, and gorgonzola.

I watch her sleep. She looks exhausted, even asleep.

I thought I was okay with her being gone all this time, but I'm so happy to have her here, in daylight hours.

I feel inspired to brush my hair, change my shirt and underwear, open a bag of cereal. I watch the rest of the parade from her seat, with the window rolled down. I can smell spent firecrackers, corn dogs, and gasoline. I feel all right. I feel we are marching in the right general direction. We just need to move the van. And roll down the windows more often. It smells like dish soap and sweat again.

The final float in the parade is sponsored by the Marina Beautification Committee and is made of three thousand blue lilacs, according to the sign hanging from the bumper. The same sign reads: REBEAUTIFY THE MARINA GREEN YARD-SALE FUND-RAISER, JULY 16. No mention of ridding the area of homeless squatters. That's not Independence Day–appropriate, I bet.

Cal

"There she is, up at the front." I point, jumping a little, which I know Jeanne Ann would make fun of if she saw. Mom and I have just finished the school tour and are in line for registration. Mom, thrilled about her decision to send me to Marina Pacific Middle School, has still pointed out all the inefficiencies. Like how there should be three lines, not one, and "we should get to be in a special, expedited line because we completed all of our paperwork in advance." Jeanne Ann said she'd join us, but she didn't show up at our designated meeting place. I was sure it was over: She'd moved out of the city without even a goodbye. The entire tour I felt like a puddle, like someone could walk right through me.

Then I saw her in line.

"There," I say again, so relieved. "See?" I think Mom thought I'd made her up. I haven't told her much, just that a girl named Jeanne Ann exists.

"Where?" Mom says. There are at least forty families ahead of us in line, snaking through the gym.

I lean to the right for a better view.

"See the girl in jeans with the red T-shirt, and the lady in green next to her?"

Jeanne Ann is not in her usual overalls, which is kind of shocking and probably a good sign. Her mom is in a baggy sweatshirt over white jeans that don't quite hit her ankles. Her hair is pulled back in a tight ponytail, which is making her face look . . . sharper.

"Red shirt. Red shirt. Oh, yeah. I see her. Proud face," Mom says, craning. "I can't see the mom . . . Wait, whoa, now I do. She's . . ."

"Large," I finish. "She cooks. Professionally."

"Really?" I think Mom's impressed.

"You guys own a lot of the same cookbooks," I say.

This is the longest conversation Mom and I have had in two weeks. There's been no Julia Child, no classifieds; just shared early-bird dinners and occasional lunches, with conversations that end shortly after they begin. I've nearly forgotten how we used to be. Now she seems most interested in measuring me, to see if I've "grown" in the ways I'm supposed to. I can't keep track of how many times she's said "We are really making progress!"

We are?

"She wanted to work at Greenery," I add.

Mom squints for a better look. "Really?"

"But she wouldn't fill out the work-history forms."

Mom clucks. "Right. Mac told me something about that. Well, it's a bad sign when they don't want to fill out those forms. Mistakes they don't want revisited."

On this and only this, I think Mom's got it right.

Jeanne Ann

MOM MUST BE TWO FEET TALLER THAN CAL'S MOM, BUT THE way his mom stands—upright, like she's leading a cavalry—and the way Mom stands—curled in, like she's carrying a cavalry on her back—they're practically even.

We pass them as we're leaving. Cal jumps out of line to grab my elbow.

I wish I'd ducked. Cal is making introductions. Lizzie—his mom's name—is smiling hugely, looking us up and down like she's deciding whether to let us into her club. I guess it's a good thing that Mom made me take off my overalls to wash them.

"I missed the tour," I say to Cal, stating the obvious. I am surprised by how bad I feel at not meeting him. I pretty much promised I would. "Mom got the day off and . . ." *She had to sleep in . . . and take her uniform and stuff to the Laundromat . . . and sleep some more.* She and I haven't had the conversation about where she's working yet, and what the plan is going forward. I keep trying to start it, and then something gets in the way.

"I told you you'd meet a friend at work," Lizzie says, shifting her gaze to Cal. "You see?" She winks at him like they share a secret.

She has the same wet eyes as Cal—wide and alert—but besides that, the two look almost nothing alike. She reminds me of one of those small, muscly dogs—the ones where all the bones show through. She's got dandelion-fuzz for hair.

"We didn't meet at Greenery," he says. He steps toward her and then back, like he's fighting some invisible pull.

"Jeanne Ann, where did you meet my Cal?"

He hasn't told her. Okay. I try to be honest. "Outside."

"Outside?"

"Outside."

"Outside is nice . . ." She turns toward Mom, not particularly interested in my answers. "I hear *you're* a fan of the restaurant."

Mom looks at me, confused.

"Where did you accept a position, in the end?" Lizzie continues.

Blood is rushing into Mom's face, turning her a purple red.

Lizzie looks to Cal. "Cal, didn't you say that Jeanne Ann's mom applied to work at the restaurant?"

"Yes," he says, drooping a little. "My mom owns Greenery." He looks at me dead-on for the briefest second.

"You didn't tell them before?" Lizzie peals. "Well, no wonder you're all looking at me like I've got two heads. Cal!"

A whistle blasts just as I'm building up a head of flames. His mom owns that restaurant?

"Fellows? Jeanne Ann Fellows?!" A woman wearing a Marina Middle School sweatshirt strides toward us, accompanied by that Principal Dan guy. They stop, check a registration mug-shot against the face in front of them—mine. Then the woman thrusts some papers forward. "Incomplete registration. We need your address, here, and again here . . . and just one more time down here."

Principal Dan steps in front of her. "Whenever you're able to get it filled out," he says in a honey-calm voice that makes me want to swat him.

"Mom?"

"I told you, kid, I wasn't ready for this," Mom says, low, turning aside.

I turn too. "I thought we could use Sam's address—for now?" I whisper.

Mom's shaking her head. She's wilted with her arms crossed. Cal's studying her, like he's looking for some evidence of . . . I'm not sure what. Principal Dan is studying her too.

Nobody says anything, and as the seconds pass, I feel like the quicksand has got us and pulled us under.

"When's the latest they can give you an address?" Cal says, stepping between the paperwork and the rest of us. He and his mom have the same selling smile. I feel a warm drip of relief, starting near the back of my neck. I want to kick him and hug him at the same time.

The registrar looks to Principal Dan and then us. "August third." She seems reluctant to say it. She shakes the papers one last time. "But that's the absolute last minute. Come back and fill in your new contact information as soon as you've got it, or we can't promise you a desk on August twentieth."

Cal

I'VE LOST JEANNE ANN IN THE CROWD. *AND POSSIBLY FOR ALL time.*

Mom can't stop talking about her.

"She's got a tough-girl thing going. Right? There's a spark to her. I bet she's smart. I like her. Where are they moving?"

She keeps reaching over for sloppy squeezes and ruffling my hair. We're getting closer to the front of the registration line. My throat closes a little with every sneaker squeak on the gym floor. I can barely hear my own thoughts.

I don't want to think about Jeanne Ann's spark. It's likely smoldering right now, looking for a liar to incinerate. I really did mean to tell her about Mom and the restaurant. Eventually.

Mom adjusts her purse, tucks some untamed hair behind her ear—it just pops out again.

The girl in front of us in line sits for her registration photo, admiring her black lipstick in a pocket mirror and spit-polishing her boots before the camera flashes. She looks like she could kick my butt.

The registrar—the one who asked for Jeanne Ann's address—hands us papers, nudges me in front of the camera. The wait is over. FLASH. The camera snaps my picture before I'm ready.

There goes my life.

We walk out of the gym. I feel a little spaced out, like I've just inhaled helium from a balloon.

I scan the sidewalk for Jeanne Ann.

Mom swings an arm around my back; she can barely reach my shoulders.

"I knew this was a worthy experiment. I knew it would work out." She sounds so proud of herself.

"You want to go home and read the classifieds?" I ask, curling toward her. If I've "adjusted" in the ways she wants, maybe we can go back to how we were. I think that's what I want. I would rather read the classifieds with Jeanne Ann than anyone right now, but that option is probably totally and forever off the table.

Mom smiles, continuing like she hasn't heard. "Look how far you've come since that dark day in the Point Academy office. I'm so glad we dealt with that." She actually claps.

We begin the long walk home. Mom threads her arm through mine. "Where did you say Jeanne Ann's moving?" I hope Jeanne Ann and her mom are discussing that very thing, right now. "Because her mother is going to need extremely high ceilings."

Jeanne Ann

MOM AND I DON'T SPEAK ON THE WALK HOME UNTIL WE'RE a block from the van, and the words fill me and fill me till I just can't keep the cork in. "What did you mean, back at the school, when you said you weren't *ready*?"

Mom widens her stride so that I can't keep up without jogging.

"Sam comes home today," I say. "Right? It's been three weeks. His address is on that letter he sent." I shift to running sideways. "How come we couldn't write that address down on my registration? What's the worst that could happen? He collects our mail for a while, after we move to our own place. Then we just go back and get it from him."

Mom stops abruptly. She's shaking her head and muttering something. She turns in every direction like a compass that's lost its way, and finally settles on me. "Jeanne Ann." It's a croaky kind of bark. "Sam is not here."

"But he's coming back."

"No." She holds my gaze, but I can tell she'd rather not. "He's not. He's not coming back. If he was ever here, he's left. I can't find him."

She pulls out the worn envelope, removes the letter from inside, passes it to me. It's practically disintegrated.

"I don't understand." I can taste something bitter in my mouth.

"I thought he was here." She points to the ground. "He said he was here. He left his number in the letter. I called it after we visited his restaurant. The number didn't work. It's no one's."

"Wha—why would he lie? Why would he make it all up?" I sound calm but I'm not.

" . . . He put in these details. About the city. That only

someone who'd been here could know. About the gray-green light in the evening. And the way the air smells ... like pickles and old milk. I read it and reread. You know. You saw me ..."

"Mom."

"Pride." She sounds very sure, like she's thought about it. "You would lie like that if you wanted someone to be proud of you, if you were pretty sure they'd never find out that you made it up."

"Did he *ever* work at that restaurant?"

She shakes her head, gets quieter. "The manager said no. Maybe he visited, ate there. The return address on the envelope is a real place. I went there. It's a stationery shop. He probably bought his stamps there."

I don't know what to say. He tricked her. She tricked me.

"You told Sandy about this but not me."

"I was going to solve this before you needed to know. You worry so much. For both of us."

But she didn't solve it.

"You *still* should have told me." To passersby, I probably look like a little kid having a fit, pounding my own legs, but this is so much more than that. How do I explain it to her? It's like giving someone the only copy of a book but tearing out the final pages. Why give them the book at all?

She tries to place a hand on my head, but I dodge it. I cut ahead, cross to the opposite side of the street, and see black the rest of the way *home.*

From: Chicago Public Library, Sulzer Branch

Re. Notice of Overdue Books

Date: July 5

To: Jeanne Ann Fellows, 798 W. Wilson, Chicago, IL 60622

This is a notice to inform you that the following books, checked out on May 8, are overdue:

Mrs. Frisby and the Rats of NIMH

Frankenstein

El Deafo

Oliver Twist

Nooks & Crannies

The Lion, The Witch and the Wardrobe

The Golden Compass

The Night Diary

Hatchet

Dr. Jekyll and Mr. Hyde

The Lottery

The Phantom Tollbooth

The War That Saved My Life

The Wolves of Willoughby Chase

Roll of Thunder, Hear My Cry

A Long Way from Chicago

One Crazy Summer

The BFG

Howl's Moving Castle

When You Reach Me

Pippi Longstocking

Swallows and Amazons

The Little Princess

Born Free

Ballet Shoes

The Penderwicks

The Saturdays

Brown Girl Dreaming

101 Dalmatians

From the Mixed-Up Files of Mrs. Basil E. Frankweiler

Merci Suárez Changes Gears

Redwall

The Railway Children

Adventures of Huckleberry Finn

A Little History of the World   The Way Things Work

Zen and the Art of Motorcycle   Finance for Dummies
Maintenance

Your fine is 25 cents a book, per day, or $294.50 total.
If the books are not returned within 8 weeks, you will
be fined for their entire value. Please call this branch
library if you cannot locate the missing items or if you
need to renew. Thank you, The Chicago Librarians

JA, Now you really have us worried. Two returned overdue slips
with the "incorrect address" stamp? We called Uptown Branch,
and Uptown called Lincoln Park, and Lincoln Park called River
North, and River North called Logan Square, and no one has
seen you this summer. Honey, *you know* what happens when
you upset a crew of trained researchers . . . Yesterday, first
thing, I sent Roberta, the new desk assistant, over to your
apartment. Apparently there's a very grouchy older man living
there now . . . Apparently, he cried, "Mother?! Mother?!" when
he saw Roberta—all 24 years of her—and then slammed the
door in her face. So, *you* clearly don't live *there* anymore.
Where do you live? We're going to birddog this till we get our
answer. Prepare to be located. In the meantime, read up, as
we'll require a backlog of book reviews when we reach you.

—Head hound, Marilyn Jablonsky

Jeanne Ann

The used-book store salesman draws out a long "Sssssssssssssssssssssss" as he turns pages, looking for damage.

"She never cooked from them," I insist. *She doesn't know what she's doing*, I'm tempted to add, but don't. "They're worth more than five dollars," I say instead.

I waited till Mom left for work—wherever that is—then grabbed two of her cookbooks, *The Trill of the Grill* by nobody I've heard of and *The Way to Cook* by *the* Julia Child, and I clomped back up to the used-book store. On her book jacket, Julia Child looks exactly like the person I saw on TV. Jolly, can-do. What use is she to Mom now? Mom's lifting crates of soap off trucks, for all I know. We don't even have a kitchen.

The salesman flips another page, moving at a turtle's pace. I think he's reading the recipes instead of inspecting the condition of the book.

I pat the mound of cash in my overalls. I'm still saving the money from *my* sold books to help pay our first month's rent. But with the cookbook money, I'm going to buy myself a sandwich—a fat hoagie—and a pastry at Greenery, full price. If I can't go to middle school, at least I can eat like someone with half a brain.

The clerk scratches his scalp. "Five dollars? I don't think so." This is the same clerk as last time. "Cookbooks lose their value like all other books. Yesterday's recipes aren't today's. My mother served beef tongue when I was a kid. Does your mother serve beef tongue?" He's really smug, this guy.

He shakes *The Way to Cook* by the spine to release anything that might be hiding inside.

A white envelope falls out.

He slides it across the counter to me. "Love note?"

I stare at the return address: 798 W. Wilson, Chicago.

"That's my old address," I say.

I hesitate for half a second, inspecting the seal, then tear it open.

Dear Mrs. Child,

I like your cookbook. I've been staying late at work to make your stuff. The Chicken Marengo was all right, just like you said. I've decided to make all your recipes, even the Deviled Rabbit. Sounds weird, but I bet it's not. Not sure where I'll find the ingredients to make everything . . . I'm going to open my own restaurant, one day, be my own boss. Maybe you'll come. I'll need someone to prep the desserts. You?

—Joyce Fellows, O'Hara's House of Fine Eats, Chicago

The letter is stamped but was never mailed.

"Was I right?" the salesman asks, leaning toward me.

"Love note," I say, mostly to myself. I look at the four dollars he's placed on the counter for me, reach across, and pull the cookbooks back to my side.

Cal

"T.E.L.L. T.H.O.S.E. B.L.U.E.B.E.R.R.I.E.S. T.H.E.R.E. A.R.E. R.E.A.L. P.E.O.P.L.E. D.O.W.N. H.E.R.E. L.I.K.E. T.H.E. G.I.R.L. A.N.D. H.E.R. M.O.M."

Sandy is Morse-ing to someone, but it's not me. I've stopped Morse-ing. It's dangerous. Now I just watch. I only see his side of the conversation. I don't know if there is another side.

"O.F. C.O.U.R.S.E. I.M. K.E.E.P.I.N.G. A.N. E.Y.E. O.N. T.H.E.M."

I think he's through, but then:

"I.T. W.O.U.L.D. B.E. M.U.C.H. E.A.S.I.E.R. I.F. Y.O.U. W.E.R.E. W.I.T.H. M.E. D.A.R.L.I.N.G."

Darling?

"T.H.E. B.O.Y. I.S. H.E.L.P.I.N.G. E.N.O.R.M.O.U.S.L.Y. T.O.O. H.E. I.S. P.R.O.B.A.B.L.Y. F.O.L.L.O.W.I.N.G. T.H.I.S. E.X.C.H.A.N.G.E."

Am I "the boy"?

"H.E.L.L.O.—I really shouldn't reply but—W.H.O. E.L.S.E. I.S. O.U.T. H.E.R.E.?"

Long, dark pause.

"J.U.S.T. U.S. M.R. A.N.D. M.R.S. P.A.G.L.I.O."

I nearly trip over my own feet as I spin left, then right, toward the green house.

Mrs. Paglio? The Paglios?

But that means the guy across the street in the red van is ... And, if I had X-ray vision, I would see a cabbage-shaped person on the other side of my closet wall, standing at her window with a flashlight, exhausting her thumb, just like me.

I've only seen Mr. Paglio in his car and in the driveway, taking down the trash. Dark hair, tidy suit shaped like a butternut squash ... I think of the portrait outside the Paglios' mudroom.

Mr. Paglio. Sandy.

Sandy. Mr. Paglio.

"W.H.A.T.'S. G.O.I.N.G. O.N.?" I Morse.

Another long pause.

"M.A.R.I.T.A.L. D.I.S.C.O.R.D. C.A.L.L. O.F. T.H.E. W.I.L.D. V.S. C.A.L.L. O.F. ... W.H.A.T. W.O.U.L.D. Y.O.U. C.A.L.L. Y.O.U.R. N.E.E.D. T.O. S.T.A.Y. F.A.N.C.Y. D.E.A.R.?" He doesn't wait for her answer. "M.O.R.S.E. H.E.L.P.S. U.S. F.I.G.H.T. N.I.C.E. I.T.S. R.O.M.A.N.T.I.C."

"D.O.E.S. J.E.A.N.N.E. A.N.N. K.N.O.W.?"

Sandy, Mr. Paglio, who is not a criminal mastermind, or a homeless person, has no fast answer to this. "N.O."—he Morses, finally—"A.N.D. F.O.R. H.E.R. O.W.N. G.O.O.D. L.E.T.S. N.E.V.E.R. T.E.L.L."

Jeanne Ann

Cal finds me on a bench the next morning near the vans. I've brought a stack of Mom's cookbooks, to see what other secrets she's keeping from me. I feel different from yesterday. Like the sun might rise at night and go down in the morning. Like I can't trust anything.

Mom's cooking food named Marengo.

She wants to own a restaurant, not just cook.

There is no sock-matching Sam in San Francisco.

I was wondering when Cal would show. It'll be easier to punch him if he steps right up.

Cal's mom owns a fancy restaurant.

I don't really know what to do with all this deceit.

I'm studying my fists. *I really want a hoagie. I really want a couch. I really want to hit something.*

I sneak a look at Cal, sitting at the far end of the bench, biting his lip to keep from speaking.

Smart move.

In the field to our right, the Bumblebees play capture the flag, but the game is temporarily suspended: Bad Chuck has stolen the counselors' megaphone and is darting around the cones, making loud reverb sounds that ring out across the green.

"It's my mom's restaurant, not mine," Cal bursts out.

I flip open one of Mom's cookbooks and scan a page like I don't hear him.

"Your mom could apply at Greenery again. Mac will understand. Mom will understand now that they've met. They'll skip the work-history forms."

"It's not the forms." I don't look up.

"It isn't?"

"She doesn't want the job."

"She doesn't?"

"No." I flip the page to a picture of a man slicing open a fresh fig. "She wants it, but she doesn't." I shake my head at this sentence. "Haven't you ever wanted something that took a lot of steps to get, and you just felt you should get to skip the steps and have it, because you deserved it?"

"Um."

"Also, she's got a job already."

The fig in the book looks like a human heart. This book's not by Julia Child, who's normal and funny. She says stuff like: "The only time to eat diet food is while you're waiting for the steak to cook." The book with the fig picture has sentences like: "We lunched on foraged fiddle ferns, swelled soufflés, and heirloom lettuces tangled like exquisite limbs." *Who writes like that?* "Exquisite limbs" reminds me of novels I had to re-shelve at the Sulzer branch library in Chicago, in the romance section. On those covers, muscly men were always running through fire, rescuing ladies with flowing hair—and the book covers advertised "*passionate* love affairs." Mrs.

Jablonsky says romance novels are for people who believe in "extreme" happy endings. What does it say about Mom that she likes practical Julia Child *and* this "exquisite limbs" junk? Is it another reason I'm living out here?

A field away, Bad Chuck puts a counselor in a headlock. By megaphone he announces that he wants a two-hundred-dollar ransom for this person, "cash."

I feel like I've been kidnapped too, in a way. Would anyone pay my ransom?

"I think my mom wishes I were more like that kid," Cal says.

Cal's trying to change the subject, make me smile. It's almost working. I hide behind the cookbook, but I can feel him staring at me.

"I screwed up," he says. "I thought you wouldn't like me if you knew we owned Greenery."

He may be right. I might not have. "Who says I like you?"

"Um. I do?"

It's true that his lie is so much smaller than Mom's—it's like a gnat next to a dinosaur. I can't work up the same froth.

"No more secrets," I say, smacking his hand, because I need to hit someone and touch someone too.

"No more secrets," he says, wobbling a bit as he does.

Cal

I SCOOT CLOSER ON THE BENCH. SHE'S NOT AS MAD AS I THOUGHT she'd be. I think she was even keeping an eye out, maybe wondering when I'd show.

"Have you watched more Julia Child?" she asks, still not turning all the way to face me. She's looking at her mom's cookbooks.

"No. Not since you were over."

"I wasn't over."

"Right." *Right.*

"She's okay." Jeanne Ann picks at the wood of the bench, pulling up a long splinter. "The next episode is about eggs."

"How do you know?"

"They announced it at the end of the last episode," she says. "You watch them in order, right?" She finally looks up, concerned. She was really paying attention.

"You want to learn how to make eggs?" I ask.

"No. Yeah. I just wanna see. How Julia does it." Jeanne Ann's face is suddenly tight, not quite angry, but definitely on the verge of something.

Back at the house, Julia Child fills the screen, a giantess waving around a spatula. "The egg can be your best friend," she explains, "if you just give it the right break."

Jeanne Ann is in the doorway, legs outside, arms in. I should tell her about Sandy right now while she's in a decent mood. Get it over with. *Sandy is Mr. Paglio. Sandy is not your*

227

homeless neighbor. And it's all for your own good, I promise.

Now doesn't feel right. Never feels more right.

I can see she's making mental notes as she watches the screen. Her lips are moving. About an hour in, she calls me over with a tilt of her head and slaps a piece of paper in my hand. "No secrets," she says, before she lets go.

It's a letter—*whoa*—from her mom to Julia Child.

Jeanne Ann

Mom, if you could have your own restaurant, what would it be?
—JA

CAL'S HOVERING IN THE DOORWAY, READING OVER MY shoulder as I write to Mom. I've chucked several bad first drafts. I want to keep it short. I want a question that gets me everything. He keeps tearing fresh sheets from his sketchbook for me. It's nearly dark. My butt hurts. Before this, we watched twelve Julia Child episodes.

Cal keeps saying "This is a very big deal, a very big deal." He's pacing. He thinks Mom's letter to Julia Child shows that she's serious about cooking.

"I told you she was serious," I say.

"Yeah, but you also said you had no idea if she was good."

"She could be serious and not good."

"That's true. But she doesn't write like someone who's not good."

I agree with that. Her letter to Julia Child, though unsent, is very . . . confident. Like they're equals.

"Jeanne Ann, listen," Cal says, pulling me up to standing. The trees are swaying their last daylight shadows. "You need to get out of the van into a real place. You need a real address."

"I know that." I can't help it, I snap at him a little.

"You also need your mom to cook, like she wants to. At a restaurant."

"Thank you for helping me keep the facts straight, Cal." I am tempted to stomp on his toes.

"I'm not trying to make you feel bad. I'm just trying to say, you want this. Being part of a restaurant is—it's good. The doors are always open and you go and it's like you've been written into a long story that repeats and repeats. And it's always warm and clean." His voice is getting louder. "And it always smells good. And you're always meeting new characters who love it too." He's waving his arms around his head like he's having some kind of religious experience. "And you're taken care of. Completely and always. If I fell off my chair at Greenery, hit my head, slept for a hundred years, and woke up, there'd be a waiter in a tie hovered over me, sprinkling water on my face, and he'd be just as friendly and helpful as the waiter from a hundred years before. And he'd be carrying the same ingredients—onions, garlic, butter, salt—because they're in everything good. And he'd ask me if I was okay and tip me right into my chair and sweep a napkin across my lap and fill my water glass and do all of that in exchange for a little money at the end of the night."

"Cal—" He is not describing O'Hara's House of Fine Eats. He is describing another planet of restaurant.

"Outside the restaurant"—he keeps going, keeps pacing, but faster—"there are loud cars and people marching with their heads down. I could collapse on the sidewalk and people might walk right by. I could be thirsty and no one would think to pour me a glass of water. I could be cold, and no one would offer to turn up the temperature. Not even for—"

"Cal," I interrupt again. "Calm down."

"I'm just saying—I just want you to know—it's all worth it. It'll be worth it."

It's been a long day. My eyes are gritty and throbbing. "I heard you. You sound—" *Passionate. Delusional.* Cal's life is not my life. I'm not going to tell him I've never even eaten at a place that made me feel the way he feels. "Can we drop this?" A ten-ton weight has settled onto my back. I start edging away.

He slows his pacing, blinks at me. "Wait! Let me walk you back," he says, hurrying to get in front of me. When we get to the Carrot, he jams his hands in his pockets—like, *Good night*—then asks, out of nowhere, "Who do you imagine you'll be when you grow up?"

I think he wants me to say *president* or *astrophysicist*—like in some movie of the week about perseverance. But I sigh and say, "University librarian," because that's what I've always pictured in my head. "What about you?" I ask reluctantly.

"I don't know. A few things."

"Well, I already know you aspire to be an emperor penguin. What could be more embarrassing than that?"

"Okay: fireman."

He's more like a firehose than a fireman—but I get it. I get why he'd want that. "Nice. You could save my library from burning."

He smiles. He has the goofiest face. It makes me laugh—I can't help it. For a second at least, it lets me forget how clueless he is, how bad things are.

I open the door, slide into my seat, roll down my window. It's like one long exhale of hot air in here.

"You should eat at Greenery with me." He's thrust his head through the open window and gotten right up close. Too close. "You should experience it."

I turn away, doodle on one of my earlier drafts.

"Greenery is . . ." He looks like he's trying to grab the last word out of the air. "How about tomorrow?"

"No thanks."

"Why not?"

"Cal." I don't really have a reason. It just sounds like a bad idea.

He's bouncing on his toes. "Let's go find her and see what she thinks."

"Who?"

"Your mom. She'll want you to eat at Greenery."

I've got better reasons to find her than that.

Cal

The next day, after lunch, Mom catches me on the kitchen phone, making calls.

She waits, leaning on the counter, staring at me, while I wrap up.

"Thank you," I say to Principal Dan. "Thanks so much."

"Are you kidding? Thank *you*. So glad you called. We'll take care of this. You were right to tell me," he says. "It's a big deal."

"Okay."

I hang up. I smile at Mom. I listen to the fridge whine and rumble. She's back early from a shift as lunch maître-d'.

"Who was that?"

"Nobody."

"Cal."

"Principal at my new school."

"Cal. Be serious."

I shrug. "He's nice."

"Really?" she says, still disbelieving. "What did you talk about?"

"Stuff. School. Did you know that everyone gets free lunch, no matter what?"

"Yeah, they mentioned that on the tour."

"And they're getting rid of the metal detector for security next year. He said it makes kids feel like they're in prison."

"That's what you talked about?"

At the end, yes, but it's not why I called. I'm not telling Mom why I called. "Yeah," I say.

"Cal."

"What?"

"Who was that, really?"

I hit the redial button on the phone and hold it up to Mom's ear. "Marina Pacific Middle School, Principal Dan speaking." I hang up. I hope he'll think it's a butt dial.

"Wow." She crosses her arms and tilts her head to look at me. "I'm so impressed."

When the staring goes on a little too long, I ask it: "Can I get a reservation at Greenery?"

"For whom?" she says.

"Me and Jeanne Ann."

Mom's eyebrows are way, way up, suspicious or curious or both. "Maybe. Why aren't you wearing your new jacket?"

"I'll go get it. I thought I could take it off in the house."

"You can. Never mind. But wear a suit on your date."

"Okay. It's not a date, though."

"Get yourself the corner table."

She follows me out to the living room.

"You and Jeanne Ann spend a lot of time across the street, hanging out in the grass, I notice."

I stop.

Has she figured something out?

"I like that you have an outdoorsy friend. All your old friends were indoor animals."

"Yeah. I guess." She hasn't figured anything out.

"You do errands for Mrs. Paglio. You called your new principal, and you're going on a date. What a turn of events, Cal! How do you feel?"

"Okay. It's not a date."

"Jeanne Ann's good for you. A good influence."

"Yeah."

Once again, Mom doesn't know what she's saying, but she's right anyway.

Jeanne Ann

Mom's here?

This has to be a mistake. Cal's brought me to that restaurant from a few weeks back, the one that resembles a luxury apartment. The walls are upholstered—like couches. The lady guarding the front door hisses just like before: "We wear white," and "This is *no* place for children." Is this all she can say?

Mom's first audition was here. This is where she made the killer eggs that didn't win her a job. Or maybe did, but she definitely didn't take it. Or did she?

I plunk my elbows on the front desk. This is the place connected to the phone number Mom left. Cal made the call, took down the address. It is not a dump. It is not a restaurant to be ashamed to work at.

"Is there another place with your same phone number?" I ask the guard-dog lady. This just has to be a mistake.

Cal steps up beside me. "We're trying to find someone who works here," he says, for the fifth time—she has kept us waiting while she answers the phone and smiles for patrons who carry thick wallets. He doesn't give her a second to answer this time, just grabs my arm and tugs us through to the dining room.

The main restaurant is small and windowless, with high

leather booths in four corners and four small tables in the center of the floor. All of the tables are filled with diners eating lunch, and everyone is whispering and sitting straight, like sharpened pencils.

Cal appraises the place calmly. He grew up in a dining room not so different, just bigger, with better light.

A waiter blasts through, carrying a steaming tray of something.

Cal looks from the waiter to me, then nods in the direction of the swinging kitchen door. He leads as we slip through, nearly colliding with a chef, his frying pan, and a blue flame that has leaped off the stove on the other side.

The kitchen is a quarter the size of Greenery's, with low ceilings and a gray-green glow emanating from the floor. I don't remember it feeling this small before, but maybe that's because there were only three of us in it the last time. It feels a little like a spaceship cockpit, crammed to capacity with bodies and knives.

"Get those kids out of here!" someone barks. I turn in time to see the chef with the too-short legs striding toward us with a serving fork that resembles a spear.

Maybe we should've thought this through.

I do my best to look around while running, but I don't see anyone who looks like Mom.

Cal hits the exit door in back before me, and I only get a second's glance at the little room we've just passed through, a kind of storage area where shoes are piled against a wall and a large woman with her back to us leans over a steaming crate of plates, one hand wiping remnants of food into a bucket, the other blasting water into an open dishwasher.

I know those legs, that back, that ponytail. I know this woman.

The fork-wielding chef is within striking distance. Cal is calling to me to follow him; he's tugging at my overalls.

I don't remember how we made it out or down the hill. I don't remember opening the door to the Carrot. I don't remember falling asleep, or pulling Mom's cookbooks on top of me. But they're here now, and they're making it very hard to breathe.

Cal

Someone is leaning on the doorbell. By the time I race downstairs, it's jingled about fifty times.

I throw open the door. The afternoon light is blinding. I blink, squint, and just make out the blurry outline of a lump on the doorstep and a figure standing behind. "Jeanne Ann?" I say. She hasn't spoken to me since we found her mom yesterday afternoon, washing dishes.

"Why can't I stay and play with the Giraffe?" the lump wails. It's not a girl's voice. "He likes me. He doesn't like you. He told me."

"Shhhh," pleads the figure behind the lump. And, then the scene comes into focus. Mrs. Caspernoff is standing over Nathan, fingers clamped to his shoulder. "Hi again!" She lifts her eyes to mine, shows me all the teeth in her head. She's gotten adult braces since the last visit, or maybe they were hidden before. They make her look more ruthless. "I was hoping to speak to your mom again," she says, "on behalf of the Marina Beautification Comm—"

I slam the door.

"Who was that?" Mom pops her head into the living room from the kitchen.

"No one," I say, which seems to satisfy her, because she ducks back into the kitchen, just missing the howling that has begun outside: "Yay! Slam it again! Do it again!"

Jeanne Ann

JA, if I had my own restaurant? It'd be tiny, a few tables. Far from anyplace, so you'd have to really want to get there. There'd be a piano in one corner and only two items on the menu. Everything would be cooked by one person— me. I'd walk the food out to the tables. I'd watch the customers take their first bites. They'd know my name.

—Mom

P.S. You'll be there too.

I don't know what day it is when I finally stumble outside. The sun is starting to fade, pulling at the shadows. Sandy is squatted by his camper van, cringing at a yellow clamp attached to his right front wheel.

"What is that?" I say, my voice scratchy and kind of flat from too much solitary confinement. I step closer. *Am I dreaming or awake?* I think I spoke to Mom in the middle of the night. I think I said, "You smell like dish soap" and she said, "No, I don't." I definitely remember her coming in. She placed her hand on my head and held it there. I remember dreaming that we lived at the bottom of a well, with no bucket to ride to the top. I think that was a dream. But it's true. We've reached bottom. Or maybe we've always been down here and I've only just noticed.

The yellow clamp on Sandy's wheel looks like a giant can opener.

"The Pretty Committee got its way today." Sandy swings his arm out toward the swarm of Blueberries congregated in the grass near the bacon-scented shed. Every few seconds a member of the committee carries an object out of the shed— a wicker basket, a bag of potting soil, a shovel, a string of lights, an urn—and deposits it on the lawn under the sign that reads PRIVATE: MARINA BEAUTIFICATION COMMITTEE GARDEN SUPPLY ANNEX. Bad Chuck, nearly hidden behind a rusty bird bath near the shed, leaps out and points his water gun at a wooden duck. His mom appears a moment later, her ponytail whipping around with her head, and yells something that causes Bad Chuck to drop the nose of his gun. The committee must be prepping for its yard sale/protest against us.

Sandy sighs and holds up a slip of paper and reads from it: *"A vehicle with five or more delinquent parking citations may be temporarily immobilized, also known as 'booted.'"*

I kneel for a closer look. "You can't move?" My head is too foggy, I can't figure out if a boot would be bad or good for us.

"I cannot move the camper till I pay my outstanding tickets. And if I don't pay soon, they'll impound it." *Bad for us. Definitely bad.*

"They can do that?" *I slept through this?* I've been mostly hiding out since I found Mom washing dishes.

Sandy lowers himself into a lawn chair beside his table and slides a peach in my direction. He's had fruit and bread and scraps of food for me every day since Mom started her job. Even "booted" he's giving me food.

Bad Chuck suddenly appears at my side, a warm, dirty hand on my leg: "My mom says you *live* out here." His water gun hangs limp from its strap as he looks back toward the Blueberries. His mom is shouting after him. "She says I'll end up living outside if I keep being bad. She says you're here because you got in *lots* of trouble."

Sandy, listening, dumps a cup of tea on the ground. I've never seen him waste tea. "This is all very upsetting," he mumbles over Bad Chuck's head, in the Blueberries' direction. "They're poisoning the minds of youth." He sets down his cup with an agitated *clang*.

I sneak a look at the other vans—eerily quiet and still like usual—and fall into Sandy's spare chair.

"You like it out here, right? That's why you're here?" Bad Chuck says, tugging on my overalls, his eyes pleading.

I can't deal with this.

I shift over slightly to eyeball Sandy's suitcase, which is always somewhere near his right hip. "How will you take your trip if you're booted?" I ask him. "Does your friend have a camper van too? You could just leave your van here and bring your . . ."

His arms are crossed high on his chest, but he follows my gaze to the suitcase. "My tea?"

I must not hide my surprise well, because his eyes grow wide. "What did you think was in here?"

Stolen watches. Gold ingots. Tens and twenties wrapped in rubber bands. I don't answer.

"Cereal," Bad Chuck shouts. "I think, cereal."

Sandy picks up a magazine, sets it down, rubs his nose, tugs at his fingertips, coughs. He looks like he's suddenly fighting off a case of hives. "I should probably tell you something, Jeanne Ann . . ."

"It doesn't smell like cereal, though." Bad Chuck is on his knees, sniffing the zipper of the suitcase.

"Nathan!" His mom is standing about twenty feet away with her arms out, like she would like to tear her son away from us, if only she could reach. "Come here this minute."

"His name is Nathan?" I whisper to Sandy.

"What did you think it was?" Sandy whispers back.

I shrug. Not Nathan. Not tea in the suitcase either.

"Young man!" his mom yells again, more panicky. "I'm counting to three. One . . ." She pauses as she looks us over. I'm tempted to give Bad Chuck a hug and really freak her out.

The kid plops to the pavement at my feet, arms crossed, legs crossed, like in protest. His mother crosses her arms to match. I cross mine. It's a standoff I'm not that interested in winning. But I don't want her to win either.

With one eye on Bad Chuck's mom and one on me,

Sandy continues to whisper, "I've wanted to broach this for a while, Jeanne Ann . . ."

Something tells me I don't want to hear whatever it is he wants to get off his chest.

I hold up a hand to cut him off. I wave to Bad Chuck's mom with the other. Her face kinda freezes.

Sandy reaches over and sandwiches my hand between his palms. I get an up-close look at his fingernails—clean, trimmed neatly. Hmmmm. "Here I am, finally committed to leading the life I've always wanted," he goes on. "Nothing in my way. I've retired. Responsibilities begone. I've revved my engines. All I need is my friend, my companion to decide she wants it too. And then, unexpectedly, I find myself sidetracked by something bigger than the open road. Something right in front of me. And there it is: If you are alive, you are responsible, and if you have your eyes open, you don't get to choose what you see."

He peers through his fur, a heavy look. I'm having a hard time meeting his eyes. They're clear and fully concentrated on me. They don't seem like the eyes of a man giving a nonsensical speech. They seem like the eyes of someone who sees me.

I take a giant bite of peach and turn away. The juice goes all over the place. I lick my wrist to catch some. It tastes like heaven around a pit. Sandy drinks tea, donates food, cares about my well-being. And, then . . . lives outside, gets "booted."

I can feel Bad Chuck's mom watching me. I can feel Sandy watching too. "Good peach?" he says. I nod. All of Sandy's donated fruit is amazing. I sneak a peek at his face. He's pulled up just the right side of his smile, and the serious look from a moment ago has slid off, replaced by his grin. He brushes his own hands together like he's just made a decision about something. "I got halfway through my speech. That's a decent night's work," he says. "I can continue it some other time. You'll listen some other time, won't you?" He lowers back into his chair. "I always say, do not disturb a good peach."

I nod for lack of a better response. Maybe he's the Robin Hood of San Francisco, a good criminal . . . Maybe I've been too hard on him . . . Or maybe my brain is too jangled to think straight.

Bad Chuck is tugging on the cuff of my pant leg, trying to get my attention again. His mom is still twenty feet off, but her attention is diverted. "The Blueberries are moving the big *thingy!*" Bad Chuck bounces on his butt a little. "I saw it. I think it's a spaceship. It smells like breakfast too. But not cereal. Mom kicked it earlier. It was stuck inside the shed."

"On three, heave!" A group of five Blueberries push a huge tarp-covered box out of the shed. The ladies just make it through the shed door, then collapse on the grass. Someone's taped a sign to the "big thingy" that reads: $4 OR BEST OFFER.

With the money they raise from all this junk, the committee will double down their efforts to get rid of us.

Sandy peeks around his magazine to glance at the commotion. He pats Bad Chuck on the head. "Did I mention your friend Cal has come by a few times?"

"My friend?" Bad Chuck says.

"*My* friend," I bark, then surprise myself further by crossing the street and banging on the Rubik's Cube door. When it swings open, Cal is there, a pencil smudge on his nose. I'm not sure why I've come and then I'm suddenly absolutely sure. "I thought we'd—I'd—lose too much," I'm saying, "coming into your house. But I woke up just now"—I breathe deep—"and realized we'd already lost it."

Cal

"DON'T SAY ANYTHING," JEANNE ANN ORDERS, PUSHING PAST ME into the house.

She loops through our living room, then back to the staircase by the front door, pausing to scowl, then marching up. I follow her as she mutters and *grrrs*, moving in and out of rooms upstairs, finally stopping inside the door of Mom's bathroom. She gives me a look that makes my tongue tuck in at the back of my throat. Then she shuts the door and the water starts to run in the bath.

She pokes her head out a second later and looks at me for several seconds, not speaking. Steam rushes out over her head.

"You changed your mind about coming inside?" I say, careful not to sound too happy. I am so happy.

She shakes her head; she can peel off a layer of skin with that stare.

"No. I didn't change. Everything else did." She closes the door.

I have many more questions, but I don't ask them. I just sit. "I'll be right here," I say. "Anything you need."

Jeanne Ann

I'VE USED FOUR KINDS OF SHAMPOO, AND THREE conditioners.

I've emptied the tub and refilled it twice.

I am scrubbing till I can see a reflection in my skin.

"Everything okay in there?" Cal yells through the door.

Yes. No. I'll never be this comfortable again.

The tub is the size of a small indoor pool, tiled white. There are shiny pendants dangling from a chandelier above and a paradise of blankets and cushions and overstuffed chairs in the attached bedroom—his mom's, I assume.

"I'm fine."

He's just outside, probably with his ear smashed against the door like an octopus sucker.

There's a moment of quiet, and then he says, "Jeanne Ann, are you . . . is your mom in trouble?"

I swat at a large bubble floating across the water, sending it airborne. It lands on my pile of dirty clothes by the toilet.

I hear a thud on the other side of the door. "That was me," he says, "kicking myself. It's none of my business." Another thud. "But she *could* be . . . you know, on the lam," he says. "And you could be, you know, her accomplice."

I smile half-heartedly. He's seen too many movies. But I suppose I am an accomplice. Was one. Coming here, to his house, feels like breaking away.

"Yeah? What crime did we commit?" I say.

He thrums his fingers against the door.

"Maybe you robbed a series of banks in Utah and Nevada. You dressed as nuns. And . . . you've got all the money in your spare tire . . . which you'll soon trade with a smuggler, who will take you across the Pacific to Hawaii . . . in a speedboat."

He's trying to make me laugh. "I've always wanted to see Hawaii."

" . . . And, you want to be near the money at all times, so you live in the van . . ."

I rub the soap into my too-long fingernails.

"Why *are* you living in a van?" Cal asks. How long has he waited to ask that hot potato? He taps out a new rhythm on the door.

I wash between my toes for the fifth time, then behind my ears for the tenth time. Would it be so bad if I pocketed a toothpaste tube from that overstocked cabinet above the sink? Would they even notice in this giant house? Does that even count as stealing?

"Jeanne Ann?"

I don't answer.

"Did you hear my question?"

"Yes." But it's *my* question. I ask it in my sleeping bag every night, staring at a rusted ceiling. I ask it every morning when I wake up, stiff on a deflated pad. I ask it when I'm trudging to the public bathroom with the overflowing garbage cans and the sinks that only run ice water.

"I like your version of things," I say, bursting a bubble with a slap. I'm adding to the waterworks, suddenly. I knew this would happen. "Let's stick with that."

Cal

HOW WILL I EXPLAIN THIS TO MOM IF SHE WALKS BY? SHE IS JUST downstairs, working in the kitchen. I will probably tell her the truth. It's way overdue.

Jeanne Ann exits the bathroom in her overalls—she's back to the overalls—with a towel wrapped around her head. She sniffles, rolls her eyes upward like she's praying for something. I think she's trying not to cry.

"It's okay," I say. But is it okay? A crying Jeanne Ann?

"No, it's definitely not okay," she snaps. Her eyes are really red. Maybe she already cried. "We left Chicago . . . we lived like this . . . for nothing."

"Not nothing."

"My mom's a dishwasher. She's supposed to be a cook. At least in Chicago she *was* a cook."

I want to say: *If you hadn't left Chicago, I wouldn't have met you,* but the best I can do is open and then close my mouth.

I get her to follow me to my room, point her to a beanbag chair. She sits—"Oh"—and then abruptly stands.

"What?"

She gestures to my walls.

"Oh. Yeah." She's the first person—besides me and Mom—in here in a long time.

"That's a lot of wings." She's standing in front of one of my sketches, my self-portrait . . . with wings, which is next to my Greenpeace ship with wings, and my Rosa Parks with wings. I'm still perfecting that one.

"They're heroic," I say. "I mean, they're supposed to be."

"Wings?" She sniffles.

"Symbols of superhuman strength or physical courage. You know, like Hercules, Eleanor Roosevelt, Mother Teresa . . ."

"They had wings?"

"No . . . yes . . . in spirit. Here." It's no fun to explain this. I'm happy she's seeing my stuff, but I don't want to talk about it.

"They're kind of intense, the wings," she says.

"I guess."

She wipes her nose on the back of her arm and looks at me, nodding, like she's solved something. It feels like an X-ray. I look away. I look around. I snatch up the purple skirt and matching blouse with wave patterns that Mom had in the garage in a "donate" bag. I've been collecting clothes, waiting for a chance to give them to Jeanne Ann. "Keep them," I say, feeling bold.

Jeanne Ann looks down at herself.

Her face closes up and she pushes Mom's clothes away. "I gotta go," she says. "This was a bad idea."

"Wait! No, it wasn't." She's already out of the room and halfway down the hall. She stops and turns; she's gone the wrong way if she wants to get downstairs. "Don't leave." I step into the hall. "You've come all this way."

She has to slow down to go around me.

"I made a reservation at Greenery," I continue, talking fast. "We could—you could taste what your mom thought she'd be . . . why you're here."

This stops her midstride.

Jeanne Ann

CAL STARTS TALKING ABOUT THE GREENERY MENU, THE dishes that Mac, the chef, makes best, and he just won't shut up. He thinks Mom would "actually really like it." He says it's the sort of food Mom aspires to make.

I don't know what's wrong with me—I should be running out of here, but I don't. I'm stuck. The house is warm and the rug in the hall feels like marshmallows between my toes. The bath has turned my legs to mush, and my eyes burn with too much shampoo and too much time in the van feeling sorry for myself and Mom, who will not give up but cannot win.

Mom's washing dishes. Washing food off people's plates that she should be making and I should be eating.

I'm hungry. For something hot, with sauce. The food Mom buys is fine, but it's never enough and it's cold. Cold. I don't want to be cold anymore. Cal says if I don't like the restaurant, if I am uncomfortable, I can just leave. He tells his mom we're going, and she says, "Of course!" Just like that. "Of course!" She was downstairs the whole time I was in the bath—and didn't even notice. Cal says she sometimes doesn't look up when she's distracted by work. She's looking up now. Looking so hard at me, I think she sees it—what we are.

Does she pity me? Do I care anymore? I don't think so. She's dressed up for a fancy event and wears a gowny thing that trails across the floor. She looks like a doll wrapped in a rug. No offense. She's hunting for her purse, so she can go. Cal pulls me aside, offers the skirt-set combo again, and I take it and change. I'm in his mom's clothes. Something has definitely cracked inside me. I stepped into his house and now I'm on this slide that will not end, and I'm not sure I want it to.

I'm not Mom's accomplice anymore. But I'm not sure what I've become instead.

Cal

"Greenery sparkles," Jeanne Ann says, looking up from her book, elbows on table. She doesn't sound exactly impressed. But so far: no scowls. She only agreed to come if I loaned her a book, so I found my copy of *Dune*. Her face got tight when she accepted it. I don't know why I didn't loan it sooner. She finished the library books the same day she started them.

We're seated in the corner booth, where the floor-to-ceiling windows meet. We can see everything from here: bubbling wine in the high-stem glasses, silver buttons on sports coats, gems in ladies' necklaces, glassy chandeliers, even the first brush of sunset glancing in.

"Yeah. I could never draw this," I say.

I'm glad Mom's got an awards banquet tonight—she gave her blessing and watched us walk down the driveway and across the street before she shut the front door—but I also wish she were here, refereeing the floor, so nothing spins out of control.

"Yes, you could," Jeanne Ann mumbles, nose back in the book. "You can draw anything."

Jeanne Ann's wearing Mom's wave skirt and the matching

blouse, and her hair is up in a bun, curls popping out in every direction. Every few seconds she looks up from *Dune* and cases the restaurant.

I want to say something, but I'm not sure what, so I show her the I.D. that the middle school just sent in the mail—my eyes are closed, but my hair is over them, so it's sort of a wash. I hope it'll make her laugh. She cracks the mildest smile.

"We give the mayor this table when he comes," I say, tapping my plate with my sketchbook. *I can draw anything . . .*

"He brings his vegetarian girlfriends," I continue. "We're hoping he settles down with one of them." Jeanne Ann reaches across to my plate and places a finger on my butter tab. She stares deep into my eyes: "*Don't* tell that one at your new school," she says. "You gonna eat that?"

Jeanne Ann

THE FOOD AROUND HERE LOOKS LIKE THE PICTURES IN Mom's cookbooks . . . minus the steak and gravy. No one will bring me any, is the problem.

"Do they always make you wait so long for food?" I'm chomping on ice from my water glass. I've eaten all the butter slabs on the table. Cal says I was supposed to wait for the bread. Whatever.

I adjust my skirt. It's too small; I have to leave it unzipped at the top so I can breathe, but the zipper is itching, and my

feet are hot in my high-tops. At least there's the book—*Dune*.
I can't decide if I'd rather live on a barren planet and wear
a suit that recycles my pee, or in a van, on Earth, with no
good place to pee.

Cal's introduced me to the waiter—or as he calls him, "the
server"—the busboy, and the person in charge of wine, who
has a serious winking problem.

I unroll the paper menu. The main dish is called fricassee. It sounds like a disease, but I bet it will taste good. I get
to finally try gorgonzola.

"You okay?" Cal asks.

I am weighing the differences between the bag of non-
perishable grocery-store food under the front seat of the
Carrot and this menu. I wonder what Mom would say if she
were here, with us, if she'd admit she liked it. Or if she'd
say one thing and mean another.

"Hungry," I say. "So hungry."

"I can fix that," he says, waving his arms. "I can actually
fix that."

Cal

MAC SETS DOWN TWO SALADS—FLUFFY MOUNDS OF GREEN
dotted with slices of grilled peach and chunks of blue-veined
gorgonzola. I love this salad. Mac makes it look like art. She
gave us extra-large servings. We are doing this!

"Nice to see you again," Mac says, beaming at Jeanne Ann. Mac knows everything. Yesterday, when I asked her why a great cook would ever take a job as a dishwasher, she looked at me cockeyed and then slurped up a big sip of coffee to give herself a second to think. "'If I can succeed, I can fail—dodging one means skipping the other,'" she said, like she was quoting someone. I didn't understand what she meant, but when I told Jeanne Ann, afterward, her mouth opened slightly and she asked me to write Mac's exact words down.

"On a date with our patron saint." Mac pats my back now. "He's not the greatest at counter service, but man, can he take care of a gal."

My toe connects with her shin too late.

Jeanne Ann

"IT'S NOT A DATE," CAL SAYS AGAIN. HE'S REPEATING IT FOR me and Mac, the chef lady, and anyone nearby who will listen. "Not a date."

His squirm is a tiny bit hilarious. He's sucked his head so deep into his neck, I think it's going to disappear entirely. While it's out of the way, I get a clear view of red and blue lights, blinking and swirling on the other side of the floor-to-ceiling windows. They're reflecting off the window glass like fireworks.

I stand and lean forward for a better look. The lights are so urgent.

"It's not a date," Cal says again, tugging my sleeve. "*Really*. I mean—well, Mom says it is, and it can be, if you want, but . . ."

I pull away and take a step toward the windows. Mac turns to look out the windows too.

"Let's just eat. The food's getting cold. Ha. The food is already cold." Cal scoots out of the booth to come around to my side. "*Please*."

I can hear him saying something else, but it's crossing and snagging with the . . .

Oh, no. No, no, no, no, no!

I dodge past the wine server who winks too much and tear out Greenery's front door.

"Stop!" I yell, flying over faded chalk arrows, now pointing in the wrong direction. "Don't tow us!"

I wave my arms, jump into view. The man inside the tow truck sees me and hears me—I know he does—but he rolls up his windows. The front of the Carrot has already been raised; it's attached to a giant metal hook; only the van's back wheels touch the ground. "Please!" I bang on the door of the tow truck. "Just give us a ticket like last time! Don't tow us."

The driver revs his engine and begins pulling away from the curb. I have to jump onto the sidewalk to avoid getting my toes run over.

A traffic cop pulls into the lane behind the tow truck and gives me the barest sideways glance, his flashing lights spinning circles, reflecting off the water and every remaining pane of glass.

Cal

THE AIR'S GONE STILL AND STICKY. EVEN THE PASSING CARS SEEM to glide by in slow motion.

I sit beside her on the curb.

I let another van get towed.

This is my fault. If we'd been with the van instead of at Greenery, I would've talked the tow driver down. I would've bribed him. I would've . . . done something. I don't know what, but something.

Jeanne Ann

"I HAVE TO WAIT HERE," I SAY TO CAL, TWISTING TO LOOK at the streetlight above. It can't decide if it wants to be on or off; every ten seconds, I lose sight of my hands.

"Until your mom gets back?" Cal says.

I nod.

"I'll wait with you."

No. "Your mom will worry if you don't go home."

He thinks about that.

"Come with me, then. We can keep watch from my room."

I sit up straighter. "I can't. My mom has to see me—here." I point to the ground at my feet. She has to see me, and I have to save the spot. This is our corner of everything.

Cal digs something out of his pocket and hands it to me. Two slices of fresh bread wrapped in a napkin, two tabs of butter, and the menu. "Mac has doggy bags with your name on them."

"Thanks." I should not have gone to his house for a bath. I should not have accepted his invitation to dinner. "That happened so fast."

He stands, shuffles.

"Yeah," he says.

I find myself staring at his ankles.

"I'll stay," he says.

"Okay." He's wearing tan loafers with lime-green socks. "If it'll make you feel better," I whisper, studying the folds in his socks, the inward turn of his feet, the warmth of his night shadow over me. I think I have never paid closer attention to anything in my life.

Cal

WE SIT BACK TO BACK AT FIRST. THEN SIDE TO SIDE. THEN SHE rests her head on my shoulder. I don't like the circumstances, but I like this feeling. A white parking ticket flaps at us from under Sandy's windshield wiper. Is he home with his wife tonight? I hope so. I hope they're together, making up.

"Cal?"

"Yeah."

"You're a really good person."

"Nah."

"Don't argue."

"Okay."

"Promise me, when you start middle school, the first week, you won't speak to anybody unless they speak to you first. Don't try to make a friend. Don't stalk. Just observe. Draw. Keep to yourself. Be mysterious."

"Okay."

"It's all gonna work out."

"Sure."

Her head gets heavier on my shoulder. But I can handle it.

Jeanne Ann

It's four a.m. by the time we board the 30 bus, switch to the 19, and wait while the night-shift driver is replaced by the morning-shift driver. Mom sits upright and at attention, with her purse propped up at her hip, a corner of dishwasher smock hanging out the top.

She hasn't said much since she found me sitting on the curb. She sent Cal home, pulled me up by my armpits, and walked us to the nearest bus stop.

"We should've listened to the kid," she says now, as the new bus driver revs the engine, adjusts his mirrors, makes the sign of the cross. We're in a row near the front. There are three people napping in the bus's way back.

"Yeah," I say, leaning against her. "They really do tow."

Our seats vibrate as the bus rumbles through a tunnel.

"This is it," Mom says over the noise. "This is it, for now."

It's the answer to almost every question I've got.

The bus grinds uphill like it's using muscle to climb—just like Cal and me on bikes—then whooshes and shudders on the down-slope. We pass through neighborhoods I've never seen before. They look nothing like the neighborhood we're living in. Each one could be its own city. One stacked with skyscrapers framed in lights and the next stair-stepped with skinny houses in rainbow colors. Every hill we slip down makes me wonder where the bottom of the city is, when we'll hit it. Have we already?

We sway in our seats. Mom's hand rests on top of mine.

"What's with the outfit?" she says.

I look down at myself.

"I got invited to dinner."

She snorts. A comforting sound. "I wasn't sure what to be more worried about when I found you—the van or your clothes."

She gently turns my chin toward hers. She inspects my face, neck, arms.

"I'm fine," I say, rolling back and away.

She touches the fabric of my skirt. "A loaner, from his mom," I say.

She raises an eyebrow.

I pull the menu from my pocket.

She tucks it in her purse, occasionally pulling it out to read, occasionally looking out the window, occasionally flicking her eyes in my direction.

"Fricassee is old-school. It's basically leftovers in a dressed-up stew. French. The French get away with everything." She puts the menu away. Takes it out.

"I had to leave before it was served."

"And the salad?"

"Doggy-bagged."

She nods. "Too bad." She sounds sincerely sorry.

"How come we never eat food like that?" I ask.

She covers her mouth with the menu. I think she's not going to answer, but then she says, "Don't want you to get a taste for something I can't provide." It comes out quick but sure, like she's known this for some time, and it makes me wonder what else she's going to reveal. She sets down the menu and rubs the corners of her eyes.

The bus stops, and we step out into the gray light of early morning.

The pay window, a block on, is pocked with dents and scratches; it has met its share of angry visitors. A small pane slides open as we approach.

The total bill comes to $844—the tow plus the previous two parking tickets. They won't give you back your vehicle if you have outstanding tickets.

All of our money—from the books, the windshield, Mom's job—is stuck in the van in my overalls, where Cal and I stopped to unload before dinner. But if Mom got paid tonight, if she worked overtime—like eighty hours instead of forty this week—then maybe . . .

She slides a wad of cash through the slot.

I hold my breath and close my eyes. If we can afford to pay to get our van back, I won't eat anything but peanut butter for the rest of my life, and I'll never leave the van without our savings on my body . . . I shouldn't have in the first place.

When I open my eyes, a voucher appears through a slot near her head, accompanied by the sounds of a printer, powering up and down.

Mom says we have enough to retrieve the Carrot, get the tire patched, buy a gallon of gas, cross town, and re-park. "Ninety-eight dollars in tips," she says, explaining. Saved by tips! I'm going to be the biggest tipper if I ever have the chance.

But we're no closer to that $1,500 rent, plus down payments.

No closer to a couch.

Much closer to pb&j for the rest of my life.

This is when Mom should say we're going back to Chicago, when she should say this isn't working.

I wait for it.

I wait for it.

I wait for it.

Cal

"**I** go home one time," Sandy says, holding up a finger to the yawning moon, "*one time*, and look what happens."

We've moved his lawn chairs to the vacant spot, on top of the motor-oil-stained cement, and are seated in them. It's so barren and cold without Jeanne Ann's van here. The sun is just starting to raise its orange eye.

"They'll come back," Sandy keeps repeating. It's been four hours since they left. How long does it take to get across the city from the tow lot?

"Why *did* you go home?" I rub my eyes—they feel woolly. I haven't slept yet. I got Sandy and returned to the vans. I wonder if Mom checked in on me when she got home from her banquet last night. I don't think so. There would be a SWAT team in our driveway right now if she knew I was not in my room.

Sandy leans toward me, elbows on his thighs. "Because my wife is beside herself. I live in a space one-seventeenth the size of my real home." He flings his arm out toward his house. "To her, I'm behaving irrationally. To me, I've just retired. I'm old. I'm going to die one day, and I don't want to waste another minute in that house. She doesn't under-stand. She wants to live out her days attending smoked-fish luncheons with master gardeners. She wants to think about the symbolism of orchids. The road doesn't offer the refinements she says she requires. She's angry that I'm making her choose."

I don't understand either. "You're dying?"

"We're all dying." He combs his fingers through his beard, glances at the yellow clamp on his tire that prevents him from going anywhere. I don't think it was part of his living outdoors plan. "If you keep that in mind every day, Cal, you'll be much less scared of the little stuff."

"I think they're going back to Chicago," I say. That doesn't feel at all little.

"That would be okay," Sandy says.

"No, it wouldn't!" I hate how I sound. Like a baby. But it's the truth. I take a breath. "I'll never see her again."

Sandy lets go of his beard and adjusts his chair so he's knee to knee with me. He reaches over and places a hand on each of my shoulders. "We will help them get back on their feet, Cal. After that, they should go where life is best for them."

"I didn't help enough. Not with them. And not before either. Or before or before or before."

Sandy mushes up his forehead squinting at me. "You saw those other tows too, eh?"

"Yeah."

Sandy nods. "I still hear that parrot."

I snap my eyes to him. "Me too."

A figure emerges from behind a tree at that moment—Gus—and shakes the dew from his battered raincoat. Sandy looks up and twinkles his eyes and Gus twinkles back. "He lost somebody he can't get back," Sandy says, lowering his voice.

"How do you know?"

"He told me."

I stare at Gus as he works his knitting needles out of his pocket. He's found some yarn and is making something with it.

Why did I never think about the knitting before? Who does he knit for?

Why?

I'll get him more yarn.

. . . I will ask him if he wants more, first.

"I find it's more tolerable if you spread the blame around," Sandy says, watching me. "Blame the city for not leaving them be, and the landlords for charging sky-high rents, and the tow truck drivers for being too good at their jobs, and the people in the vans for not thinking far enough ahead. And then, way down at the bottom of the list, me and you."

That sounds a lot like not feeling bad at all. That sounds like an excuse. "I want to blow up this parking spot. Make it impossible for anyone to park here ever again." I lean my head into my hands. This hurts so much more than it ever did before. And it's not even my own pain. It's Jeanne Ann's. Or maybe it's not. Do I even know how Jeanne Ann feels? I try to really imagine it. I'm not sure I can. And that only hurts more.

"That's one approach," Sandy says. "Blowing it up. But there's a better way, I bet." He waves at something behind me. "We'll figure it out."

Jeanne Ann

"THAT'S YOUR DATE?" MOM ASKS AS WE IDLE AT THE STOP light, opposite our spot. Sandy is waving. Cal has stood up.

"It wasn't a date."

"The kid's wispy."

"You mean tall?"

"Naw. I mean weak."

This annoys me.

"He's not."

She rolls down her window and takes a deep breath of warm air.

"I've been reading your cookbooks," I say, testing.

Mom runs her hand over the dashboard, fiddles with the radio dial that's never worked.

"Can you make that stuff, in the books?"

The light turns green, and we lurch across the street, coming to a hard stop in front of our parking spot. Cal jumps to the curb with his chair. Sandy shakes his teapot.

Mom revs the engine, puts the van in reverse, and prepares to back in.

I study her profile. "Mom?"

She sighs—"Jeanne Ann"—looks at me quickly, scrunches up her face—is that a glare, a shrug, a wince? "It would be better if you forgot about those books."

I fold my hands in my lap.

She honks a quick blast to signal our return.

She knows that *I* know that I cannot forget about books.

PLACE

From: Chicago Public Library, Sulzer Branch

Re. Notice of Overdue Books

Date: July 13

To: Jeanne Ann Fellows, 798 W. Wilson, Chicago, IL 60622

This is a notice to inform you that the following books, checked out on May 8, are overdue:

Mrs. Frisby and the Rats of NIMH

Frankenstein

El Deafo

Oliver Twist

Nooks & Crannies

The Lion, the Witch and the Wardrobe

The Golden Compass

The Night Diary

Hatchet

Dr. Jekyll and Mr. Hyde

The Lottery

The Phantom Tollbooth

The War That Saved My Life

The Wolves of Willoughby Chase

Roll of Thunder, Hear My Cry

A Long Way from Chicago

One Crazy Summer

The BFG

Howl's Moving Castle

When You Reach Me

Pippi Longstocking

Swallows and Amazons

The Little Princess

Born Free

Ballet Shoes

The Penderwicks

The Saturdays

Brown Girl Dreaming

101 Dalmatians

From the Mixed-Up Files of Mrs. Basil E. Frankweiler

Merci Suárez Changes Gears

Redwall

The Railway Children

Adventures of Huckleberry Finn

A Little History of The World

Zen and the Art of
Motorcycle Mai . . .

The Way Things Work

Finance for Dummies

Your fine is 25 cents a book, per day, or $351.50 total. If the books are not returned within 8 weeks, you will be fined for their entire value. Please call this branch library if you cannot locate the missing items or if you need to renew. Thank you, The Chicago Librarians

Jeanne Ann, You're very good at disappearing. You're very good at most jobs you set your mind to, so it should not surprise me that you're good at one more. Perhaps too good. We've got fifty librarians on the case now, one for each state in the union, and none can seem to locate you. Very slippery, and more than a little worrisome. We'll have you the moment you enroll in school; that's what we're all telling ourselves, between hand-wringings. Wherever you are, hang in there. I know this letter probably won't reach you, but I'm writing it anyway. Desperate times. Find the nearest library and hunker down.

—One of Fifty, Marilyn Jablonsky

Cal

"Come over. Let's watch Julia Child."

"Can't," Jeanne Ann says. Which is what she said yesterday and the day before that.

She's sitting in the driver's seat of the van, dividing her attention between the rearview mirror and the windshield. I'm in the passenger seat but facing her. It's got to be a hundred degrees in here. Freak heat wave. My hair sticks to my forehead like pasta to sauce.

Somehow, Jeanne Ann looks cold and alert. She's got a metal spatula in her lap. I feel scared for any tow truck driver who approaches.

"Icy lemonade *and* Julia Child?" It's hard to make anything sound enticing with my tongue hot-glued to the roof of my mouth.

The Paglios said that bribery is a perfectly acceptable way to motivate someone in a situation like this. They said I should try everything. Food, books, cash. Since the tow, Jeanne Ann's back to micro-bites of peanut butter. She and her mom are nearly broke again. Sandy's regular snack deliveries are the day's bright spots—at least for me. He bulks them up as much as he can without blowing his cover. I've decided I'm glad she doesn't know who he really is. He's our secret weapon in disguise.

A siren blares, and Jeanne Ann rockets to the back window, pushing back the curtain.

"Can you see it?!" she yells. "I can't see it."

"It's an ambulance," I say quickly as it turns right into the parking lot by the piers.

"Ambulance," she repeats, hands over ears, face two shades paler than a moment ago. This is the third siren in less than an hour. She can't get much paler.

Jeanne Ann returns to the driver's seat and gazes at the houses across the street.

"You've got to move the van," I say.

She blinks her eyes so slowly it almost looks like she falls asleep for a second, but then they're wide again. "This is it. We . . ." She doesn't finish the thought.

"Come on," I say. "We can watch the van from across the street."

She shakes her head and fiddles with the key in the ignition. "It's too far. They could tow us like that." She snaps her fingers.

"You'll go stir-crazy in here," I say. She hasn't left the van except to use the restroom.

"Too late," she says, staring dead ahead, like she knows how this story ends.

I don't think it's too late. But it's hard to argue with someone so sure.

Jeanne Ann

I SWEAR I CAN HEAR CAL THINKING OF SOMETHING ELSE TO offer. This is his millionth visit. He doesn't get that it's over, he can go home, no more making the best of it. Things are back to the way they were. Rock bottom. He guessed it the other day: I *am* Mom's accomplice. She *can't* make this work without me. My job is the van, keeping it safe. We are as tangled as my hair.

"How about the library? I'll get you more books," he says.

"No thanks." Mrs. Jablonsky would not approve of my borrowing books on someone else's card. "I shouldn't have accepted before." *I'm sorry, Mrs. J.*

I abandon the front seat and flop onto my sleeping bag. I need to give him back those library books. I'm surrounded by pots and pans that fell off the ceiling rack during the tow, laundry that we can no longer afford to wash at the Laundromat, cookbooks I wish I'd never opened. I pat the front pocket of my overalls. The remaining money won't last long if we keep getting ticketed and towed. Before she went back to work, I told Mom we needed a minimum of three thousand dollars. She agreed—"to go forward or . . ." She can't bring herself to say "back." Three thousand dollars. It sounds impossible. Like paddling a canoe to the moon. Mom thinks she'll have enough in three weeks if she works back-to-back eighteen-hour shifts. The restaurant may as well fit her with a bit and yoke her if she's going to work that much.

"How about takeout Chinese? We can eat it right here. I'll get extra fortune cookies," Cal says.

It's harder than ever to look at him, those wide eyes. He just sees possibilities. I mean, fortune cookies? Ha. I'll only believe mine if it reads: YOU WILL NEVER SLEEP IN A REAL BED AGAIN.

"You can't fix this, Cal." I push the library books into his hands. I wish he would quit trying.

Cal

"Save the Marina! Say no to squatters! Save the Marina! Say no to squatters!"

The Marina Beautification Committee is marching circles in the grass, chanting slogans and waving signs. I count fifty people, most in blue aprons and gardening hats. They're close enough that we can see their sneers. Nathan is out there, whacking the backs of his mom's knees with his sign. And—oh. I breathe in fast. Mrs. Paglio too. Why? She should be *protesting* the protest. She's only on that committee to get Sandy home—that's what Sandy says. And she wants Jeanne Ann and her mom to park someplace where they won't get towed. I don't think she's thought through where that magical place is. It's not near here.

At least Mrs. Paglio isn't waving a protest sign. She's looking a little lost, actually.

We are sitting around Sandy's table, wishing the ocean would sweep up the protesters and wash them away. The grass around us is littered with stuff: pots and rakes and gnomes—anything related to gardening that the Beautification Committee could sell for its fund-raiser, which ended right before the protest began.

"Ech," Sandy says, pulling at the neckline of his DILL WITH

IT T-shirt. "Terrible. Disgraceful." His face is crumpled, like he was forced to drink spoiled milk.

The students who live in the RV at the back of the line have looked up from their books. They're watching the protest. The bike messenger is poised over his bike seat, unsure whether to stay and guard his home or flee before things get nastier. The guy with the can collection locked to his fender is sitting in his front seat, hands on the wheel, windows shut tight. Even tourists are slowing down to see what's going on.

"We *are* an eyesore," Jeanne Ann says, matter-of-fact, without looking up from her book. She smacks a metal spatula against her thigh.

She's here, outside, because of the book in her hands and the food that Sandy has put out on his table. That's what it took to get Jeanne Ann four steps from her ignition—*Superfudge* and actual fudge. I bought the book, used, so she couldn't make excuses about upsetting the laws of the library and because she said, all those weeks ago, she loved it. It may even be her original copy—I got it from the same bookstore. She keeps examining the binding for signs that it was previously hers.

Sandy is watching her every move, blinking like his eyelashes have been stuck together all morning, like he's seeing her for the first time. She's just turned her chair away from the protest and pulled her book closer to her nose, so she doesn't have to watch.

"That's it," Sandy mumbles, pushing out of his chair.

"Oh, jeez," I say, as he marches into the green. "What's he—? Where—oh."

He reaches the edge of the protest and then sort of dives into the middle of their circle.

"I love that woman! Now stop this nonsense right now!"

I suck in a breath so fast, I start coughing.

Jeanne Ann is slow to react. She raises her head like she's just noticed a change in air temperature. Then she sets her book in her lap. Then she twists around to look at me. "Was that . . . ?" She stands. I'm trying not to look in Sandy's direction.

"I love that woman!" Sandy yells again, so that now I *have* to look.

Beside me, Jeanne Ann is climbing onto her chair for a better view, stretching her neck. "*What* did he say?" Sandy's surrounded by blue aprons and confused faces. "What's he . . . ?"

He lunges for the person standing still among the protesters. Mrs. Paglio. Then he dips her backward and kisses her, like in the movies. I pinch my eyes shut. The crowd gasps.

"Oh, gross." Jeanne Ann has covered her mouth. "That poor woman!"

This is the beginning of the end. I can just feel it.

Jeanne Ann

"Holy holy holy!" This is nuts. "That's the lady who wants us out of here, right? Kissing our Sandy?"

Cal has his eyes shut, shaking his head. He's clearly as baffled as I am. The Blueberries in the green can't seem to hold their signs straight. Their chants have dimmed and their line has broken in about three places.

"Is she the one he wants to drive around the world with? His 'friend'? Holy holy holy. I did not see that coming. Did you see that coming?" I reach for the fudge on the table without thinking and eat it. I'd like some popcorn too. The big commotion has passed, and now Sandy is weaving around shovels and broken pottery, marching his prize toward the crosswalk. "Cal?" I hear furious pencil-shading instead of an answer. He's not watching. I lean toward him, tap his shoulder. "The movie's not over! Look up. Cal! This is—"

He lifts his head. His cheeks, splotched with red, make him look like he's melting from the inside out, the heat just reaching his skin.

"Are you okay?"

He nods but doesn't answer. I think he's in shock.

I yank on his sleeve and swallow a snort. I didn't think it was possible, but I laugh. Which reminds me. I scan the road. No tow trucks. Even better, some of the Blueberries are packing up the chipped pots and going home. "Sandy romances the neighbor and the protest collapses. Maybe he *is* our Robin Hood."

Cal adjusts in his seat. "Robin Hood?"

"Don't look now—they're at it again!" I cover Cal's eyes. Sandy and the lady with thick ankles and the white whip of hair have reached her front door and are kissing between admiring glances at the sunset. "I can't watch! I can't *not* watch!" I look away and then back. "My neighbor is having a fling with *your* neighbor!" But even as I squeal it, I hear the strangeness. Why—why would the woman in the giant green house let someone like Sandy kiss her? He's nice. She's not. She lives in a house. He lives on the street.

Cal clears his throat, removes my hand from his eyes and maybe holds on a little longer than he needs to. He bends back over his sketchpad. "Last year," he says, "I touched a girl's hair." He continues his shading, head way down. "Her locker was right below mine. She was crying because her boyfriend dumped her—he dumped her like three times in sixth grade. Her hair was always so close to my hands."

"What does that have to do with anything?"

"She slapped me." He lifts his head.

"Good."

"I was trying to be nice."

"Touch your own hair next time."

"I'm just saying, things get—they aren't always what they seem to be." He's mumbling into his shirt collar.

I am about to snap back, *Some things are exactly what they seem to be*—but here's Sandy, returning from across the street, flip-flops smacking the pavement.

"Well, that worked," he says, brushing his hands on his pants. He looks very proud of himself. "A public display of our common humanity. Can't very well protest after a kiss with the enemy camp."

"Who—?" I start to ask, but Sandy veers right, into the open grass, and away from me. He returns with a chipped ceramic mermaid. "This is the stuff they couldn't sell. Freebies." The yard sale, staged in the grass around the shed, was cleaned up in a hurry, and more than a few items are still on display. "Now they have to give it away or pay to have it taken to the dump." He looks excited, like he's going to score something of value.

"Great. Maybe they left a hat box full of cheeseburgers," I say, uninterested in this change of subject. "Sandy, how do you know that woman?"

"Who?"

I point across the street, though I don't think I should have to.

Sandy grins. "Oh, her?" He scratches at his beard. "She's a neighbor deserving of love," he says, like it's a universally well-known fact.

Cal nods in agreement. They are edging toward each other, evening shadows crossing over their faces along with something else.

"Oh, come on!" I scowl at Sandy, then at Cal—they're shoulder to shoulder like merged bobbleheads. "When did you and the lady start your—?" I make a kissing noise.

"That's none of your business," Sandy says, smiling, one eyebrow way higher than the other. He's carrying his chipped mermaid like it's a baby and walking toward his van. "I think I'm going to turn in early. Such a busy day." He splits off from Cal.

"Wait!" I'm not letting him go without answers. I'm right behind him, at his side door, when I notice it: His wheel is no longer booted. The yellow clamp has been removed.

"Hey," I say, mostly to myself, turning to see if anyone else sees it. I touch the tire. "Hey!" This time I'm louder: "Where'd the boot go?"

I turn to find Cal. He's got his melting expression back on. I turn to Sandy. His raised eyebrow has crashed back down to meet the other.

Cal

It gets worse.

Sandy's door slides open and the woman we joke is Sandy's partner in crime—hair bandana, buckets—steps out, whistling.

"Who *are* you?" Jeanne Ann asks, like she's been waiting a long time to ask this question.

I try to scoot Jeanne Ann away from the door, but she's not

having it, leaning instead toward the woman and the warm glow inside Sandy's van.

"Who *is* she?" Jeanne Ann has turned to Sandy. I'm not entirely sure, but I can guess.

I pull my new middle school I.D. from my pocket and hold it out. A distraction. "Here ..." I tap at it. "Remember how funny I look?" Jeanne Ann glances down briefly, annoyed. I reach quickly for my other pocket. I'd planned to save this for later, but—"Yours is so much better," I say, thrusting it toward her. "See. Your eyes are wide open."

That works.

She snatches the I.D.

Jeanne Ann

"*THAT* IS A FINE LIKENESS," SANDY SAYS, LEANING IN QUICKLY to admire the photograph, then nodding at Cal with what looks like surprise.

"How'd you get this?" I say.

Cal is taking his hands in and out of his pockets. He looks both nervous and pleased with himself. "Um. Remember when we met the principal—Principal Dan?" He waits for me to nod. I don't. "Well, I talked to him. He knows about"— Cal rotates his head around—"and he wants to help." Folded papers materialize from Cal's back pocket. "We got three classes together too." He holds the papers side by side. "Math, English, and PE. We can probably get more. He said we could have as many together as we'd like . . ."

I look past the papers to Sandy's camper van. I've got a clear view of the interior now—a shiny two-burner stove, counter-height refrigerator and dishwasher, oval dining table with a plush red wraparound booth, ceiling skylight, suspended bed, a door marked LAVATORY. And dangling from the rearview mirror, a framed picture of a lady who looks a lot like the victim across the street.

I catch Sandy's eye briefly. He looks away, says, "How does everyone feel about dessert? I'll just hop over to Greenery, get us a full assortment."

I feel Cal tug at my elbow again. "We don't get as many elective choices as I thought we'd get, just Spanish and . . ."

I'm hearing their voices, but the tuning is off, like scratchy radio signals.

"Who's the lady?" I point to the woman with the bucket and the bandana, now walking across the street.

Cal's got his lips locked and tucked.

"*That* woman?" Sandy says. "That's Priscilla."

I shake my head, touch his tire with my toe. "And what happened to your boot?"

Sandy holds out a peach, dancing it back and forth. Did he pull that out of a hat? "Snack?" he says.

"*What* is going on?"

Nobody answers. Sandy sighs as he lowers himself into a lawn chair. Cal stays where he is, a few steps behind the table, arms locked at his sides.

"Priscilla is our cleaning lady. She cleans here and then she cleans"—Sandy pulls his mouth sideways—"across the street. At my house." He indicates the green house with the hotel driveway. "My wife lives there . . . for now."

The scratchy radio signal in my ears roars.

"And I paid for my parking tickets," he continues. "The San Francisco Municipal Transportation Agency accepts major credit cards and removed the boot early this morning."

If it's possible to feel your own blood sloshing inside you like spilled milk, I'm feeling it now. I squeeze my I.D. between my fingers till the edges cut into my skin. The address on it reads: *Greenery Restaurant, C/O Jeanne Ann Fellows, 1 Marina Vista Blvd., SF, CA.* The school thinks I live at the restaurant? I turn toward Cal.

He blinks his long, translucent eyelashes at high speed. Sandy grins, but I narrow my eyes and he pulls the grin straight. It's very quiet as I watch the cars stream by behind them. I run a finger over Sandy's hood, examine the finger for dirt.

"You pretend to be homeless?" I turn to Sandy. "Does my mom know?"

"No, she doesn't. And I don't pretend—I never pretended to be anything. I do live out here, temporarily, until I hit the road."

"You called meetings. You palmed money from people passing by. You—you complained about the neighbors across the street and sold them weird smoothies! You dress . . . *badly*." I lurch forward and tug on his beard. "*Is this even real?*"

"Ouch. I call meetings because I want to keep tabs on you. I don't palm money; I give it to people. I complain about the neighbors across the street because they are a spoiled bunch—I know this firsthand. My wife loves smoothies, and selling them is an excuse to give you money and for me to visit her. She isn't pleased with me. I do *not* dress badly. I dress comfortably." He uncurls my fingers from his beard. "Yes, real."

"You have a bathroom!" I swing around to Cal. "He has a bathroom in his camper!" Cal looks like he's mid-choke. He won't meet my eyes.

And then I get it.

"He lives in the green house," I say to Cal, more quietly, "next to yours." The roaring in my ears turns into a high-pitched whine. "You knew?"

Cal

"*You knew?*" she says again. It's a terrible combination of words.

Jeanne Ann's eyes are bulging. I step toward her anyway. "I

289

didn't know," I say. "Not at first. And then I figured it out. Just recently. I know you're mad. We just . . . you wouldn't have let him help if you'd known. And you needed help."

"You know I'm *mad*?" She raises her hands overhead, opens her mouth and lets out a sound, a howl crossed with a groan, that makes my teeth hurt.

I think she's going to march away, but instead she slaps her school I.D. on the table.

"I don't want this. I don't want anything from you, either of you. Tell Principal Dan. No more fliers, no more food, no more visits, no more."

"You'll skip school?"

She shrugs like it's no big deal. "You promised not to keep secrets."

I did. I did. But I had to. "Wait." I turn toward Sandy. "Tell her. Tell her why." I swing back to Jeanne Ann. "Your mom wasn't doing anything, so I—"

"Leave my mom out of it."

"But you shouldn't be out here!"

"You shouldn't care so much."

I step closer. "I thought you'd be happy—about the I.D., I mean. About that part."

She smiles, but not the good kind. "'Huzzah! You're helpless! I told the principal. Now he pities you too. Look at all my good deeds! Now I can go to heaven! My name is Cal!' That kind of happy?"

"I didn't mean it that way. I meant it . . . I was trying to . . . Don't you *want* to be rescued?"

Jeanne Ann

"ARE YOU KIDDING?" I SAY TO HIM.

Cal looks mortally wounded, but then steps closer anyway. "No," he says. "I thought—I thought everyone wanted to be rescued."

If he says more, I don't hear it over the sound of my van's door slamming behind me.

Cal

I visit Principal Dan the next morning and tell him the plan flopped. I don't know how I made it up the hill to the school. Guilt weighs a hundred extra pounds. Principal Dan says, "A long shot is still worth a shot." He hands me a memo with my assigned locker number while I'm there. He has one for Jeanne Ann too in a sealed envelope. I try to give hers back but he won't accept it. "Worst-case scenario, you claim two lockers for seventh grade instead of one," he says.

I unload thirty dollars' worth of change in parking meters and outstretched paper cups on the slog home. Then I read my memo:

To: Cal Porter, 202 Marina Vista Blvd, SF, CA

Re: Lockers at Marin Pacific Middle School

Welcome, incoming seventh grader! We are pleased to inform you of your locker number. Lucky #45. The combination is 32-17-12. Don't panic if you lose this or forget. EVERYTHING IS UNDER CONTROL. In other words, your locker number is on file in the office. See you in 44 days.

—Principal Dan

EVERYTHING IS NOT UNDER CONTROL.

I rip it up.

... I tape it back together.

Jeanne Ann

I come close to Cal's house, then veer off. I avoid the Carrot. I avoid Sandy.

Today I feel truly homeless.

The bars over the library door tell me it's closed before I can get past the bowing trees to the sign that lists the hours. There's the guy in the yellow raincoat and red rain boots, Gus, sitting on the steps, mumbling. Like always, he nods at me. I stop. Where does he sleep? He doesn't have a van. I look at him. Really look. He has white hair and deep grooves in his forehead. He pats at the pocket on the outside of his coat like there's something valuable in there. I look down at the pocket I'm always patting. I nod back.

I wander down to Greenery, passing the middle school—43 *DAYS TILL SCHOOL STARTS!* Inside the restaurant, waiters—*servers*—fold napkins, straighten tablecloths, dart from here to there. Everyone with something to do. They'll open for dinner soon. The light is turning down in the sky.

I stand at the water's edge, pick up a rock, and throw it in the direction of the Golden Gate Bridge. It falls short by a mile. An actual mile. But the throwing feels right. Stupid bridge. "Stupid bridge!" I scream it and throw until my shoulder aches, and I start to feel less angry and more dumb.

Only when I'm standing in front of the Carrot again, arm

sore, feet on fire, do I realize what I've done: I've walked away, blocks and blocks and blocks away. We could've been towed. I could be truly, truly homeless right now.

I bang a fist on the van's hood. "Sorry," I say. But I'm only apologizing to myself.

Cal

I'm staring into an empty soup pot in the Greenery kitchen, overhearing Mom and Mac assess my damage:

"He's been like that all day," Mac says. "I can't get him to talk."

"Well, that's not really what I had in mind for him here," Mom replies. "Has he been wearing his jacket?"

They're behind the bakery counter, peeking into the kitchen through the swinging door that separates us.

"He looks . . . forlorn," Mom says.

"I think something's happened with the girl," Mac says.

Nothing's happened. Jeanne Ann hasn't spoken to me in eighteen hours.

"Jeanne Ann? That's too bad. What'd he do? I like her," Mom says.

"Her van got towed, then there was the protest, and now something with school I.D.s."

"Whose van? What protest?"

I don't have to look to know Mac's pointing out Greenery's windows.

"The girl drives?" Mom gasps.

I hear Mac whispering.

"Oh!" Mom exclaims. "I had no idea. That poor girl."

They tiptoe away. I resume staring into the empty pot. I feel just like it.

Jeanne Ann

I'm left with Bad Chuck—I mean Nathan, which sounds a lot like "nothin'" if you say it fast enough. I think I'll stick with Bad Chuck.

We're seated on a bench in the grass. Behind me, the van feels so impossibly small. Around me, the city is so huge.

Bad Chuck's made his way to me from the shed, where his mom and a small group of women in blue are gathered. He says he "escaped" the Blueberries. "They are so mad about you. They don't pay attention to me," he says.

They've left all the unsold gardening stuff in the grass. For a beautification committee, they seem weirdly unconcerned with their own litter.

I watch Bad Chuck walk over to the tarp-covered box just outside the shed and kick it to show whose side he's on. I appreciate the loyalty, even if he *has* chosen the losing side. He comes back hopping on one foot. "That hurt. But it still might be a spaceship." He slips his hand inside mine. It's warm and sticky with who knows what, but I find I don't mind. A hand, even Bad Chuck's, is a nice thing. This is difficult to admit, but there, I have.

"Don't you want to see what it is?" he says.

"Nah," I say. I don't really care. It looks like a mid-sized U-Haul trailer, the kind you hitch to the back of a truck. If the

Blueberries wanted to sell it, they should've uncovered it.

Bad Chuck tugs me to standing and I let him. I don't have a lot of fight in me. He holds a finger to his lips and raises his knees to show we should move on tiptoes.

I smell it before we reach it. Bacon.

I groan. The timing is just *super*—like hail followed by sleet when you're caught outside without a jacket.

Bad Chuck, watching me, sniffs, practically wiping his nose on the tarp. "I told you," he whispers. "It smells like breakfast, but not cereal—the *other* kind."

I step toward him, pulling on the tarp till I can see the rusty structure beneath. There are two wheels. A hatch in back, wide enough for a person. Two windows. A griddle. An order window. Well, now the bacon makes sense. "It's not a spaceship," I grumble—and the smell is killing me. I hope the people at the dump come to pick it up quick.

Cal

"Cal! Cal? Have you seen my purse?!"

Mom races past the front door twice before she spots it. Then she happy-squawks, mumbles something, and climbs the stairs. I'm standing next to my desk, looking out the window, listening. Outside, across the street, Nathan is on top of the boxy cart thing, pumping his arms like he's king of a castle. Jeanne Ann is on a bench nearby, reading a book—probably *Superfudge*, because that's all she's got. Occasionally she looks up to scowl.

"Found it," Mom says, out of breath, leaning into my room. "It was right in front of me. You put it there so I'd find it, didn't you?"

I shrug. "I always know where your purse is." I flip closed my sketchpad. I don't want her to see what I'm working on.

She eases into the room, perches on the corner of my bed.

"I'm late for work."

"Yep."

"There's a tomato guy coming in. If I'm not there, Mac will buy too many of the red ones with the stripes. They're the mealiest ones."

"Uh-huh."

"Hey, Cal?"

I lean into the window. There's something . . . Jeanne Ann is sucking on her finger.

"Mom!"

I think Jeanne Ann's given herself a cut. A cut could get infected.

"What?" Mom leaps up from the bed, looking ready to dive on a grenade.

I want to run past her. "I have to get a Band-Aid," I say. And antibiotic ointment. But it's also true that I know I shouldn't and that these things are not welcome. I know I need to stop. Or I need to not stop but come at it all differently.

"Mom!"

"What? Did you cut yourself?"

I shake my head. I still don't know where to go with this. I want to—

"Mom!"

"What?" Mom glances behind her. She looks how I feel—utterly confused. This is like being trapped in the middle of the crosswalk when the light turns green for oncoming traffic. Go back? Go forward?

"Cal, honey. You've got me worried." She edges closer.

"What's new?" I hold out a hand to stop her. Her words sting. As usual.

"Mac says—I hear—I think I can help. I could—"

"You can't do anything. You keep trying and you keep getting it all wrong. You just—you aren't paying attention."

"I'm sorry about that. We need to talk about that. But this is—different. I can—"

"No!" I say. "You can't."

She's quiet for a second. "What hurts you hurts me, honey," she says in a soft voice that reminds me of when I was younger. "That's our bond. That's my motive here."

What hurts you, hurts me.

I slow the words down. Replay them.

I understand. Too well.

Mom, me.

Me, Jeanne Ann.

I feel Mom wanting me to look up at her, but I'm still buzzing.

"Mac says you are a lifeline to that girl—Jeanne Ann."

"Yeah, well, she doesn't want a lifeline," I say, though I don't totally believe it. "And neither do I," I announce. I don't really believe that either but it sounds good, and I blow past Mom anyway, unsure of what it is I'm meant to do next.

Jeanne Ann

The air feels different this afternoon. Not biting cold, not sticky hot. Blue sky. It must be seventy degrees. Mom calls seventy degrees "God's temperature." She doesn't believe in God, but I know what she means—this temperature requires no extra effort. It's like breathing or blinking or sleeping.

I grab a wad of paper towels from the bathroom, wet them, and wipe down the Carrot's interior, unzipping the sleeping bags and dangling them out the open windows to air. Mom still doesn't know the truth about Sandy. She's been coming in too late and leaving too early for me to tell her.

Outside, Nathan is back on top of the food cart, playing Lord of the Manor with an invisible sword. I can hear him through the window. "March on the Blueberries at dawn!"

I think it's maybe the reason I feel a tiny bit better.

I am tempted to climb up there too, see how it feels to be above it all. Or at least aboveground. If the cart were a little closer to us, we could almost call it our outdoor kitchen. A kitchen that'd give us tetanus, for sure. It's so covered in black grease and rust, shards are falling into the grass and dyeing the turf a funky orange. I'd be worried for Bad Chuck's safety, except that *I'm* not his babysitter. His mom, at the shed, is, and she doesn't seem concerned. I'm not surprised the Blueberries want it gone. I'm more curious about how it ended up with them in the first place.

And us? How did we end up where we don't belong? Where do we go now?

I glance at Sandy's van—silent for days—and at Cal, up in the Rubik's Cube.

Cal

"At least she's got something to occupy her time," Sandy says, fists on hips.

"At least she's not alone," Mrs. Paglio says, tapping her mouth nervously.

"It's terrible," I say, plain.

They nod in agreement.

We're watching Jeanne Ann from the Paglios' living room window, two stories up. Mrs. Paglio has served lunch—little sandwiches with the crusts removed and colored toothpicks poked through—but I'm not hungry. I haven't been hungry for days. We're lined up, three in a row, with a sandwich each, and I remember what Jeanne Ann said about me watching from my window. It's not right. We should close our eyes. But that's not right either. We have to look and listen. The details matter. And if the reason is right, we should be allowed to do something.

"Half the Beautification Committee feels wretched, and the other half is undeterred," Mrs. Paglio says. "It's far more complicated when we know who we're shooing away."

Sandy sighs. "You should hear yourself."

"I'm just reporting," Mrs. Paglio says testily.

"I can't watch," I say. I turn away from the window, but then turn right back.

"That's it," Sandy says. "I've got to get back down there."
Sandy's been sleeping at home—his big home—to give Jeanne
Ann space to cool off. It's made Mrs. Paglio happy. It's made
Sandy anxious. They watch Jeanne Ann together from their
big window, ready to pounce if even the wind blows her hair
the wrong way.

"If you go back out there, you're not setting foot in this
house again," Mrs. Paglio says, stretching her body straighter.

"Is that an ultimatum?"

I don't like it when the Paglios fight. I wish they'd remember
their big wet kiss from five days ago.

"She needs a basket of hot rolls with butter," Mrs. Paglio
says. "I can send her those. You stay here."

"That came out hard-hearted, dear. She needs a lot more
than hot rolls." Sandy, without his grin, is a very unpleasant
sight.

"I am the furthest thing from hard-hearted! You know what
I mean. We can do just as much good for her over *here*."

The Paglios are glaring at each other.

"You see why we prefer Morse?" Sandy whispers, leaning
toward me. "Talking, texting, calling—it's all too fast. You jab
back before your thoughts are together. Deadly. Change the
subject for me, would you, Cal, before I say something I'll
regret?"

"Why was there a food cart in the shed?" I say. It was
already on the tip of my tongue.

Mrs. Paglio chuckles. "We were supposed to clean it up

and sell it, twenty years ago. One of many ill-formed ideas."

"I'm glad you didn't," I say, watching Jeanne Ann. We are all looking at her again.

She's got both hands pressed against the food cart, as if feeling for a pulse, and her lips are moving, like she's giving it advice.

Somehow, the sight is reassuring.

Jeanne Ann

"Here's the thing," I coo, holding a hand to the black and sticky griddle. It reminds me of some of the greasy surfaces at O'Hara's House of Fine Eats, which I officially miss. What were we thinking, giving up that security? "I didn't like the looks of you at first. But you've grown on me. You saw a lot of bacon in your day. We'd have been good friends."

Cal

Jeanne Ann: meet me at greenery 9:30 am. I want to show you something. It's important.

Jeanne Ann: meet me at greenery at 11 am.

Jeanne Ann: meet me at greenery at 3 pm

Jeanne Ann: i'm sorry for everything.

She's ignoring my notes. She's ignoring me. I don't know what to do. I am standing in front of the bathroom mirror, looking at myself. My bow tie is crooked and rumpled. I slept in my clothes last night. Abraham Lincoln and Winston Churchill—heroes—wore bow ties. I bet they didn't sleep in them. Or maybe they did. They had bad days. They made mistakes too.

I drag myself to the kitchen to assemble a care package Jeanne Ann won't accept. The sunlight coming in through the stairwell windows is too bright. Maybe I could offer the care package to someone else across the street. Gus, maybe. All this focus on Jeanne Ann, I should focus on other people again too. Ask them what they need.

I pass Mom on the living room couch, elbows on knees, opera glasses pressed to her face, staring out the big front window. I rub my eyes to make sure I'm seeing correctly.

"What are you doing?" I stand over her.

"Where's her mom?" Mom says, making a note on a pad of paper. It looks like a log.

"Whose mom?"

"Jeanne Ann's? I never see her mom out there." She adjusts the focus on the opera glasses, stands, walks to the window.

"Her mom works. She's washing dishes. What are you doing?"

"Paying attention." She lowers the glasses, looks at me, then raises the glasses again. "I'm a little nervous about the cart. She seems—"

"Attached." I join Mom at the window, but keep a few bodies' distance between us.

"Very."

"Yeah." We stand there quietly looking. Just looking.

"She glances up at my room sometimes," I say.

"That's encouraging."

"Is it? Maybe she just has a cramp in her neck and turns her head this way to stretch it."

"Maybe . . ." Mom says.

"Probably she's looking."

"Yeah, probably." We rest our foreheads on the cool glass. "They picked a beautiful place to park," Mom says.

"That's why they stay."

Mom doesn't say anything.

"And maybe for a few other reasons," I add.

"Maybe."

"They don't want to be rescued," I say. "It's not something people plan on wanting. They're not . . . projects."

"That's true." Mom pauses, then hands me the opera glasses. "And sometimes people don't even know anything is wrong." I think she's staring at me, but I don't look.

"That's what I painted—at Point Academy—on the wall." I tap the window. "It was big. Six feet by five. The vans. And the water and the bridge. And some wings. Jeanne Ann wasn't there yet, so her van isn't—wasn't—in it. There was a green van, with a parrot, in that spot. Before."

Mom is quiet for a while.

"How long have you—how long has all this been going on, Cal?"

I smile. "Remember when I wore those footie pajamas?"

Mom's mouth falls open.

"Cal—"

"They're out there! We're in here!" I let that sink in. "With the mural, I wanted you to see what I saw. You and the whole school. It was going to be this big reveal. Get people talking—"

Mom puffs out a tired sound. "It was a big reveal all right."

I give her the stink-eye, something I picked up from Jeanne Ann. Mom gives me the stink-eye back. Hers is almost as good as Jeanne Ann's.

"It still revealed kind of a lot," I say. "Like, you don't know me very well."

"You hid something big for a long time, Cal," she says, "and then you sprang it on me and expected me—everyone— to get it."

"And then you totally overreacted."

"I acted on the advice of your dean and my instincts as a mom." Her voice is starting to go up.

"I don't even have that dean anymore! That's how much you overreacted!"

Mom pinches the top of her nose, like I'm giving her a headache. "Okay. Tell me: What about your friends?"

I raise the opera glasses and fidget till the view is blurry. "I don't think they were friends. I think we were all just waiting in the same place, at the same time, to find friends, and the waiting near each other looked like friendship."

"That's a very interesting theory." Mom's crossed her arms.

"It's Jeanne Ann's."

"Smart girl."

"She hates me now. So . . ."

"She doesn't hate you."

"She should hate her mom. Her mom planned really badly."

"Yeah, she did. But I bet her mom hates herself plenty with- out Jeanne Ann piling on. Or you."

That's an interesting theory.

"Jeanne Ann needs to go to school, and I got her regis- tered. But I didn't ask her first."

We hold each other's gaze. "That doesn't sound so bad. I'd have done the same thing," Mom says.

"Yeah, that's the problem."

Jeanne Ann

Bad Chuck is standing so close, I can feel his hot breath in my ear. I'm leaning against one of the Carrot's wheels, unfolding Cal's paper birds. Some have notes inside, others don't. I've counted fifty so far. I think I'll leave a few intact and perch them on the windshield next to Mom's notes. Extra pairs of eyes.

"Nathan! Nathan!" Bad Chuck's mom, down by the piers, has just finished stringing up a new BEAUTIFY THE MARINA sign, and is looking for her son. One more turn of the head, and she'll see.

"Where's the Giraffe, anyway?" Bad Chuck says, trying to read what Cal's written. "He's more fun. He's never around anymore."

"You shouldn't call him that."

"Giraffe? Why not?" Bad Chuck yanks up a fistful of grass and throws it.

I squint at him and at the afternoon sun that's set the water behind him ablaze. He's really not a "Nathan." "I dunno. Maybe you should."

He swings himself around and lies flat in the grass, his head near my hip. "My mom says I can't live out here with you. It's no fair."

"Nothing's fair." I glance at Sandy's van. He's back, but

he's avoiding his outdoor living room, which is just fine with me. He can go to his big house if he needs a living room.

"She doesn't know what I need."

Moms.

Out of the corner of my eye, I see one of my van neighbors, the bike messenger, whacking a small carpet against his fender, dust flying. Sandy introduced him to me—Horatio. I look at the rusty cart I've taken under my wing and wonder how it might look without the top layer of crud. Cleaning helped the Carrot.

"Mom says I can't take care of myself. She says running fast is *useless* unless you're a puma," Chuck says.

"Or a bank robber."

"Did you know there's no dessert or TV out here?" he says.

I nod. "None."

He shoves his finger in his nose. "That's terrible."

I nod.

We both stare at the sky over the water. It's ridiculously beautiful. I can't stand it.

Crapinade.

"You're the only one who tells the truth, Chuck."

He's simple. I know what I'm getting.

"Yup. I'm the good guy," he says, beaming his gap-toothed smile out over the bay. "Who's Chuck?"

Cal

Sandy finds me at Greenery, folding and unfolding napkins behind the counter.

"Listen, Cal, I need to do something. I'm leaving you in charge." He slides a five-dollar bill across the counter and points to a croissant under the glass.

I just stare at the money. "What do you mean?"

"I mean, I have to go someplace for a few days."

"Now?"

"Day after tomorrow. You can handle things. I've just come to tell you. And to get a croissant. Mrs. Paglio will do whatever you say. She's a very amenable person when I'm not involved. I've prepped her. You'll see."

"But . . ." I consider grabbing ahold of his wrist.

"A day, maybe two. Up the coast. I think it'll be good for everyone. If I'm missed, wonderful. Maybe things will repair themselves. If I'm not, well—we know which way destiny was leaning."

Mac walks by, sees the five dollars on the counter in front of me, and stops. Sandy knocks on the glass again to indicate which pastry he wants. Mac looks at me, looks at Sandy, waits a beat, then grabs the croissant and puts it in a bag.

"Jeanne Ann won't talk to me ever again," I say, resting my elbows on the counter and my chin in my hands.

"Doubt that. Jam, please. Raspberry."

Mac looks to me, sighs, then places a plastic container of jam in Sandy's bag. She takes the cash to the register.

"Helping is so complicated," I say.

Sandy reaches across the counter to pat my hand and grab a napkin. "Most people never even try."

"We were becoming friends," I say.

"You were already friends. You are *still* friends," Sandy says.

Mac brings Sandy his change, and Sandy drops it in the tip jar. *Clink clank clank.*

Sandy looks back at the long line behind him. "Trust me on this."

"I don't know what to do." I lean over the counter. I must look desperate. "Don't leave. It's a terrible time for you to leave me in charge."

"First rule of business: Go back to what worked before."

"But nothing worked."

"We wouldn't be having this conversation if nothing worked. You just hit a snag. Don't hit it again."

Jeanne Ann

Mac, the chef at Greenery, shows up with a toolbox in the morning. "I hear you've got some bad wiring."

"I do?" I look at the Carrot. I'm sitting in the grass, tearing up an old T-shirt for a rag.

Mac nods at the rusty cart that's turned my hands gray and permanently sticky from all the scrubbing. I think it's always going to resemble something dipped in a deep fryer and left out in the rain for twenty years. I'm not making much progress. The soap from the bathroom isn't industrial strength. It barely cleans me.

"Who sent you?" I say.

She doesn't answer, just nudges past me to the cart, which she proceeds to push farther into the green, away from the shed, like it's a big bag of paper towels. Then she stands beside it with her legs spread wide, arms crossed.

She spends the next several hours tinkering with mechanical parts under the griddle. I scrub away at the tiny floor space behind the griddle and the hatch, and pretend not to watch her. The bacon smell is everywhere now. Gus in his yellow raincoat sits on a nearby bench and watches for an hour, while clicking knitting needles together. I can't tell if he's making oven mitts or amoebas.

Mac doesn't say a word until it's nearly dark out, which

surprises me, because I figure she's here to press for details. She didn't even bring food.

"I'll come back tomorrow, at lunch. Some parts I gotta get."

"Wait. Parts for what?"

"To make it work."

"It can work?"

"What do you think I've been doing all day?"

I don't know. I don't even know what *I've* been doing—but the hours have passed, and the sun has risen and set, and I'm still doing it.

"Eventually, you're gonna want it to work, right?"

I didn't know that was an option.

She hands me Cal's jacket and some red paper folded in the shape of a bird. "A hello from Cal," she says, and gestures toward his window as she grabs her tools and starts away. I look up—he's there, in the middle of the Rubik's Cube, pretending not to be looking down. "He's not gonna quit till he knows you're all right," she says.

I tuck the jacket between my knees and tear open his card. There's nothing written inside, only drawn. "What's his obsession with wings, anyway?" I say, mostly to myself.

Mac sighs, turning back. "Duh. All the best superheroes fly."

Cal

"Remind me what I'm supposed to say to her?" Mom says. She's standing inside our front door, holding a bucket of chicken away from her body like the drumsticks might leap over the edge and avenge their deaths.

"Tell her: School starts in twenty-seven days, and Cal says: 'The book club is still seeking members.'"

"'The book club is still seeking members.' Right. Right." She presses her ear, sealing the message in. "Are you sure we can't just give her an artichoke quiche instead of this? I could ask Mac to make it extra cheesy." She peeks inside the bucket and makes a face like she regrets doing it. "Poor hens."

"Mom." I try to sound firm.

"And what if she rejects it?"

"Just bring it back. We'll give it to someone else." This is the approach I've settled on. I'm not going to stop helping. I don't think she actually wants me to stop. I think she just wants to control it. So I'm going to follow her lead. If she says no to this, then I'll just try something else, and something else, until she says yes. I'll let her decide what and how much, but I'm not going to just give up, because I don't want her to just give up.

Mom's halfway down the driveway when I remember the

key. "Wait!" I run back to the junk drawer in the kitchen, then race to catch up.

Mom and I discussed the key-offering a lot yesterday. I said Jeanne Ann was unlikely to go for it, but we set up the spare room and stocked the fridge anyway.

Mom balances the bucket on one hand and accepts the key with the other. She stuffs it into her pocket, then smooths over my eyebrows, and pulls down my shirt to get rid of the wrinkles.

"Go," I say. But Mom just stands there, staring at me.

"I will do as ordered . . . if you give up the beige." She scans me up and down.

"What?" I try to spin her around. "The beige is fine. It's a form of expression."

"It's a form of blah."

"I give all color to my art."

"Uh-huh. Well, thank you for explaining."

"Do you think Jeanne Ann finds the beige blah?"

"Oh, yeah, definitely." Mom whips around to face the street.

"Maybe I should've kept the leather jacket," I say to her back.

"Mmm. I don't know. It looked kinda clownish. Not my best idea. Maybe try something else. Something *you* pick out."

"Mom."

She shrugs and raises a hand in apology as she walks back down the driveway.

"Hey, can I quit the job at Greenery?" I call after her.

She nods, turns sideways, yells: "Mac says you're the worst employee we've ever had. She's very proud of you."

I sit on the front steps and watch her go.

"And my paint and pens?" I yell before she's reached the bottom.

"Cal. Let me deliver the chicken."

I'm pretty sure that means yes.

Jeanne Ann

Something is wrong. There's an engine idling close to my head. I hop to the back window in my sleeping bag, knocking over an empty chicken bucket, and push back the shade. Sandy's headlights are on, and he's standing in front of his van, folding up his table. He's never folded up his table before.

I step outside and hug my elbows. The sun has barely risen, and the fog lies low and thick. I expected to find Mom beside me when I woke, but she's wasn't. She's already left for work—of course. I do the math: To get in eighteen hours, she has to leave before sunrise. That's six hours a day more than she worked at O'Hara's House of Fine Eats.

Sandy folds a chair.

He stacks the chair on top of the folded table, then he makes trips from his "living room" to his sliding side door, carrying furniture as he goes.

He stops to acknowledge me, looks down at his T-shirt as if he's lost something that might be found there. It reads: DIM SUM AND THEN SOME.

"I need to take a drive, clear my head." He runs his hand through his beard. "Ends up that great kiss was not the solution to all my problems."

I rub the sleep out of my eyes but keep my head mostly

down. "See ya." I kick his tire. It's the first I've spoken to him in nine days.

He's looking across the street when I pick my head up again. I follow his gaze to the house next to Cal's. His house.

"That's it?" he says. "'See ya'?"

I kick his tire again.

"Well, we'll have other opportunities to talk," he says. "I'll be back. Soon. I just need to feel the road move beneath me for a few days. My wife—Mrs. Paglio—and Cal are here to help while I'm gone."

He fixes me with a weak smile.

"You have a magnificent scowl," he says. "I'm sorry you're still mad, but I understand."

My fists are balled. "I—thought we were the same."

He nods.

"No, not the same." I feel my nose sting and my chin start to shudder. "I thought I was *better*."

Sandy stares right back at me, eyes wide like he's prepared to take all the poison darts I'm blowing his way. "You are, Jeanne Ann. You are. I should've told you about me and the missus at the start. It wasn't right. And I got Cal in trouble in the process."

I look past him, at his camper. "I bet you have hot water in there too?"

He nods. "With a Jacuzzi setting."

"*Ice* is warmer than the water in the public bathroom."

He looks down. "I thought about sharing."

"You did not," I snap.

"I did. Would you have come inside if I'd invited you?" he asks.

I consider this. "No way."

"That's what I told myself. I also told myself I'd offer you a room in the big house if anything should happen to that van of yours."

"Would you, or would you just *think* about it?"

He holds out a key. It dangles from a chain. It's the second key I've received in the last twenty-four hours. This one's got a charm to go along with it—a plastic book; I've seen charms like it at the gas station, but I get the sense Sandy went out of his way to find this one, to make the match. "I would," he says. "The room is yours if you want it. I'd have offered it much sooner, but then you and your mom might not have accepted any help at all."

I squeeze the key. It's light as a feather and weighs a thousand pounds, just like Cal's. I tried to give Cal's back—and the bucket of chicken—but his mom was adamant that I keep it. I'll never use it or Sandy's, but I cannot deny the feeling they give. It's like seeing two seats at the end of musical chairs instead of none.

"Do you believe me now?" he says.

I watch him pack up the last items. I listen to the *slap, slap, slap* of his ratty flip-flops and then, as his side door slides shut, his rolling suitcase circling the van one last time.

Sandy comes to stand near me. "Try to be nice to that boy." We both look across the street. Cal is backlit in his window. It looks like he's drawing. "Maybe he started in the wrong place. But he's getting it now. And his only sin is liking you too much . . . and being a soft-bellied goof, like me. We're not going to let anything happen to you while you're parked here. If that annoys you, so be it." That's pretty much what Cal's mom said too, the last part. Sandy places a plastic bag in my lap. "Good food."

I stare at his van's headlights, swirling with dust and gnats. He walks toward the driver's-side door.

"I approve of your restoration project, by the way."

"What?"

"Where others see junk, you see treasure."

Oh, the cart. "I just see grease."

"What is grease but the residue of past meals? What are meals but fuel for man's greatest achievements?"

I roll my eyes, which is, I realize, my forgiving him. Sandy grins, knowing.

"First rule of life: Keep your hands busy."

He seals himself inside his camper and rolls down the window.

"Hey, Sandy."

"Yes?"

A seagull lands on his hood and flaps its wings without actually going anywhere. It's saying what I can't: *Don't go. I'm here.*

"Don't forget your tea," I say.

"That-a girl."

Cal

I stand at the window and watch Sandy pull away, and then, an hour later, watch a puke-green van pull into his spot.

Smoke drifts from cracks in the windows.

Snort, snort, hrrrrr. It grumbles in place. Then, around 7:30 a.m., the engine cuts out and is replaced by a terrible banging, like all the instruments in the world have been played at once, as loud as they'll go.

Crapinade.

We knew someone would pull into his spot.

But we didn't plan for this.

Jeanne Ann

I wake up to Mom coughing. It's 8:30 a.m.

She's never still here at 8:30 a.m.

"Mom?"

"Kid," she croaks. "Nice to see you. Build me a roaring fire, would ya?"

She coughs again. A deep, wet rattle.

"You're sick."

"Very."

I kneel beside her. She never gets sick.

"What can I get you?"

"Sleep, hot orange juice, a massage, ten days on the beach in Mexico."

"I can get you the first three." I roll down the window for fresh air.

"Careful. We'll hear the trash music even louder with that open."

She's right. I roll the window back up.

"Those are the new neighbors. Sandy needed to take a drive."

"He told me. Can't win 'em all."

Can't win any of 'em.

I put a hand on her forehead. It's hot. "You're working too hard."

"Yes."

"We can't keep this up."

"No." She shuts her eyes. "As soon as I'm better, we're out of here."

I don't usually look out this window at night—on Mom's side. It's too much. All the big houses. All the stuff I'm not sup-posed to want, but do. Tonight, though, I'm wide awake, and there's no one to talk to. And maybe I need to see the lights on in the houses across the way.

Mom's asleep—exhausted—and I don't want to wake her, not if the music hasn't. She's slept away the whole day, through sirens and the new neighbors playing their gui-tars and drums, full blast. I've nicknamed their band the Headache. They're between sets, and the quiet feels kinda panicky, because I know the noise will start again, but when? I wonder if Cal's been hearing it and what he thinks. His lights are off, but maybe he's up there, sitting in the dark, or maybe he's moved on.

We're finally moving on.

I'm not the only one awake. Sandy's wife is up. She's on her second floor, pacing. She's got a lamp on. This morn-ing, she brought me cleanser, rubber gloves, steel wool—for cleaning the cart—and purple flowers. "Morning glories," she said, holding out the flower pot. "For affection." I don't understand how she can be kind *and* want me gone at the same time. I don't think she knows Sandy gave me a key to the house. When she was here, she said, "You're getting the best of my husband." She seemed sad about it but maybe a little bit proud too. I'm not sure what to make of her.

I reach into the top pocket of my overalls and remove the keys—one from Sandy, one from Cal's mom—dangling them from my finger. I will never get to use them now—but I can feel the relief in my shoulders, behind my eyes, just knowing I could have. It's like a stone has melted. I don't have to be here, in this van. I could be there, across the street. They are not going to let anything happen to me. No matter what. No matter how far down we go. As long as we're here. I know I said I didn't want their help, but I— Maybe, if we stayed a little while longer, I could convince Mom to let us use a key. She could sleep inside on a bed . . .

I roll down my window a teensy bit, then Mom's. I know this is risky. The bay sounds nice uninterrupted—the little heaves of tide that jiggle the boats that creak and bump and set the wind chimes singing. The Headache will drown it out again in a moment.

Mrs. Paglio—Sandy's wife—stops her pacing.

I shine my flashlight on my hand and raise it.

Across the street, a flashlight snaps on in a dark room in the Rubik's Cube, like it was waiting, waiting, waiting for just this moment to signal back. We could almost be regular neighbors, passing messages through the night.

Tomorrow I'll return the keys.

Cal

I haven't slept one minute when she rings the doorbell at seven a.m. I watched her walk over, like a snail with second thoughts.

"You wasted a lot of paper on these birds!" she barks as I throw the door open. She's holding up one of my winged origami notes. She's wearing the jacket.

These are the first words spoken *by* Jeanne Ann *to* me in approximately 216 hours. Not: "You made it all worse!" or "Get a window shade and leave me alone!"

Maybe that's still to come. But the jacket . . .

She strides past me, into the house, looking around like she's seeing it for the first time. She removes her shoes and heads upstairs, slowing down. At my room she stops and rolls her bare toes through the carpet. "You guys could sell tickets to stand on this rug," she says. She's got streaks of grease on her hands and under her nails, and her hair is so matted, it looks like it wouldn't move in a brisk wind. Her eyes are red, but they're bright.

"Are you okay?"

She shrugs, curls her toes tighter. "Mom's sick. She can't work."

"I wondered."

She nods and kinda shuffles in place. "At least I can leave the van now." She half laughs, shoving her hands in her pockets, though we both know this isn't actually funny.

I stay in the doorway and she sits on the corner of my bed, bouncing a few times.

"And, we're leaving. So—so I thought I should return the—this." She pulls our key from her top pocket and holds it out between us.

Sandy said that leaving might be the best thing for them, but I didn't think it would actually happen. It feels terrible.

"But—when, where are you going?"

"I dunno. Mom's too sick to plan. But she knows she wants to leave as soon as she's better."

"Do *you* want to leave?"

She shrugs. "I never wanted to come here in the first place."

"Yeah, but—" I can see her leaning away from me, so I drop it, change course. But I'm not taking that key back. "You got all my messages?"

She nods, pulls another paper bird out of her overalls pocket. It's a little flat but mostly intact.

"You believe what I wrote on them?" I say. "That I'm sorry and—"

She's not quite smiling, but she's not doing the opposite either. "If you're going to apologize like a dope, I'm going back to the van." She's still holding out the hand with the key, but I can tell that her arm is getting tired. "I can't take any more sorries. You screwed up. I get it. You were trying to help."

"I really was." She looks mildly amused. "So—"

"Yes, I'm over it," she groans. "Too tall. Too brown."

"Beige."

"Too nosy. Too charitable. Yes. Over it. I missed you."

"You did?"

She steps toward me and swats at my elbow. "Sandy said I should be nice to you."

"He did?" That's embarrassing, and not really what I was hoping for.

"And the chef lady—Mac. And your mom."

"And that's the reason you're here?"

"Nah, I told you, I had to return the key."

"You could've put it in the mailbox. You must've wanted to see me."

She says something in the direction of the ceiling and takes a step toward the door like she's going to blow past me, but I can tell it's a fake-out. "You know, you're really infuriating."

"I know."

"And intrusive."

"Yeah."

"And you don't know when to stop."

"Or even how to start," I add.

"Yeah, and that," she says, but she doesn't sound all that mad about it.

I yank on my shoes, skip tying the laces, grab my backpack.

"Sandy gave me the keys to his house too," she says. "I

gotta return those too." She turns like she's leaving. I fall in behind her. She looks back, annoyed, and stops.

"He told me he might give you keys. I thought you'd throw at least one of them back at us. Two felt safer," I say.

She squints at me like she's surprised I know that. She pulls out Sandy's key. "You guys mean business."

"How could you not know that?"

She shrugs and walks to the window instead of the door, leaning her forehead against the glass. The fog has settled gently on the hoods of the vans. The orange one looks permanent today, like it's been glued in place. "You let that parrot get taken."

"That was before."

"Eventually, you'd get distracted, forget about me."

"No. We won't."

I stand beside her. I think she believes me.

"What are you going to do with that thing?" I ask, pointing with my forehead at the food cart down below. It's actually shiny in a few places.

"It's not mine. Why does everyone keep asking me what I'm doing with it? I don't know. Nothing."

"Does it work?"

She waits a beat before pouncing on a reply. "I just want it clean. When it's clean, I'll be done.'

"Okay."

She crosses her arms. "So, what's this thing you have to show me?" she says.

"Tomorrow. I'll show you tomorrow."

"But you put your shoes on."

"So I could be ready for whatever you're doing next."

She stomps the perimeter of my room, pretending to be massively inconvenienced. It makes me smile.

"Your heroes," she mumbles, cruising past the portraits on the walls.

"Yeah." I watch her follow the wall around.

"Wings."

"Yeah."

"Shouldn't it be capes?"

"Wings are more permanent. They can swoop down, pick you up, take you places."

"Uh-huh. Makes sense. Man, you're weird."

She points to the big poster—just finished, just pinned up across from the door. "Who's the girl?"

I can't tell if she's kidding.

"Don't you recognize her?"

She turns back to the portrait, makes the quietest squeak of recognition or horror or both. "Gimme a break."

"You don't like it? I've been working on it for a while. You saw some of the sketches."

"It's ridiculous. My head's the size of a rhino."

She flops, legs crossed, onto the rug and stares up at her herself, obviously pleased.

"It's one of my best." I like the way the hair blows back, curling like vines, and the same curling pattern is repeated in the wings. "You know, your name doesn't suit you," I say, looking back and forth between the portrait and the girl. "You're more of a Rosalind."

"Mom jokes that my name is French," she says. "But it's not. It's as close as she could get to Gee Whiz. That's how she felt when she found out she was pregnant with me. Like *Gee Whiz, how'd this happen?*"

She smiles, but just with the corners of her eyes.

"Why'd she tell you that?" It's not very nice.

"It's the truth. She always tells me the truth." Her face darkens a little. "Except when she doesn't know it yet."

"Or when the truth might improve later," I add.

This brings up Jeanne Ann's royal chin. She likes my interpretation.

"Your name doesn't suit you either," she says, swinging her legs to face mine. "Cal is a cowboy name."

"It's not my full name. My full name is Callebaut."

"Calabow?"

"It's a kind of chocolate. From Belgium."

She snorts. "La-dee-da." Then she gets serious.

"Cal. Callebaut."

"Yes?"

"We can't sleep down there another night."

Jeanne Ann

"THIS IS NEVER GOING TO WORK," I MUMBLE TO CAL, hanging back. He's brought everyone over to the back doors of the Carrot. I can't believe Mom actually opened up.

"I'm not going anywhere," she rasps now, looking for me in the group. There are tissues erupting from her sleeves like pillow stuffing.

"Tea in the morning"—Mrs. Paglio leans in, smiling—"white horehound flowers, a bath. Mr. Paglio doesn't appreciate comforts like those anymore."

Mom looks at Mrs. Paglio through slitted eyes, then at me like, *Who is this person?*

"You'll just catch more of a chill in here," Cal's mom says.

"No." There's an edge in Mom's voice now. "I'm not going in one of the houses. I—"

"I told you," I mutter.

"Can Jeanne Ann sleep over? Just Jeanne Ann?" Cal edges forward.

Mom looks at me and closes her eyes. Her whole body settles down. "She's just going to get sick in here with me."

The words push me and pull me. But I go.

Cal

Jeanne Ann isn't one hundred percent sure, but she comes back home with Mom and me. We set her up in the den, across from my room. She seems eager to take a bath and go to bed, so she can get back to her mom as soon as the sun is up.

I know that makes sense. Her mom's the priority. But I wish Jeanne Ann could enjoy being here.

She told us we could wash her clothes. Mom and I sort through them while Jeanne Ann is in the bath. I separate out the colors and Mom squirts a special detergent on the clothes with the most stains, then throws them in the wash.

"I keep wondering about the rest of Jeanne Ann's family," I say, holding up a shirt for a final inspection. "Her mom has a mom. Where's she?"

"Maybe they argued. Maybe there was a big misunderstanding," Mom says.

I turn to face her. "Maybe they never made up. It must've been a really bad fight if she can't call her now."

Mom squirts another shirt, slides her eyes toward me.

"Let's never have one of those fights," I say.

Jeanne Ann

I wake to a feather lightness in my limbs, like my muscles are not connected to my bones.

It's the mattress beneath me. I'm in Cal's house, in a spare bedroom. This is the first morning in over a month that I've woken up on something other than metal. I'd be panicked if I weren't so comfortable.

The clock on the desk says five a.m. It's ringing softly, almost like a ringer in a dream. Cal set it to do that. He said it was a pleasant way to greet the day, like brushing your face with a feather.

It's still dark, but gray-dark instead of black. I throw off the covers and walk to the window on the other side of the room.

The van is still there. Mom's still inside. Alone. It's probably too early to go down. I don't want to wake her, or worse, scare her. I'll go down when the sun is up.

My stomach growls while I dress. There's a pile of clean clothes on the floor by the bed. The clothes smell like soap. I am tempted to lie back on the bed and cover myself with my clean wardrobe.

But I'm too hungry.

I dress and make my way to the top of the stairs.

I'm an invited guest here.

I still have the key to this house.

Cal said I should make myself at home.

I tiptoe down. I can feel the nearness of food. The refrigerator gurgles just for me.

"Hello?" I whisper. Every light is on down here.

"Hello?" I whisper again.

One of the cabinets is open, and the oven light is on. I smell something baking. Cookies? I edge toward the scent.

A sack of sugar stares back at me from the counter.

"Coffee cake—sour cream and walnut," I hear behind me. Cal's mom—Lizzie—is standing in the kitchen doorway. She steps toward me. "I know you want to go soon. I thought you should wake up to something sweet." She's pulled her dandelion fuzz into a ponytail atop her head. A smock—green, with the restaurant logo—is dusted with flour, protecting her pajamas. She doesn't seem mad to find me down here. "Does that sound appealing?"

"Uh, sure."

"It'll be ready in a few minutes. Milk?"

"Uh, yeah. Yes, please." I'm not entirely comfortable with Cal's mom.

She pours me a tall glass.

She cocks her head to study me, then raises her eyebrows way high, like I'm supposed to say the next thing, but I don't know what it is.

A buzzer saves us. She pulls on mitts and extracts the cake. We hover over it, inhaling the steam. "That will be good," I say, admiring the swirls of yellows, browns, and tans in the crumbly top of the cake.

"Yes, it will," she says.

For a small person, Lizzie takes up a lot of space.

We both have our elbows on the counter and our chins resting in our hands.

"I thought you didn't cook."

"Oh." She dips her head and scratches her scalp with all ten fingers. "Did Cal tell you that? I don't cook at Greenery. That's true. I gave that up after Cal was born, so I could be around to, you know, raise him . . . whatever that means. Ends up you can be around and still bungle all that . . ." She trails off, pulls a tissue from her pajamas, blows her nose, starts up again. "I don't cook at home much either. But, of course, I know how. I mean, I'm really quite good. Sometimes, when you're really, really good at something, you don't want to do it at all, unless it's your best work. Know what I mean?"

I nod. "When I'm writing a report on a new book—to tell the librarians if I think they should carry it—I don't want to be interrupted."

"Yeah. Yes. You get it."

I continue staring into the cake. I would like to make something that smells this amazing and looks like it will fix everything that has ever gone wrong in the whole world. It sounds corny—but who knew you could pass time so comfortably, just staring at a cooling cake.

When the steam clears, Lizzie unclamps the metal band

around the cake, exposing the full glory. "We should really wait till it cools to eat it," she says, then, ignoring herself, pulls out a chair for me and cuts two slices, one for each of us.

"My mom doesn't bake," I say, through a hot mouthful. I'm trying not to shove the entire thing into my mouth at once. It's like eating a small butter island. "She thinks baking is for prisses."

Lizzie makes a *hmfff* sound. She takes a sip of her milk. "Everyone in the kitchen is the same: slaves to fat, fire, and time. No prisses survive. I know. I've hired a few by mistake. Has your mom ever baked anything?"

I bring my shoulders to my ears—dunno—I can't recall ever waking up to this smell. I'm not even sure our oven worked.

"Well, I've only met her twice, but if I had to guess, your mom's just scared of what she doesn't know."

I turn that over a few times while Lizzie cuts me another slice. "I didn't think Mom was scared of anything till we got here."

She pours me another glass of milk, taller than before. She watches me drink it.

"You might like baking," she says. "It's for precise minds. You can't really improvise. You have to have a plan and stick with it."

She's looking me over, that same judge-y up-down that she gave me the first time we met.

"What?" I'm annoyed.

"Nothing. It's just, the oven's still on. You could make something."

I catch myself halfway into a shrug and stop. "Okay."

She starts pulling down more ingredients. Butter, salt, baking powder.

She slides me a cookbook—Mom has this same one—and I start paging through. I stop on a familiar picture, slide the recipe over to her. "Can I try this?"

The recipe is for buttermilk biscuits. The picture reminds me of *I Capture the Castle*—the girl in the book ate biscuits over the sink and felt rich, though she was poor. I think hers were the English kind of biscuit, which is more like a cookie. But still.

The cookbook says buttermilk biscuits can turn out like "hockey pucks" if you don't make them correctly. They absorb gravy. They pair well with ham and eggs. I like ham and eggs.

"Excellent choice," Lizzie says, skimming the recipe. She grabs a few more ingredients, then taps the page.

I move closer to her.

"It's all there, on the card. You can't mess it up if you know how to read."

I go slowly. Lizzie hovers. I don't know why, but I'm excited. The recipe says to measure everything out on a cookie sheet and mix the ingredients with my fingertips. It feels like I'm playing, like I'm a kid in a sandbox. This isn't cooking. The flour moves like sand. The butter squishes, forming little flakes and pebbles.

I step back, raise my batter-caked hands overhead. I've read the directions carefully but this can't be right. My pile has gone from dry to sticky/clumpy. I thought I was going slowly, but it all happened so fast. No wonder Mom is scared of baking.

"Good, good, stop there. A few more turns and you'd be in trouble," Lizzie says. She pokes at the batter. "This is perfect."

"It is?" It looks like mashed potatoes.

"Yeah. Now you roll it out."

I like the feeling of the rolling pin, its weight—it's more powerful than it looks. When I've got a not-too-lumpy disk—less mashed potato, more tacky Play-Doh—she hands me an empty jar, upside down. "This is my favorite part."

I discover it's my favorite part too. Perfect circles. Press. Press. One. Two. Press. Press. Three. Four. It's hard to believe this will become something edible. But I don't care. Perfect circles. Look at that.

I think Mom would like this.

"What time is it?" I say, quickly pulling back my hands. I run to the living room window before she can answer.

I tap the window, leaving a flour dusting on the glass.

Lizzie follows me. Here I am baking when I should be taking care of my mom across the street. The sun is up.

"She is working so hard to get you out of there," Lizzie says. I nod. "She'd want you to stay until the biscuits are cooked. I know it."

Lizzie puts the biscuits in the oven and comes back. I have to stay near the windows now.

She sits down beside me on the rug. I don't know why, maybe it's the smell of butter, the warmth of the room, but I tell Lizzie about Mom. The job interviews that went nowhere, but didn't have to. The dish-washing. The cookbooks and the unsent letter to Julia Child ("Really?" Lizzie says. "Ambitious.") The Hydras at O'Hara's House of Fine Eats. The food we ate at home, and the food, I've come to find out, we didn't eat.

She asks questions. I answer. She nods a lot. I wait for her to tell me what to do. Cal says his mom likes to tell people what to do. I might enjoy being told what to do, at this point. But if she's making a list of ways to adjust us, she's doing it silently in her head. Eventually, she gets up and excuses herself, and I think that's the end of the conversation, but she comes back half a minute later with a thin newspaper, and flops down again. "Have you ever read the classifieds, Jeanne Ann?" she asks, paging through to the back. "After a long week, I find them wildly distracting."

I walk two finished biscuits to the guest room, sit down on the floor, plate in lap, facing the window.

I have to juggle the first biscuit from hand to hand to

345

avoid burning myself. It is seriously attractive, I think. Golden brown on the top with flaky layers along the sides. It looks like a picture in one of Mom's cookbooks.

Cal enters, sniffing. I offer him one.

"Your mom and I made them," I say.

His eyes go wide. He is nodding and smiling, crumbs falling out of his mouth.

"Are you going to try yours?" he says.

"Gimme a second. I've never fed anyone before."

Cal

"What can I do now?" I whisper. We're just outside the van. Jeanne Ann's holding a green box filled with biscuits for her mom.

"I don't know," she whispers, her back to the van. I don't think Jeanne Ann's ready for life back in her own box.

"So, you're still gonna leave when she's better?"

"I guess."

"Will you stay at our place again tonight?"

"I don't know."

A car honks just as she's squeezing the door handle. We turn to look. It's Sandy in his camper van, idling at the stop light. He waves. Jeanne Ann raises a hand and watches him turn the corner. I can't tell if she's happy or sad.

"He can't go home," she says, almost like she's talking to the sidewalk. We both look at the green van in his spot.

"I want you to stay," I say.

She rolls back her shoulders, opens the door. "You just want a friend at middle school."

I smile. "You do too."

Jeanne Ann

The fever makes Mom say nutty stuff. Today I thought she was asleep when I cut my finger on a pineapple can. "Crapinade," I hissed, biting down to stay quiet.

"Don't say that," she muttered, eyes closed.

"What? Why?"

She groaned. "I picked it up from family. Then, one of my stinkier boyfriends started using it."

"My dad?"

She hesitated and I thought she'd fallen back asleep. "Maybe." She started to snore.

I don't know if any of that is true. There's a lot of fever-mumbling that I don't think I should be hearing. Like: "I'm so tired. Was I this tired in Chicago? I could do it all by myself there. But here, it keeps going . . . I can't get off . . . I understand Chicago. We were better off in Chicago . . . I thought wishes grew on trees out here. Sam's letter . . . But it's just like anyplace."

I think of Mrs. Jablonsky and her bowl of butterscotch candy at the library. Some things were better in Chicago. Much better. But then I think of the water streaming through the bedroom ceiling that the super wouldn't fix, and waiting for Mom outside the library in snowstorms, and grimy O'Hara's House of Fine Eats, and Mom's faraway eyes when she looked at that poster in the old travel agency or down at the expressway from our bedroom window.

Maybe San Francisco *is* just like anyplace. "We don't really know yet," I say to her sleeping face, surprising myself. "We haven't really stepped inside."

Cal

All day and half the night, the green van behind them screams and shakes with sound. "White noise," Jeanne Ann says, when I ask if it keeps her up. She hasn't slept at the house again. She says one time was enough. I don't believe her.

I supply orange juice, cough syrup, cough drops, soup.

"Have you told her about your project?" I whisper when I drop off supplies. I pass them through the open window.

"What project?" She's reading a book, *The Secret Garden*. Used. Hers to keep. From me. Unfortunately, she won't look anyplace but the pages now. She's leaving San Francisco, a page at a time.

"The food cart," I say. Jeanne Ann has been polishing it a few hours every day. I've come down to help. Mac too.

"It's just something to do till we leave."

I don't think that's all it is, but I don't push it.

Sandy's camper van glides by in slow motion as I'm walking home. He still can't find a parking spot. It's been days. He only wants the spot behind Jeanne Ann. "I knew you'd take care of everything," he hollers, idling at the stoplight.

"*What?*" Where's he getting his information? Nothing is taken care of. Jeanne Ann and her mom can't make it here. I can't make it better. Added up, it's only a smidge better than being towed.

But he continues on without further explanation, disappearing behind a curtain of fog.

Jeanne Ann

Mom is starting to show signs of improvement. She sits upright. She accepts a stale biscuit and hot soup. She notices the grease box outside. Bad Chuck is running circles around it, while all of the Bumblebee campers chase him.

"When did that show up?" Mom says, leaning out my window for a change of pace. "Who made this biscuit?"

I set down the laundry I'm folding. The biscuit she's eating is four days old. I look out the window to the cart. There's still a two-inch dent over the gas tank that Mac couldn't bang out, and some ugly rocks stuck in the tires. I've been steel-wooling and polishing—always when Mom's asleep. Mac and Cal have come by to help. Mrs. Paglio supplies lemonade—she brings it out in a crystal jug with matching glasses; she says it's the only civilized way to serve lemonade. Mrs. Paglio is fancy, but lemonade is lemonade, and she's sharing hers.

Scrubbing the box with the neighbors has been less difficult than listening to Mom's chest rattle.

"What do they serve?" Mom takes another bite of biscuit, holds it up to her nose, splits it down the middle, and examines its innards.

"Who?"

"The guys stuffed inside that cart?"

"Nothing. It's just empty, abandoned junk." Mom has a side view of the cart; she must think there's a sign on the front.

"It doesn't look like junk," she says.

"It doesn't?" I look over at it and—

Oh.

Mom takes the last bite of biscuit, brushing crumbs from her enormous hands. "Can we get more of these?"

Cal

Jeanne Ann's mom, Joyce, is outside, running her hands over the now-sorta-okay-looking food cart. I drop my paints and roll my desk chair backward. "She's up! She's up!" I shout to Mom as I bolt downstairs and out the front door. I whisper the same to Jeanne Ann once I've crossed the street. But excitement fades as I realize a healthy Joyce means a soon-to-depart Jeanne Ann.

"Yeah, I guess so. I guess she's really up," Jeanne Ann whispers back, pulling at her lower lip.

We watch Joyce run her hand over the griddle, then walk around to the hatch door in back. She stares at the cutout, half her height, and snorts, but she folds herself in and stands hunched over the griddle.

I pull out my sketchbook and stand at the order window for the best view inside. I find a blank page—there aren't many left; the sketchbook is falling apart—and begin laying down lines.

Jeanne Ann pushes through the hatch, squeezing into the area under her Mom's left armpit.

"What's he doing?" Joyce says.

"Sketching us."

"Why?"

They're both resting their elbows on the griddle and looking up at the clouds and the swooping seagulls and the clear
blue that they've been waiting for.

"Don't worry. He'll make us look good."

Jeanne Ann

Mom is gone when I wake up. She didn't mention going to work—she says she was automatically fired for missing three days in a row—but maybe she's arguing her way back in to earn a few days' wages before we leave. We're going to need money for gas and food and a down payment on an apartment.

Her purse is still in the van, though.

"Mom?"

I find her outside, messing with the cart again. A cyclist whizzes by. It's a weekend morning—the farmers' market has begun in the lot behind Greenery—and the playing fields are starting to fill with runners and bikers and tourists.

"It works," she announces, spitting on the griddle. It sizzles.

I guess that chef lady, Mac, really did it, really crossed the right wires.

Mom runs her hands over the knobs, opens and closes and opens and closes the oven doors, checks the warming drawers—that's what Mac called them—then does a thing with her hands that can only be a mime of cooking.

She jams her hands into her pockets and pulls out crumpled bills. She thrusts them at Cal, who—surprise—has just arrived, eager to be of service. He hands over a basket of warm biscuits his mom made. Apparently, she has been at the oven, waiting all morning for us to get up too.

Mom seizes Cal's sketchbook and thrusts it at me. The pages are falling out. She grabs his wrist, forces the money into his hand. "Be useful. Buy me some paper plates, a carton of eggs, a good aged cheddar, salt, pepper, chives, and a crusty loaf of bread—no, these biscuits will do—and butter, lots of butter."

Cal starts to speak, but she interrupts.

"I'm gonna make us breakfast," Mom says.

Cal

WHEN I GET BACK TO THE VANS, JOYCE—JEANNE ANN'S MOM—IS sharpening her knives like she's about to go into battle. She's talking to Jeanne Ann—probably about what interstate they want to take back to Chicago to avoid duplicating the route they took to get here. Jeanne Ann is nodding. I approach slowly.

"Finally," Joyce grumbles, grabbing the food bag out of my hands. "Change?"

I dig fifty-four cents out of my back pocket.

"I gave you twenty bucks and you come back with *this*?"

"It's all from the farmers' market. Extra fresh." Eggs and cheese and butter, practically right from chickens and cows. "It'll taste better."

"I know that." She storms off to prepare, mumbling. I can't

tell if she's really mad or if, like her daughter, storming off is a kind of thank-you. I fall into the grass next to Jeanne Ann, who's got *The Secret Garden* open.

"Crapinade," she mumbles. She's lying on her back with the book over her face. My sketchbook is lying next to her, pages askew.

"I got salt and pepper from Greenery. I saved big on those." I feel like I need to defend myself.

"Mmm-hmm."

"I think breakfast is gonna be good. Don't you?" She doesn't answer. She's very still. "Jeanne Ann?"

She rolls toward me. "I wished for this," she whispers, daring to smile, then shoves her face deeper into her book.

Jeanne Ann

I GUESS THIS ISN'T A TERRIBLE FINALE. WE'RE ENDING WITH a proper breakfast, which is how our stay should've begun. And, maybe we'll be able to sell the food cart for more than four dollars now that it's cleaned up. It does look decent. Maybe it'll pay for our trip home. The Beautification Committee *should've* taken the time to clean it up. They didn't know what they had.

Cal's brought over a picnic blanket and is lying next to me, stretched long, his hands under his head, which makes him appear massively overconfident about something. If he continues whistling, I may have to take some drastic action, like throwing his sketchbook into the air and letting him chase down the pages.

"Somebody open the package of plates!" Mom shouts, finally, when she's ready. Cal jumps up first.

Cal

A SKATEBOARDER IN A FADED 49ERS T-SHIRT GLIDES TO A STOP IN front of the cart, while I'm juggling plates. "Excuse me." The skater pokes at my shoulder, first slowly, then like a woodpecker. "Excuse me!"

I've got a plate in each hand and one balanced in the crook of my arm. We're all getting the same thing: two scrambled eggs mixed with cheddar and chive, and a biscuit on the side. A picnic in the grass is the plan. Me, Jeanne Ann, Mrs. Paglio, Mom—she's coming in a second—and Joyce, who's still cleaning the griddle, in case any of us wants seconds. Her face is its own sharp tool, warding off critics.

"Excuse me! How much for one of those?" The skater is a little too close to the plate in my left hand. He's thrusting a wad of cash in my direction. Everyone is handing me cash today. The guy reminds me of a Greenery breakfast customer—hangry, impatient, wanting to get fed, *now*.

Jeanne Ann leaves Mrs. Paglio on the picnic blanket to come see what's going on. I look at Joyce. Joyce looks at the skater's knee guards with disgust.

"Twelve fifty!" a voice screeches behind us. "Don't take a penny less!"

Mom arrives out of breath, still in her pajamas and a Greenery smock, with hair that looks like an electricity experiment. She's carrying another tray of biscuits. It looks like they've come straight from the oven. Her feet are bare. I don't think the skater cares; he opens his wallet again and pulls out another wad of ones, laying them in Mom's palm. "Keep the change," he says. Joyce looks at the money like it's dirty kitty litter, then stands upright and "hmphs."

I surrender one of the plates to the skater, then watch as he gets smaller and farther away.

"What just happened?" Jeanne Ann asks.

"Business!" Mom says excitedly.

"Twelve fifty?" Joyce splutters. She cracks two more eggs into a bowl, automatically. "Twelve fifty? We didn't even give him utensils."

"Was that my plate?" Jeanne Ann protests, but not loud enough for the woman with the baby in the stroller who's just pulled up and is tugging my sleeve.

"Hi. Oh, wow, a new food cart. You guys. Those eggs look amazing. And biscuits." She's talking like she already knows us. She steps forward and backs me against the cart with her high-speed talk. "What do you call this place? Are those

360

homemade biscuits? We love biscuits." I adjust my balance, careful not to drop the plates. She leans over her baby and taps his nose. "I'm going to take a picture. This is so cute. No signage. Very cool." She's eyeing the two plates still in my possession. I look to Joyce and Jeanne Ann for direction. They lift their chins at the exact same time, a signal to proceed.

Money is exchanged, the baby gets half the biscuit and promptly mashes it against his face.

"What are we doing?" Jeanne Ann asks.

"Let me tell you what *I* think," Mom says, placing her hands on Jeanne Ann's shoulders.

Joyce interrupts her. "Cal." She shoves twenty-five dollars into my hand. "Resupply. Run," she orders.

Jeanne Ann

MOM COOKS HER EGGS LIKE JULIA CHILD. TWENTY TO thirty high-speed whisk-turns in the bowl, a tablespoon of butter for every serving, no more than three eggs cooked at one time, and the whole thing's done in thirty seconds or less, on a plate, sprinkled with salt and a "wap" of pepper (Julia's word)—then out to the customer. That's exactly how Julia does it too.

"What?" Mom snaps, watching me watch her.

"Nothing," I say. "You really know what you're doing."

"It's just eggs, kid."

"Mom." She looks up, adjusting her jaw back and forth, like she's caught out. The muscles in her arm flex, then release. "Don't say that. You know what you're doing."

"Fine." She wipes her knife clean with a towel that looks suspiciously like one of my clean shirts.

"Say it."

"I *know* what I'm doing."

Cal

WE WILL TURN TWENTY-FIVE DOLLARS' WORTH OF RAW EGG INTO three hundred dollars' worth of scrambled. I feel the weight of good luck in my hands as I carry the cartons back. These are golden eggs.

Of course, Mom and Jeanne Ann will need to bake more biscuits to go with them. I think Jeanne Ann likes baking. And I'll need to buy more cheese, butter, herbs, oh, and paper plates—when there's more money to buy with. Mom could offer to pay for those things, but I don't think Joyce would accept. I know she wouldn't.

I wonder if this is the start of something, and if they might stay a little longer, to find out?

I pick up my pace just as the wind picks up its own. I was ordered to run, but running is hard with fragile eggs. A stack of papers flies past, swooping through the air on a burst of wind. It looks like sketch paper. My sketch paper . . . *Hey.* I watch two sheets fly higher and higher, like in a dance. They're accompanied by a sound, a low moan that gets louder the higher the papers go. I spin around. I set the bags down.

It takes my legs several seconds to get the message from my brain to run, to acknowledge what I'm hearing. SIRENS. I look back just once as I go. My sketchbook has taken flight, and I've abandoned forty-eight delicate eggs on a sidewalk teeming with large, crushing feet. Also: flying paper resembles flapping wings.

Jeanne Ann

WE ARE SERVING OUR FIFTH AND SIXTH CUSTOMERS—TWO skinny women who claim to know the location of every great biscuit in town—when I look up and see paper whipping in the wind, smacking walkers in the face, sticking to their pants legs. Cal's sketchbook papers—picked up on a gust. I lurch out the hatch door and grab for a sheet. Miss it. I reach for another. Miss.

Mom doesn't notice a thing. I see Cal streak by—his heels rising and falling fast—and the first crazy thought I have is: *He's found another penniless girl to save.*

Then a crash of sound and color. Red. Wailing red.

Where did it come from? Did we not hear the sirens over the biscuit-loving customers? Is the exchange of goods for money that deafening?!

This time I am only steps away. But the area is busy with farmers' market comers and goers, weekend runners and bikers, wobbly babies holding tightly to barking dogs.

"Pardon me. Excuse me."

I hurdle over and around.

Move, move, move. Oh, please. Not again.

"Not now!" *We are about to leave!*

Over a wide pit in the grass. Around a picnic table. Onto the sidewalk.

The hook on the back of the tow truck is already rising, already attached to the Carrot.

I can hear the *beep-beep-beep* of the tow truck's mechanical arm, the clang of the chains—then the brake lights flicker.

"Stop! Don't tow it!" I barely hear myself over the sirens.

I stand where the tow driver can see me, arms out, palms out.

Am I having some effect? The driver is honking. Honking like crazy.

I place a hand on the hood of the tow truck and a hand in the air. Then I slide forward along the hood. When my hand reaches the headlights, I look down, and there's Cal.

He's lying in the street, arms and legs spread wide, like a snow angel.

"Cal!"

"Hi!" he yells back, waving.

The truck inches forward.

"Hey!" I bang on the hood. The truck driver points down and leans into his horn again. He sees Cal.

I take a breath and step into the road. I smell asphalt, tar, and engine exhaust. I crawl until I'm beside Cal, then lie down. I feel the vibrations of the engine in my skull and the heat streaming off the truck. Cal grabs my hand and squeezes.

"About time," he yells, smiling.

"You're unbelievable," I yell back.

"You're welcome!"

"Let's pretend *I'm* saving *you*," I shriek.

"You are!" he replies.

Cal

Mrs. Paglio races home to get her phone. She never takes her eyes off us.

She calls a friend, who calls another friend, and before too long a local news truck arrives with cameras and microphones and those giant roving spotlights that kinda look like dinosaurs.

We learn this order of events later.

Sandy finds a parking spot—about the time the cameras arrive—in the middle of the street, right next to us. He adds his honks—high and whiny—to the honk symphony. We are blocking traffic. Then he gets out and stands at our feet.

"Scoot over!" he shouts, scratching his beard.

He wiggles between Jeanne Ann and me, which, I'll be honest, dulls some of the joy of his arrival. I peek over to check on her. Her hand grasps at air.

"This is living!" Sandy declares, waving wildly to his wife across the street.

Then he grabs our hands and locks them together on his belly. This time, Jeanne Ann gives mine a squeeze.

Jeanne Ann

TURNS OUT, LYING IN THE STREET FOR AN HOUR DRAWS A lot of attention. Especially if the lying causes traffic to snarl, cops to sweep in, and news cameras to roll.

Dusk is streaking the sky purple and orange, and we are about to watch TV footage of the morning from our new parking spot: Cal's driveway. After the tow truck let us go, we reversed the van up here and went right back to selling eggs. Now we've returned and are counting our money. It totals $360. I've checked my math three times.

Cal watches over my shoulder. We're sitting on the Carrot's back bumper, legs swinging. *It's just camping ... in a van ... in my friend's driveway.*

I fold the money and stuff it into my overalls, surprised

and satisfied. Mom cooked and no one can tow us. No one can ticket us for not feeding the meter either. Because *there is no meter*. We're invited to stay here as long as we want. I think we may stay a few more days. Maybe longer. If we have a few more days of sales like today, we will be rich in no time. Rich for people living in vans.

Mom is warming to our new location, in her way. She's standing off to the side with her arms crossed, muttering: "This will never work. We can't stay here." But she doesn't have a better plan, and she actually entered Cal's house twenty minutes ago—"I gotta use the girls' room"—and came out with her hair brushed. Everyone is trying not to stare. Also, Mom keeps accepting popcorn from Mrs. Paglio, who's been ferrying the snack over from her house—down her driveway, up Cal's, back and forth, back and forth. Sandy's sitting cross-legged on the ground, hugging his own giant bowl. He and Mrs. Paglio are swapping long, deep glances.

Lizzie is hip to hip with Cal, inspecting him for cuts. "An axel was three inches from my boy's head," she says about every minute. Cal flexes his arm muscle idiotically every time.

"Ready?" he shouts, pointing the remote control. The TV newspeople sent us a video of all their raw footage from this morning; Mrs. Paglio made that happen. I motion for Mom to sit next to me on the bumper. She drags herself over reluctantly. Because no one wants to test to see if Mom will go inside again, the adults have rigged up a television outside, propped up on a square of butcher block just in front of our toes. The van sinks when Mom rests her weight on the bumper. "I really don't like this," she says.

"I know," I say. "But I do. I wish Sam-who-left-us-hanging could see this."

She takes that in silently, leans over me like the teapot in the song, and checks my head for injuries. "Don't be mad at him. He and I are the same."

"No way."

"He's back at O'Hara's or someplace like it. Sweating to prove himself. Getting underpaid and overworked by the Hydra. Feeling a little like he deserves it." She drops my hair. Her face is serious and a little sad. "You're all future, Jeanne Ann. Sam and me, we're all past."

"That's not true. You got us here."

"Here is a driveway, kid. Before this I almost starved us." She looks up at Cal's house. "If this is an improvement—and I think *maybe* it is—then you're the reason." She pushes herself off the fender. "I'm going to be over there, working on doing better for us."

She returns to her spot on the side of the driveway, while I weigh the bad and good of what she's said. Cal gives me a look, scooting closer to fill her empty space. I nudge him with my shoulder. I know he heard. He stays quiet, though, just turns and hits PLAY.

The screen fills with a close-up of Cal and me and Sandy lying in the street, then jumps to a shot of a policeman writing a four-hundred-dollar parking ticket, then to a crowd of men and women congregated around our vans— a flash mob, who knows where they came from—marching with signs that read: WE PAID FOR THE STREETS, LET US PARK ON THEM!

Then the narration begins.

"'Park in Peace' protests have sprung up across the city today as the selfless, dangerous, and defiant acts of two San Francisco kids and a retiree sparked the collective rage and frustration of an entire city. With city rents skyrocketing, living in a car, van, or RV is often the only option . . . but only if City Hall allows long-term parking . . ."

Mom snorts. Sandy throws popcorn at the image of San Francisco City Hall.

Onscreen, the TV interviewer, a woman with blue eye shadow and glossy lipstick, asks, "Now that you've got your home back, what will you do?"

She places a microphone in front of my nose. I am standing beside the Carrot trying to get gravel out of my hair and squinting. I am obviously not thinking clearly, but the effect is good. "Make more biscuits?" I say to the camera.

Back on the driveway, Lizzie reaches over Cal and pats my knee.

Onscreen, the TV lady interviews us about the move from Chicago, the days and nights in the van, the tow. The camera pans the intersection. It takes in Cal's house, the line of parked vans, the bay, Greenery, and the Golden Gate Bridge.

Then it zooms in on our cart. There's Mom, beating eggs and gently pushing them across the griddle. There's me, moving biscuits to plates with a spatula. The longer the camera is trained on us, the more customers arrive to find out why. The TV footage captures some transactions:

> Customer 1: "I'd like two orders of the eggs, hold the cheese."
> Mom: "No cheese, no order."

> Customer 2: "Can I get the biscuit, no eggs?
> Mom: "Nope."

> Customer 3: "I'll have the eggs, dry, herbs on the side, biscuit warmed."
> Mom: "You'll have the eggs the way I serve them. She"—Mom pokes me with her thumb—"handles the biscuits."

> Customer 4, Bad Chuck's mom: "Do you have a license for this business?"
> Mom: (Silent.)
> Bad Chuck's mom: "You know butter is very unhealthy."
> Bad Chuck: "I love butter!"
> Mom: "Is that your son?"
> Bad Chuck's mom: "Excuse me?"
> Mom: "Give the kid a free meal, Jeanne Ann— extra butter."

Customer 5, Mac: "I'll take it however you make it."
Mom: (Silent. Proud.)

Customer 6: "Hey, you give discounts to garage
    bands kicked out of their garages?"
Mom: "You drive a puke-green van?"
Customer 6: "Yeah, I guess?"
Mom: "No."

The interviewer with the blue eyeshadow fills the screen again, smiling so hard, it looks like she's hurting herself. "Two chicks on a roll," Sandy yells at the screen through a mouthful of popcorn as the news camera zips past Mom and me to take in the whole bay. The narration continues: "The freedom to park in peace will allow this child and her mother to work and live in peace. And that's all you want, right, Jeanne Ann?"

The microphone turns to me again. "Well, that's not *all* I want," I say, staring straight into the camera. "I'd like a sleeper sofa, three meals a day, naps for my mom, a library card, a bathtub and shampoo, a functioning thermostat, washing machine and dryer, a street address, a front door, a refrigerator, a place to hang my clothes, a great seventh-grade teacher . . ."

My list went on and on. Nowhere on it was "move back to Chicago," Cal points out later. He notices everything.

BACK TO SCHOOL

Cal

Jeanne Ann, meet me at the Paglios': 7 a.m.

Jeanne Ann, meet me at the Paglios': 7:15 a.m.

Jeanne Ann, meet me at the Paglios': 7:18 a.m.

"**S**he's not getting my notes." I peek past Sandy—Mr. Paglio—but I see no movement in the driveway next door.

"Cream or sugar?" Sandy says, setting a teacup and saucer in front of me on his table.

"Let the boy be," Mrs. Paglio says, squeezing her husband's knee. "First day of school. He's got a lot on his mind."

Sandy wiggles his brows and leans over for a kiss: "I know all about having a lot on my mind." Mrs. Paglio offers him her cheek, smiles, and rolls her eyes. They do this all day.

We are in lawn chairs in the Paglios' horseshoe driveway, tucked into the shade cast by Sandy's camper van and a big, leafy tree. The chairs are new—cushioned, with recliner settings; Mrs. Paglio insisted. They have decided to live in their van, in their driveway, until "bigger decisions are made."

"I like those wings you've got on the oolong," Sandy says,

tapping the new sketchbook in front of me. I'm working on the food cart's expanded menu. Customers have demanded a beverage option. "They can drink from a hose" was one suggested solution—Joyce's—and tea was the other.

"Get him off me!"

We all turn toward the voice—Jeanne Ann's—a driveway over. My driveway. She's adjusting something on her new bike, and swatting away Nathan, who's trying to climb aboard. His mother is racing up the driveway after him with what looks like a bowl of cereal.

"I thought we were all having tea over here," Sandy says, pushing himself to standing. I can't tell if he's really upset or just pretending.

"You keep saying that, and I keep telling you, it's their first day of school. Leave them be." Mrs. Paglio is speaking with binoculars pressed to her eyes. She's spying on the new crop of vans across the street, confirming that all is calm and mostly right, which she will report back to the still huffy co-chair of the Marina Beautification Committee, Mrs. Caspernoff, currently in my driveway, trying to haul Nathan home. The two women have struck a deal. So long as Mrs. Paglio can verify that every van or RV on the block is quiet and clean, complaints will not be lodged.

"Bring me *someone*. How 'bout the adults?" Sandy points to Mac, at the bottom of his driveway, helping Jeanne Ann's mom. They're cutting a sunroof in the food cart.

The "adults" snort as I roll past them on my bike. I snort back. They are my guardians for two days while Mom's on her mountain retreat, developing new recipes for Greenery. She says she's figured out what needs her undivided attention and it's not me. She left a classified ad on my pillow before she left: "Will trade meat grinder for ride to emergency room."

Good one!

"Take me with you!" Nathan howls.

"You have a first day too. You don't want to miss it," I say, trying to get ahold of him.

"The teacher will make me sit all day!" he whines.

"How 'bout this," Jeanne Ann says. "How 'bout meet us here after school and tell us all about your horrible, wart-faced teacher and your terrible first day?" This offer shocks Nathan and me. I grab him while his mouth is still hanging open.

"Lower him over!" Sandy hollers. "I'll show him fun." Nathan's mom watches as we lower her son headfirst over the hedge that divides the two driveways. She looks unsure of what to do with the cereal bowl in her hands. "We'll return him after tea, Mrs. Caspernoff," Sandy assures her, taking the cereal bowl, then guiding Nathan toward the cups on his table. "Now, young man, first rule of growing up: Act out when no one is watching."

I'm not sure I agree with that rule.

Jeanne Ann

I RUN BACK TO THE VAN ONE LAST TIME, TO MAKE SURE I'VE got everything. Mom meets me there and lifts my chin gently upward and orders me to have a good first day.

"Okay." I think we're both surprised this is happening. In San Francisco. And that we are smiling—mouths stretched wide, as far as a smile can go. We have caught a break. Today it feels officially real. We still live in a box, but it's actual living, not barely scraping by. I pull away; she pulls the other way. Neither of us is entirely comfortable with being entirely comfortable.

Cal is pretending to inspect the gears on his bike. He has someplace he wants to take me before school, which is why we're leaving early and why he is so impatient to go. I like making him wait. I receive more notes that way. I am saving them under my sleeping bag. I will be able to tease him mercilessly about them someday. Even the word *someday* makes me uncomfortable.

I push off on my bike—a garage-sale find, twelve gears, mud guard, rear basket—and Cal pulls alongside.

"Principal Dan says we should come in through the back entrance."

"Principal Dan?"

"Yeah."

"I thought we were going someplace *before* school." I was

hoping for a donut shop. The climb is starting. I grind into the pedals. I hate this part.

"You'll see."

The ride up is only three long blocks, but it puts me in a bad mood. I can't believe we're going to have to do this every day. It's like starting the day barfing.

Cal hands me a peach as we walk our bikes onto the sidewalk, toward the back of the school. "From Sandy," he says. "I told him you'd be crabby about the uphill."

I swipe the peach out of his hand.

"Greetings, Earthlings!" Principal Dan is sitting on a step in back. It looks like he's been waiting for us.

Cal shakes his hand, which seems a little formal. I just nod. I still don't like that the principal knows about Mom and me.

We lock our bikes, then follow Principal Dan as he practically skip-walks around the corner of the building, stopping in the spot over the basketball courts and puddles where Cal and I first inspected the school, weeks ago. There are still rusty hoops and faded lines; fewer puddles, though.

Principal Dan swings open a door in the fence. We descend stairs into the playground. "This way," Cal says, tugging my sleeve. "Remember this?" We're standing in a bend in the yard, where two buildings meet. There's a shrub underneath a barred window, providing shade. "You said we'd read here?"

Yeah. I did. It's the same as before, but now we're in the corner looking up instead of above it looking down. Across from us, like twenty long strides away, is a slab of the large retaining wall that surrounds the yard. And hanging from the slab is a white sheet.

Cal and Principal Dan look at each other and snicker-giggle. I get the sense they've been talking for a while about whatever this is. I look from face to face and scowl. I don't think Cal is going to be a fireman when he grows up. I think he's going to be a goofball head of school like Principal Dan. "You do the honors, Cal," Principal Dan says.

Cal walks over to the sheet and pulls.

Underneath is a mural that is clearly Cal's work—the signature wings. But there are no human faces in it. Just a street scene with a bazillion red-and-blue wings holding up an orange van.

"Oh, jeez," I say, leaning in for a closer look. "Is that our block?"

"Yeah," Cal says, looking pleased with himself.

"We like it," Principal Dan says. "A lot. Massive improvement to the exterior—painted with real verve. We can't believe Cal's previous school would object to such an evocative work."

"They called it graffiti. It's not graffiti," Cal says.

I don't say anything. I'm not sure what to say. The painting makes me feel tight. Like a hug that goes on too long.

I will have to get used to it. Like I got used to Cal. I give myself two months.

Principal Dan pats Cal on the arm about fifty times on the walk back to the bikes. He offers to let us hang out in the office till school starts, but Cal says we have other plans.

"We do?" I say.

He's already pushing his bike toward the street. "I thought, since we have so much time . . ." He disappears over the lip of the hill.

"Hey!" I say, throwing a leg over the seat. "Hey!"

Whirrrrrrrrrrrrrrr!

Yes.

The fast air slaps eyeballs, chills teeth, whips skin, blurs sound.

Tcktcktcktcktcktcktck . . . Wheeeeeeee!

This is what it's like to *be* the wind.

We ride right down the middle of the street.

Cal's quiet if you don't count the sound of his pride.

"What should we do?" I yell.

Sky melts into city. City melts into bay.

"Fly!"

From: The Chicago Public Library, Sulzer Branch
To: Cal and Jeanne Ann
Re: We found you!
Date: August 17

Dear Cal,
I am writing on behalf of the Chicago Public Library. We have spent several weeks trying to track down the family living in your driveway and were so pleased to read about your heroic efforts in recent newspapers, all on behalf of our Jeanne Ann. Please share this letter with her at your earliest convenience. We've enclosed a self-addressed, stamped envelope and stationery so that she might send us a reply, describing her state of mind and the events of the past summer. We've been so very worried. Also, please give her the books we've enclosed. They're advance copies of novels that are about to publish, and we'd very much like to hear Jeanne Ann's opinion of them. Finally, we've reached out to the librarian at the San Francisco Marina Branch Library, which—according to our maps—is the closest to you. We've asked him to treat you both with special care. There will be a pillow and small desk waiting there. Jeanne Ann will understand.

—Full of relief and affection,
Marilyn Jablonsky

P.S. If this is not the best address at which to reach Jeanne Ann, please notify us of a better one.

P.P.S. Speaking of desks, please tell Jeanne Ann that I recently found the cardboard box filled with her overdue library books. I knew she wouldn't mishandle property of the Chicago Public Library, even if she is a resident of a new city and a ward of its libraries now. The box was hiding in plain sight, right where we usually find Jeanne Ann. How silly of me not to look under her desk! We found her goodbye note too: "Sorry, no time to re-shelve." Only Jeanne Ann would apologize for that.

Roughed-out Profit and Loss Statement for food cart, provisionally named "Two Chicks on a Roll":

Initial stock and restock costs, weekly

Eggs 200 eggs per day x 6 days = 1200 eggs x .50 cents/egg = $600/week

Cheese 12.5 lbs/day x 6 days = 75 lbs/week x $6/lb = $450/week

Butter 12 lbs/day x 6 days = 72 lbs/week x $5/lbs = $/360week

Tea 3 lbs/week = $80 (with our 60% friends discount)

Misc. foods (herbs, flour, salt, lemons, milk, yeast, baking powder) = $150/week

Other (fuel, utensils, napkins, menus, fire extinguisher, cleansers) = $500/week

Waste: $150/week

Total loss/week = $ 2290

Total gain/week: $12.50 per order x 100 orders/day x 6 days week = $7500

Weekly net gain: 7500-2290 = $ 5210

Monthly net gain, 4 x 5210 = $20840

Mobile food facility permit = $1000/month

Insurance = $100/mth

Food safety/health permit = $30/mth

Taxes = $1000/mth

Monthly take home = $ 20840-$2130=$16,580

Monthly rent for future one-bedroom apartment in San Francisco (with bathroom) = $3500

One-time down payment for apartment = $7000, in addition to first month's rent

Average cost of heat/electricity/per month = $250

Cost of firm and wide two-seater couch = $800

Cost of two double beds = $4000

Cost to purchase back all books sold to bookstore at start of summer = $669.50

Cost to start fund for Gus (Mr. Yellow raincoat) and neighbors, $5 a day = $35/week

AUTHOR'S NOTE

San Francisco is a magical city. But it has a problem. There aren't enough affordable homes for the people who need them. The result is a lot of displacement—families living in cars, vans, shelters, and on the street. It's a problem facing many big cities. Libraries and the librarians who run them find themselves on the front lines of the crisis, providing shelter and warmth and priceless (paper) distraction. You can tell them how much you appreciate everything they do here: https://ec.ala.org/donate, or donate to your local library.

I didn't set out to write about the American housing crisis, but that's where the story took me. I set out to tell a tale of friendship and community, and the ways we try to help one another and sometimes fall short. If you've ever tried to soothe a crying friend and been shooed away, you know what I'm talking about.

Writing this novel forced me to ask for help in ways that would've nettled Jeanne Ann and thrilled Cal. There were the early years when it was called *Fricassee* and I was "just scratching around" with the help of workshop buddies, Tara Austen Weaver and Rebecca Winterer among them. There were the pre-baby years: Thank you, David Linker, Lindsay Edgecombe, and Beth Fisher, for reading the half-baked version and *still* liking it. There was the pre-sale period: Thank you, Kerry Sparks, agent empress. And finally, the post-sale phase, which mostly involved my editor, Jessica Dandino Garrison, lifting me over her head and setting me down over and over, in a new, better place, Incredible Hulk–style. When Jess and I (and Ellen Cormier, Lauri Hornik, Nancy Mercado, and the rest of the Dial team) were eye- and brain-drained, I handed it to Aline Marra, Anika Streitfeld, Clare Luskin, Kate Nitze, Meredith Arthur, Kirsten Main, Lucy Quirk, David Sterry, and Carol Halpern, who all led me toward the light. Until I got lost again. When that happened, I tried to channel Lewis Buzbee, my first fiction teacher, circa 1999, and I reread *I Capture the Castle* and *When You Reach Me* and *Counting by 7s*. When that didn't quite work, I gave it to Renanah and Lilah Lehner, who said, "Don't change a hair on its head," which is better for self-esteem than an over-dressed Caesar salad with extra-crisp leaves. And then there were my sideline cheerleaders: Donal and Brenda Brown, Marilyn Wronsky, Gina Bazer, everyone at LGR Literary, the Waldingers of Illinois, the Waldingers under my roof, Eric Svetcov and team, my clients, and my parents. Regarding the last in that series: Everyone should be raised by a seventh-grade English teacher (Mom) who treats eating out like a trip around the world, and a prosecutor (Dad) who graded the food, A+ through F. I'm so darned lucky. Thank you.

P.S.: A shout to Kasper Hauser for the "emergency room" joke. Brilliant, adapted, and borrowed.

P.P.S.: From Jeanne Ann's high-tops to the sunny back jacket, thank you, Tony Sahara, Kristin Boyle, Mina Price, and Mina Chung for this amazing package, inside and out.

P.P.P.S.: For eleventh-hour edits and Listening Library nods, thank you Rebecca Waugh.

An impatient chef once told author **DANIELLE SVETCOV**, "You talk too much, you move too slow!" when she was peeling onions in his restaurant kitchen. He was right. So she doubled down on writing, which rewards thinking (and talking) and going slow. Danielle wrote for the *New York Times*, *U.S. News & World Report*, the *Chicago Tribune Magazine*, and others before becoming a literary agent and, now, an author. With her debut novel, *Parked*, she writes her way back to her first loves—food and friendship. You can find Danielle across the Golden Gate Bridge from San Francisco with her salami-loving family, on Twitter @dsvetcov, and also at daniellesvetcov.com